skin

deep

diana wagman

University Press of Mississippi / Jackson

skin deep

For J.I., T.R., R.S., T.M.,

and my mother

The paper in this book meets the guidelines for
permanence and durability of the Committee on
Production Guidelines for Book Longevity of the
Council on Library Resources.

Library of Congress Cataloging-in-Publication Data

Wagman, Diana.
    Skin deep / Diana Wagman.
        p.   cm.
    ISBN 0-87805-982-2 (cloth : alk. paper)
    I. Title.
    PS3573.A359S58   1997
    813'.54—dc21   96-53362
                                          CIP

British Library Cataloging-in-Publication data available

s

k

i

n

d

e

e

p

1

DO BLIND PEOPLE SLEEP WITH THEIR EYES OPEN? ARE THEY EVEN AWARE THAT THEIR EYES are open? Do they feel them blink to stay moist?

Do the blind buy lamps for their apartments? When they get home from work, using the Braille buttons on the elevator, or the thump of their red-tipped cane on the stairs and it's a dark winter night, only 5:30, but dark already, do they turn their lights on?

Perhaps at night as you're driving by in your small blue car, using your eyes and your headlights vigilantly and you look up, really just with your peripheral vision for you mustn't take your eyes from the road, and you glance quickly and notice a dark house—or one dark apartment in a building of lit up windows—maybe a blind person lives there. Maybe a blind person lives there who doesn't know about the warmth of yellow light spilling into the night; the inviting and approachable glow of a home where people sit around the dining room table eating together, laughing and glad to be home. Maybe they just want to save on the electric bill.

Blindness, being blind and the lives of blind people, was the topic Martha was currently thinking about. She spent Monday, Tuesday,

Wednesday, and Thursday mornings in her office thinking. Or what she called her office, really the back booth by the window at the Winchell's Donuts down the hill from her house. It had a cheerful red and yellow decor of hard plastic, shiny surfaces, and clean glass that she found conducive to thought. She loved the hot and cold morning smells of coffee and window cleaner, fresh baked yeast and toasted sugar that made her swallow and stretch when she came in the door.

She usually had a topic that she worked on for a few weeks. She never wrote anything down and to an outsider, an office worker picking up an assorted dozen for the secretaries, it might look like she was just staring blankly out the window. Her thinking never changed the look on her face, but she was working just the same. She would never have told anyone that's what she was doing. She knew it was in some way pointless, but it was part of her routine. Usually she looked forward to it.

Not today. Today, Tuesday, only the second working day of her week and she couldn't concentrate. She sighed and gave up. She slid a hand into the back pocket of her faded blue shorts and pulled out a newspaper clipping. The edges were straight, cut with scissors. She hadn't ripped it out of the classifieds like some people. She used both hands to smooth the neat and tiny rectangle on the light-hearted yellow Formica tabletop. She read the ad again:

"Wanted. Woman to talk to. Three nights a week. Three hours a night. Three hundred dollars per."

It was the money that made Martha pause and consider. It was so much money. In her experience, women were only paid well for illicit behavior. On the other hand, she could understand that it would be hard to find a woman for this particular schedule. Most women had children who needed them at night; boyfriends who came for dinner and then stayed; girls' night out at the movies. They couldn't give up their evenings.

She felt the muscles in her legs tighten. She was going to get up and go outside to the pay phone to call. Then she stopped. She felt a prickle on the back of her neck, a shiver of foreboding. She breathed in the reliable, innocent Winchell's smell of warm grease. She relaxed. The ad had been in the newspaper. Murderers didn't advertise.

She glanced up at the doughnut-shaped clock behind the cash register. It was only nine o'clock. She could work some more on the blind.

Instead she smiled at the young Latina girl behind the counter. The girl nodded, surprised.

"More coffee?"

"No, no thanks. Sorry. I was just thinking."

Martha never drank two cups of coffee. She never ate two doughnuts. She no longer even had to order when she came in. The girl knew what she wanted every morning: coffee with skim milk, a plain cake doughnut, two napkins. The counter girl even knew her name, "*Hola*, Martha. Hey, Martha."

Martha couldn't reply personally. She didn't know the counter girl's name. Her white name tags with the red letters kept changing. One day it said "Beatrice"; the next day it said "Maria"; the next "Esmerelda." Martha was embarrassed to ask, Is that your name? Or is that your name? Or are they all your names? So she just nodded and smiled and said thank you, *gracias*.

She wondered which nights were the three nights a week mentioned in the ad. She assumed it wouldn't be Friday, Saturday, or Sunday. And she worried about the three hours. Would she be late coming home? She didn't want to be tired in the mornings. She didn't want to feel weary and distant at Winchell's. She felt out of control in the watery haze of fatigue.

Of course she didn't even have the job yet. She could go call right now. Martha looked at the clock. Only minutes had passed. She decided that ten o'clock would be a good time to call. She would wait, work, for an hour.

Friday she didn't come to Winchell's. Friday was housework day.

She did the laundry, scrubbed the bathroom, cleaned out the refrigerator.

Every other Friday afternoon after school, Martha's eight-year-old
daughter, Jewel, came to spend the weekend. Martha and her ex, Allen,
had been divorced since Jewel was three. Martha's single greatest regret
in life was that she had ever agreed to name her daughter Jewel. Jewel's
personality matched her name; hard, exacting, sharp. Martha often
found it difficult to be with her. But physically Jewel had not an angle
or a facet. She looked more like a marshmallow. Jet-puffed. Her face
was wide and fat, her tiny blue eyes just two moist dots on the copious
plain. She had the palest skin, the veins running blue and obvious
underneath like snail trails on the sidewalk. Her too fine white-blonde
hair didn't end in a curl or a blunt cut, but wisped away like unfinished
sentences.

One of the topics Martha often thought about was how she felt about
her own child's looks. Shouldn't she, as the mother, think Jewel was
beautiful, no matter what? Or was it because she didn't see her every
day that her flaws were so apparent? Martha returned to this subject
time after time, but she had come to no conclusions.

It was obvious that Allen thought Jewel remarkable. Martha was glad
he did. He was an exemplary ex-husband. Even their divorce proceed-
ings had been fine; Allen felt so guilty that he offered everything,
demanded it for Martha. He had fallen in love with Susan, the real
estate agent who sold them their house. Allen gave the house to Martha.
Martha couldn't remember what her lawyer looked like; Allen had paid
for him too. She didn't mind when Allen and Susan immediately got
married.

Then it seemed only natural that they take custody of Jewel. Allen
and Susan were a family. Martha knew too well what it was like to grow
up with just a mom, just a single, frazzled woman playing solitaire on
the coffee table at night as you left for a party, saying good-bye, have
fun, don't you worry about me. That first night that Allen and Jewel

were gone, Martha woke up every hour staring at the nightstand where the baby monitor had been, worrying in the quiet, missing the snorting sound of Jewel's allergies. But then it only took her a few months to learn to sleep again.

From the day Jewel had been born, Martha had felt out of her element. Allen stood beside her hospital bed grinning proudly like Little Jack Horner; his baby girl the plum he had pulled from his Christmas pie. Martha held Jewel awkwardly to her nipple that very first time and shuddered. She felt her throat constrict. Every noisy suck drew not only milk from her breast, but the air from her lungs. It was all she could do not to tear the tiny thing from her and throw it on the floor.

So, nursing hadn't worked out. That was only the first of Allen's major disappointments in Martha. Martha knew he blamed her because Jewel wasn't the easiest baby. She cried a lot and threw up a lot and didn't sleep through the night until she was over two. Martha had no one else to ask; she assumed Allen was right. If she had been a better mother, she would have had a better baby. She should never have had the epidural during labor. She should have forced herself to nurse. She should have spent more time holding Jewel. She should have loved her more. But she couldn't manage it then, she was suffocated in diapers and fuzzy pink baby blankets, how-to books, and the experts' advice. Now when she tried, it just seemed too late.

Martha shook her head and forced herself to think about the blind. If she allowed herself to think about her daughter she'd get distracted.

How do blind people dream? She saw her dreams in her mind, in that cavern behind her eyes. But if you couldn't see, would your mind be elsewhere? Maybe in your fingertips, in your ears, in your chest—the places that acted as your eyes—where you felt, heard, remembered. If she were blind she wouldn't care what Jewel looked like. Jewel felt nice to hold; she was soft and smooth, pliable and giggly. She smelled good like baby shampoo and school paste and sugary candy held too long in your hand. If Martha were blind she wouldn't care that Jewel insisted on wearing clothes decorated with Disney movie characters: Beauty and the Beast, Jasmine, pale blue and pale pink with spots of metallic glitter; clothes so pastel they had no color at all and did nothing for her chalky skin and anemic hair.

Well, today was only Tuesday. Jewel wouldn't come until Friday. And maybe, Martha thought, she would get this job and with all that money they could go shopping. Jewel would like that. They could go some place small and exclusive, some place where polyester shirts printed with princesses from two-dimensional movies didn't exist.

She had to concentrate. She pushed the ad away, down by the napkin dispenser against the window. She closed her eyes and ran her hands over the butter-colored tabletop. She felt the coolness of it and the hard bumps of someone else's sugar-coated doughnut that a wipe with the rag hadn't dislodged. She tried to feel the tabletop color. If she were blind, what would she know of color? How could color be explained? Red was easy, red was the dress your mother didn't allow you to wear; the smooth vinyl seat of the bad boy's car. And blue or yellow could be explained. But what about turquoise? If you were blind you could get married in a green dress, a black dress, or any dress that felt good to wear.

Martha opened her eyes and took a deep breath, exhaling through her nose, pushing all the air from her lungs until she had to gasp to get the next breath. She had been a topless waitress for the past year. She made pretty good money and there were some nice women. But it bothered Allen. He didn't think it was a proper profession for Jewel's mother, even her only every other weekend mother. The club had been fine, not degrading in the least. It was nice to feel good about your body. She had felt proud of her breasts even though they hadn't been any good for nursing. They were small but full, and they still pointed mostly to the ceiling when she lay down. Her areolas were a beautiful dark rose, not brown like some. And not a hair. Some of the waitresses actually had to pluck the hairs from their nipples. They said you got used to it, but just thinking about it made Martha cringe.

Still, Martha hadn't made much in tips and she hadn't made any friends. Allen still paid most of her bills and when he said it was time to stop, really time, that Jewel was beginning to ask questions, Martha figured she could find something else. She was smart. She had been to college, had almost graduated when she'd gotten pregnant with Jewel and then married Allen. She could type. She just hated to give up her mornings. Allen couldn't understand that. He thought she should work a regular daytime job. But Martha wouldn't do it. That was where she drew the line. She loved waking up alone, her little house quiet around her. The sheets were cool and smooth against her bare legs; the smell of her own pillow slightly sour and metallic with sleep. She liked to lie still and think about her day. Then she would get up, put her bare feet on the polished wood floor and pad about, loving that everything was just how she had left it the night before. On Jewel's weekends, Martha woke up earlier just to have this time to herself. She couldn't imagine not having the time to take her shower and afterwards wipe out the tub; to sit in her pink bathrobe at her own place at the table. She had her rituals, her liturgy for each day. She couldn't get up and dash out the door. She wouldn't.

That was why she had been so interested in this new job when she read about it in the classifieds. She could wait to say anything about it to Allen.

The morning rush was over at Winchell's. The shop gave off a sense of relief, of a breath taken, held, and finally released. The other counter girl, not the one who knew Martha, but the one who worked from 3 until 9 A.M., was leaving. She yawned as she walked to the door. There were feet and inches marked on the doorframe to catalog criminals who didn't pay for their doughnuts. The girl's head of long, silky, dark hair barely cleared the five-foot line.

Martha thought about the girl's bed waiting for her. It would be upstairs in her mother's house, a room shared by two younger sisters already up and gone to school. The girl would peel off her sticky sweet uniform, grateful for the cool air against her floured skin. She would pull the shade down, not noticing the tiny ripped corner that let the bleached sunlight stripe her bare abdomen. She would fall into the bed that she'd had since she was a child with the same blue flowered sheets, the same gold and brown quilted bedspread. Instantly the girl would be asleep and dreaming as always of Barbie dolls and pink dream houses and of Ken driving up in his fast plastic convertible.

"Later," Martha's counter girl spoke in English to her departing co-worker.

Martha could hear the envy and resignation in her voice. She watched her rinsing the coffeepot, wiping the counter, filling the creamer. She was efficient, her busy arms free of blemishes or freckles, her pretty skin just a shade lighter than the cardboard inside the dough-nut boxes. She was good at her job. Martha was envious of her future at Winchell's.

Martha peeled her bare legs from the red plastic bench and stood up.

"I'll be right back." She wasn't sure the girl had heard her. She hoped her coffee would still be there.

Martha stood on the sidewalk outside Winchell's and felt the sun on her face and neck. It was going to be hot. The sky was white and the air thick with haze. The trees across the road had lost their color; she saw everything filtered through the pallid smog and moisture. Los Angeles in September. It was a terrible, ugly time of year. Martha walked up the melancholy strip mall to the stand of pay phones by the super-market. She passed the crowded, disorganized video store, the bad Chinese fast food, the ice cream parlor with the cracked linoleum floor. They were run-down, dirty little places to shop, but they were walking distance from her house and she loved her Winchell's.

She dialed and listened to the ringing. She was queasy, her stomach a child's bright xylophone of nervousness.

"Dr. Hamilton." His voice was deep and serious.

He was a doctor, Martha liked that. "Hi. I'm calling about the ad in the paper?"

There was a pause. She heard his desk chair squeak, give as he moved.

"Is it filled?" Martha asked, not sure which answer she wanted to hear.

"No," he replied, "no, it's not."

"Well—" Martha began and then stopped.

"I just need someone to answer some questions," he said. "Maybe have a conversation." He paused, cleared his throat. "Tell me about yourself. No, don't, wait, um . . . what other work have you done?"

Martha was prepared. "I've been a waitress, you know, a barmaid really, at a topless club, the Sweet Spot, for about a year. I went to UCLA, I majored in urban studies." She didn't tell him she still had no idea what that really meant. "I'm just a couple of semesters short—"

"Can you start tonight?"

"Tonight?"

"We'll try it. See how it goes."

Martha didn't say anything. She saw her reflection, distorted and bent in the shiny silver panel on the telephone. Her eyes looked like two long ghosts in her face. She closed them, felt the phone's buttons, the knobbly black casing, pretended she was blind.

"What's your name?" he asked.

"Martha Ward," she said and then thought, Should I have lied?

"Ms. Ward," he began, his voice raised in pitch, "it's perfectly legal. I'll pay you in cash. If you don't like me, it . . . you're free to leave at any time."

She recognized his desperation, his need to convince her to do it, to come and do it, whatever it was he was after.

"Okay," she said. Her palms were sweating; she tasted the salt on her upper lip. She wasn't doing anything tonight anyway. Or tomorrow night either. "Okay."

Things at Winchell's hadn't changed. Martha sat down, lifted her coffee to her lips. She closed her eyes and took a sip. It was only barely warm now. Tepid. She liked it that way and she rolled it around in her mouth. It had its own taste now, like the smell of pencil erasers.

How would a blind person know what they'd been served? Every trip to a restaurant would be an adventure. Would they feel the plate first? Would they use their fingers to identify and separate the chicken breast, the steamed carrots, the mashed potatoes? Or would they stab away, confident and trusting that what came up on their fork would be edible? If she ever made dinner for a blind person, she would be sure not to use any decorative garnishes.

She opened her eyes and felt assaulted by the cheerful decor. It was time to go. Tuesdays she always went to the grocery store after thinking. She wondered what to wear tonight. She wondered why they were meeting at a hotel and not at his office. She had never heard of the Hotel Belle Noche before, out on Route 1, north of Malibu. It would be a long trip home. She decided on jeans. If anything weird were to happen, she would rather be in pants. Allen had always said she had great legs, but her legs had not been mentioned when she had spoken on the phone to her new employer. Martha assumed it was some kind of psychology experiment. One of the other topless waitresses had been paid lots of money to test a new drug for depression. The drug had made the girl very thirsty and likely to giggle inappropriately at her customers, but she said she felt better and the doctors had paid her well. Martha didn't want to take any new drugs, but she was happy to sit and talk about anything. She didn't get the chance to talk to many people.

She smiled at the counter girl as she stood. The counter girl smiled back wearily. "Bye, Martha."

Martha wanted to say something about her new job. But she looked at the capable and secure counter girl and was afraid of her reaction, afraid she would spoil it. Martha could tell her about it tomorrow, afterward.

"*Hasta mañana*," Martha said as she left. She always made an effort to use what little Spanish she knew.

After her usual careful hour of shopping, she carried two bags of groceries up the hill to her house. She bent her head against the relentless sunshine and noticed her own smell, her tart and musky sweat smell. It wasn't unpleasant to her, but Allen hadn't liked it. He didn't like any smell but Chanel 22 and Crest mint gel. When she'd been first married to him she had brushed her teeth ten, maybe thirteen, times a day. She waited to shower until an hour before he got home from work. She slid out of bed in the morning before he woke and replaced her perfume.

She pushed open the door on her little house and smiled. It was such a nice house, so feminine. Two bedrooms, hardwood floors, Spanish style, filled with arches and curves, wrought iron and funny little icon niches. She thought of her house as a maiden aunt with a big soft bosom and warm brown arms that wrapped around her when she walked in. She was glad she had talked Allen into buying it even if that was when he met Susan, the seller's effervescent real estate agent. It was almost as if Martha had known the future. The house had been too small for Allen and Martha and Jewel, but it was perfect for Martha alone.

She noticed the light blinking on her answering machine. There was a lifting in her chest. Perhaps one of the other waitresses wanted to have lunch. Maybe that nice guy she'd met at the club two weeks ago had finally gotten around to calling her.

She forced herself to put the groceries away, just like always, arranging them by color and item on the shelves in the refrigerator and the pantry. Apples went in the vegetable drawer, next to the grapes, but separated from the carrots and celery. Cheeses went in the cheese compartment, but first each block was unwrapped and sealed in a new ziplock bag. On the top shelf she lined up the milk, apple juice, and orange juice. She would never put the orange juice next to the milk—the two didn't mix—they needed the apple juice between. On the bottom shelf went her little pleasures, oatmeal cookies and microwave popcorn. It was her ritual and she usually enjoyed it.

But this Tuesday she was anxious to listen to her message. She knew it might be a wrong number, a salesperson, a survey of some kind. She tried not to get excited. Only when she was completely finished with the groceries, the bags folded and put away in their special drawer, did she allow herself to turn to the small telephone table. She pushed the button. The machine gave a little shucking sound and then sighed, rewinding. It was a long message, possibly two. There was another soft shuck-shuck and then a man's voice:

This is Dr. Hamilton with a message for Martha Ward; a few instructions concerning our meeting tonight. At the hotel, give them your name. They will be expecting you. Go up to the room and let yourself in. In the room, you will find clothes to put on and further instructions. If any of this is in any way distressing to you, simply leave the room and tell them at the front desk. Otherwise, approximately fifteen minutes after you've arrived, I will knock on the door, come in, and we will commence. I hope, I very much hope, to see you this evening.

The answering machine stopped. Martha rewound and listened once more. She liked the way Dr. Hamilton sounded. His voice was masculine and precise. She wondered if he had called the Sweet Spot for a reference, although she couldn't imagine what they could have said about her. She felt a sharp uneasiness, a sense of unknown prophecies coming true.

She shook her head, her arms, shuddered away the restless feeling. She needed a change. She had nothing to save. She was glad it didn't matter what she wore. She had liked that about being a topless waitress too. They couldn't expect too much from your appearance when they supplied the tiny skirt, the high heels, the fishnet stockings, even the garter belt, and hoped it all would fit.

She set about making the food she would eat that week: lentil soup; corn bread; vegetable ragout. She was only spontaneous when Jewel was visiting. She chopped the celery and smiled to herself, hoping, very much hoping, for miraculous alterations.

2

MARTHA WENT TO THE Y ON TUESDAYS AND
THURSDAYS AND TOOK A FIFTY-MINUTE AERO-
bics class and right after that a twenty-five-minute class called "All Abs."
She loved aerobics. She loved all the other women's bodies, fat or
skinny, pear-shaped or boyish. She loved the way their forms were re-
strained, held captive by spandex. She especially loved the flesh that
occasionally escaped. A woman would jump and a curve of deviant
tissue and skin would break free and jiggle irrepressibly. To Martha it
was a moment of physical exhilaration. She could never understand the
embarrassment the woman seemed to feel; the furtive way she would
pull up or down the twisted article of clothing, tucking in the spot of
flesh, glancing around to see who had noticed. Martha herself wore as
little clothing as possible when she worked out, only a jogging bra and
very short exercise pants. She loved to feel the air between her legs.

The mashing rhythm of the music, music she would never listen to
at home, filled the cavity at the base of her throat and made her want
to say "uh!" She enjoyed feeling part of a roomful of women moving in
unison, following the prescribed order. The teacher was inspirationally
perky. Her name was Robin and that's what she seemed like to Martha:

a tiny bird, chest puffed up, proudly announcing, Here I am, look at me.

Robin would call to Martha, "Come on! Yes, you in the gray, watch me! Watch me move!" Martha had been going to this same class, almost without missing, for two years, but Robin still hadn't learned her name. Robin always spoke in exclamation marks and Martha knew that "Martha" was not a name that responded well to excitement. It was a somber name, meant for the wife of the father of our country. It was not to be shouted in moments of exuberance.

Martha's Y was in the suburb of Glendale and most of her classmates were Armenian, large dark women with prominent faces. Their noses captivated Martha; they seemed so much to carry on the front of a face. She admired the way the women threw their bejeweled arms around each other when they met before class; the way they touched each other with their long painted fingernails when they conversed; the way they all seemed to know the same places to shop, the same restaurants, the same jokes.

This day, after class in the locker room, Martha made an unusual overture. She felt good about her work that morning at Winchell's, how well she had lifted her legs during class, her new job starting that evening. She turned to the woman next to her. A splendid woman, commanding, that's the word, Martha thought, admiring her size, twice that of Martha's, and her olive skin and dark brown eyes and the maroon lipstick that had remained remarkably fresh.

Martha smiled. "Quite a workout today, wasn't it?" She pushed long damp strands of her red hair off her flushed face.

The other woman looked at Martha. There was a moment before she nodded and grunted her assent, then picked up her towel and shoes and moved over to another bench populated with her compatriots. Martha didn't mind being snubbed. She knew it was a cultural thing. They could never really be friends.

Anyway, women, girls, had never liked her. By now, at age twenty-eight, Martha was used to it. It had hurt in junior high and high school, but it didn't anymore. Boys had always liked her; mostly the bad boys with lots of leather and little parental supervision; the ones who spent their time in the parking lot and at the stone bridge over the creek. She liked the way they smelled of dirty denim and beer and cigarette smoke with a faint aroma of the baby shampoo their mothers still bought for them. Martha was good at rolling joints, even though she rarely smoked them. One boy had wanted to buy her hair.

She had thought back then that maybe her reputation had been prematurely ruined by her older sister, Audrey. Audrey had gone to the same school three years before and she was a drug head and a lousy student. Still, during high school Audrey had friends. Even a little plump, even with braces, Audrey had Margaret and Nicole. Nicole married Ron the drug dealer the summer before her senior year and dropped out of school and Margaret ended up a bona fide prostitute down at Thomas Circle, but Martha remembered how close they had been, the hours Audrey spent with them, conversations on the phone, trying on clothes, laughing about boys and their penises. Martha hadn't had anybody like that.

On the way home from the Y, Martha stopped at the mall to buy a new pair of socks. She wanted to start her new job that evening with something untouched by any other moment in her life.

She had bought new underpants, white cotton thong-style Calvin Kleins, when she started her job at the topless club. All during that first, awkward night she had been aware of them, felt them, enjoyed the fact that they were there and completely new. They had made her feel lucky.

She pushed open the glass doors to the mall from the parking lot and, as always, felt a mixture of familiarity and anxiety. Anywhere she'd ever been in America the mall had felt the same. She could depend on a mall. She knew what to expect: women pushing their babies in strollers; old people sitting on the center benches; teenagers roving, eyeing each other. The anxiety came from feeling like she could never shop enough, she could never buy enough to keep up with the amount of things for sale. The mall always made her feel as if she didn't quite know who she was. There were so many choices.

And, as usual, when she walked in the double glass doors she immediately had to go to the bathroom. What was it about the mall that made her bladder instantly fill? She could try to ignore it, but then she'd spend all her shopping time needing to pee, uncomfortable and unable to concentrate on choosing her new socks.

She headed for the nearest rest rooms, down a long hall between interchangable men's stores. Maybe her body responded to the fluorescent lights. She had read that fluorescent lights in schools were responsible for girls getting their periods so much earlier. She wondered if it was happening to blind girls too.

Martha walked down the dark hallway, listening to her sandals make dead claps against the flecked acrylic floor. She could smell the industrial-strength disinfectant.

She reached the gray swinging door marked "Women" and pushed it open. A rush of hair spray, cloying and medicinal, accosted her. A lovely woman, tall and impeccably dressed for work or a fancy lunch date, stood at the first mirror fixing her marvelous long blonde hair. Martha was struck at first with how the color of the woman's hair matched exactly the accent color in her flowing skirt and jacket. Martha avoided her own reflection, feeling shiny from the dried sweat of her workout; uncombed and faded like her shorts and T-shirt.

Then Martha noticed that the woman had a broken arm, badly broken it seemed; the cast stretched from wrist to shoulder. Still the woman was incredibly adept at working with her hair. Martha smiled appreciatively at the woman's face in the mirror.

The woman spun and glared at her. "Stop staring at me," she said.

"I'm sorry." Martha looked away, first at the mirror, no, the floor, the sink. "I was impressed with how you combed your hair. You're so good with only one arm."

Martha braved a quick glancing smile. The woman's lips curled back off her teeth showing her red, damp gums.

"You want a broken arm?" The woman bit the air as she spoke. "I'd be happy to give you one."

Martha backed away, her eyes locked on a piece of toilet paper crumpled on the floor. The woman turned back to the mirror. Martha fled. She practically ran back down the hallway. Her nose felt hot, tears were coming. Had she been staring? She knew she did sometimes. It was a bad habit, one that had gotten her in trouble before. But the woman had been so beautiful. And not much older than Martha. It was only her beauty that had attracted Martha. Should she have said something else? Should she have lied about once having had a broken arm? Should she have said she wanted to help? Whatever she had done it was wrong. She sneezed, the tears in her nose bubbling out in a wet mess. She reached in her bag for a Kleenex, but knew she didn't have one. She was disgusting, dirty, rude and that beautiful woman had known it.

Furtively, Martha wiped her nose with her fingers and then brushed her fingers on her shorts as she hurried through the mall. She couldn't buy socks now. She didn't deserve new socks. She should learn to take better care of the socks she had, to wash them more carefully, more gently. This job wouldn't work out. It didn't matter what socks she wore.

As she pushed open the heavy doors out to the parking lot, Martha felt her tears settling in her nose and eyes. She felt her face thicken like a stone head from Easter Island. An attractive businessman passed her on his way to lunch at the food court and didn't even look at her. She would look terrible tonight.

She reached her small blue car gratefully, opened the door and slid into the driver's seat. She thought of the blonde woman in the bathroom and had to fight from exploding into great growling sobs. The poor woman. Martha probably had been staring. Probably everybody stared at such a beautiful woman in a cast and the woman had a right to be sick and tired of it. And instead of appearing as a friend or ally, Martha, as usual, was just one of the ugly masses.

Martha leaned her head against the steering wheel. The familiar choking feeling started in her throat. She was the one who was deformed. Her arms deserved to be broken. The day was spoiled. She thought of her earlier pleasure speaking to Dr. Hamilton and then of his message on her answering machine. She thought of his calm, controlled voice, giving instructions but giving nothing away.

She was out of her mind to take this new job. He was probably a pervert, a psycho. He would rape, maim, or torture her. She saw the scene that night: she put on the clothes he'd left for her: a steel and leather chastity belt, a dirty T-shirt with ragged holes around each breast. He entered the dingy motel room, grabbed her, and slapped her face. He was big and ugly and he wore a caftan that had been white and was now stained and obscene.

Somehow, the scene she pictured brought her to a solemn, quiet calm. She felt herself surrender. Her hands lay open in her lap. Her throat expanded. She took an unrestricted breath.

Well, Martha said to herself, if that's what it is, then that's what it is. It doesn't matter.

She started the car, put on her seat belt and carefully backed out of the parking place. Her mind returned to one of her most familiar daydreams. She imagined her body on the cold steel gurney at the morgue. She imagined herself naked and pale, her skin the yellow white of wax beans in her grandmother's Missouri kitchen, cooked in bacon fat until limp.

" 'Fraid the beans didn't turn out," her grandmother would say every time she placed a steaming bowl on the table.

"They're wonderful," someone always gave the requisite answer. "Just wonderful. Really wonderful." A family of liars needed to say things two and three times to each other. This time I mean it. This time it's true.

Who would call her family? Who would call Allen and Jewel? She imagined the morgue doctors clustered and talking about her. In her mind they were always bathing her, gently, using cotton balls and soft squares of fuzzy cloth, almost like diapers. They would notice her youth and frown sadly over the bruises and other marks of violence they found. She listened to them murmuring to each other.

"Why did she ever take that job?"

"That Dr. Hamilton is going to fry."

"He deserves it."

"If you ask me, it's her husband who should pay. Her goddamn ex-husband. What kind of man would leave such a woman—a woman with such nice legs—"

"Possibly even pretty, if there was enough of her face left to tell."

"Exactly. How could he leave her on her own, needing to do this kind of dangerous and bizarre work, anything she could find to supplement his tiny alimony payments?"

Martha laughed in the car. She pulled onto the freeway heading home. She rolled down her window. If she thought about the blonde woman in the bathroom she felt sick to her stomach, but if she concentrated on her own dead body in the morgue she felt fine. She was okay. She was brave. She would go home and take a nap to be rested for tonight. She would need to be well rested.

3

IT WAS TEN MINUTES TO NINE. MARTHA HAD GIVEN HERSELF JUST ENOUGH TIME TO GET there and now, thanks to improved traffic patterns or tailwinds or the inaccuracies of her Thomas Guide, she was ten minutes early. She hated to be early, almost as much as she hated to be late. She sighed. Ten minutes was too early to go in, but not enough time to go anywhere else.

She hesitated in the left turn lane, then changed her mind, pulled out and drove past the hotel, looking back at it over her shoulder. It was brand new, the color of poached salmon, with a red tile roof in the current theme-park old Mexico style. It wasn't appealing, but it looked expensive.

She continued up Route 1 along the ocean. The hotel was some distance north of the beachfront homes of Malibu and sat in isolation on the highway. She drove on alone except for the dark and overwhelming sea to her left. She cracked her window, afraid to open it any further, afraid to mess up her hair.

The breeze was acrid, smelling of tar and dirty sand and seagulls. She missed the fresh smell of the Atlantic Ocean of her childhood. Bitter and salty in her mouth, but clean, a reminder of age and generation and cycles of life. Lying on her stomach in the warm sand, she would unfasten the strap of her bikini top to leave her back line free. She would dig one hand over and over into the fine, creamy sand letting the small grains cascade gently over the back of her fingers and down to her wrist. That evening she would clean the sand from under her fingernails, hold her fingers to her nose and smell the sea. Just as later in her life she would smell her husband there.

She put her window all the way up, signaled left, and made a U-turn on the empty highway. She was homesick. The Los Angeles beaches always made her that way. She wanted to go home. She wanted to go east where September meant something; the beach closed up after Labor Day and you were given a reprieve from summer. Next year, I'll learn to boogie board, next year I'll look better in my bathing suit, next year I'll wear a hat and I won't get sunburned.

She walked into the hotel. It was as she had imagined it from the outside: saturated with southwestern ambience, Mexican tile floor, natural-looking fabrics in earth tones, accents in peach and turquoise. There was the ubiquitous coyote with the bandanna around his neck sitting by the gas fireplace.

She walked over to the reception desk.

"I'm Martha Ward," she said to the popularly handsome blonde man behind the counter. He was dressed in a white shirt and a vest printed with a feeble version of Indian material. There was a hole in his left ear where he usually wore an earring; not allowed at work she supposed.

He stared at her blankly.

"Dr. Hamilton is expecting me," she said. That made it sound like it was a doctor's office, not a hotel. She was suddenly self-conscious. She watched his perfectly manicured nails as they typed on the computer. Some blondes had such wonderful skin, golden really, and smooth, with frosty white nails. The light hit the blonde hairs on the back of his hands, making them actually sparkle. What if she were a flea walking through that flaxen forest? She saw clearly the bug's-eye view: the peaceful glowing skin, the enormous hairs radiant around her. Which glorious spot could she possibly choose to bite?

The receptionist startled her when he spoke, "Of course. Room 355." He handed her a flat credit card kind of key. "Dr. Hamilton asked me to remind you that he will be joining you in fifteen minutes."

He smiled professionally.

Martha took the key and blushed. He probably thought she was a hooker. She wanted to explain to him, but she wasn't yet sure what there was to explain.

She walked to the elevators and pushed the button. She glanced back over her shoulder. He wasn't looking at her. He was busy with his own job. He was probably a homosexual; something about the squareness of his jaw, the protruding muscle in the back of his cheek gave him away. He didn't care why she was here. Still, she hated anyone to think badly of her. She would have liked to justify herself, share her confusion, laugh a little, even with the gay hotel night clerk.

He would think differently about her later, when the ambulance came, when they carried her out on the stretcher. He would tell the police she had seemed perfectly nice.

The elevator was encased in coppery metal, hammered all over with little marks like the design on the New Mexico license plate. Martha winced at her brown and spotty reflection. She looked like an Indian smallpox victim.

The doors slid open on the third floor. The hall was quiet and empty. There were no signs or sounds of occupancy in any of the rooms. Martha felt like she should tiptoe. She found room 355 and inserted the keycard. The wood of the door was light and lacquered to a smooth shine. Someone had left a long diagonal scratch in the finish, not really noticeable from any distance, but definite. It was not a mark made by mistake. Martha wondered who could have done it and with what. It was too deep for a fingernail. Maybe a regular house key, angry that the door took only flat plastic cards. Or a knife that had come up with

room service and then been left on the tray outside the door, stuck in
the sticky yellow of egg on the white plate, among the shards of but-
tered toast and smears of mixed fruit jelly. Someone walking by had
seen the knife and . . . and just couldn't resist ruining the pure, virgin-
ally blonde door. Someone like Lars, her first stepfather, who couldn't
wait to get out in the newly fallen snow and make tracks.

The red light next to the doorknob flashed green. Martha ran her
hand once down the scratch, turned the knob and went in. The room
was simple and the same flavor as the rest of the hotel. Without looking
she knew what it said in the brochure: contemporary elegance with
casual southwestern charm. A queen-size bed was against one wall. On
the bed were a brown paper bag, the top closed neatly and folded over
twice, and a typewritten note.

Martha saw the typed instructions, heard them beckoning, but she
couldn't wait. She picked up the bag. No obvious clanking of metal
chains. The bag was light, lighter than her gym bag after aerobics. She
opened it carefully, unfolding and gently pulling the bag apart. The bag
made her think of cookies and dry clothes after the rain.

She started to reach into the bag, then stopped. That would be a
trick; to put something terrible in the bag, a snake, a bomb, a scorpion.
She turned the bag upside down and dumped it on the bed. There was
nothing immediately dangerous. It was just a pile of navy blue. She
separated the pieces. Navy blue sweatpants, navy blue sweatshirt, navy
blue gloves, socks, and lastly something else . . . some kind of a hat.
They were all in an enormous size.

Martha frowned. No wonder he didn't ask about her legs. He was
expecting a hippopotamus. Had she sounded enormous on the phone?
Did he know she spent three mornings a week at Winchell's?

She picked up the note and read,

Dear Ms. Ward,

In the bag you will find five articles of clothing. Please put them on.
They are intentionally quite large. Please do not attempt to make them

smaller in any way. I want as much of your female form obscured as
possible. Please ensure that all areas of your skin are covered, i.e., the
socks pulled up and the pants over them; the same with the gloves and
sweatshirt sleeves. These are brand-new items, freshly washed in Ivory
Snow detergent. You should be quite comfortable. Lastly, please put on
the hood, making sure that your hair, if it is long, is completely covered
and that the neck piece covers your neck and rests loosely on your shoulders.

Please check yourself in the full-length mirror in the bathroom.
Should any bare skin be showing when I arrive I will not be able to
continue. When I knock on the door, if you are not ready, please simply
tell me how long to wait.

It was signed, "Dr. A. Hamilton."

Martha was glad she hadn't bought new socks. Things usually
worked out for the best, didn't they?

She took the clothes and the bag into the bathroom and shut the
door. It was painted bright white with white tile, no nonsense. There
was a white phone on the wall next to the toilet. She pulled the long
navy gloves from the pile and set them aside to put on last. She had
taken a long time this afternoon filing her nails.

She avoided her reflection in the bathroom's many mirrors. When
she was dressed in the new costume, she carefully folded her own
clothes and put them into the paper bag. She set the bag on the bright
counter, then turned and looked at herself in the full-length mirror. She
looked like a drooping blue blob. The sweatpants kept sliding down
her hips. She would have to keep a hold with one hand on the waistband through the sweatshirt. She hoped she wouldn't be asked to move
around too much. She checked the socks and the gloves—not a sign of
pale wrist or ankle flesh anywhere.

She picked up the dark hood. It was hand stitched, the stitches small
and evenly spaced close together. She imagined Dr. Hamilton would
sew just like this. Then again, lots of people did psychology experi-

ments. There might be catalogs, or even whole stores, full of these. Martha imagined rack after rack in a rainbow of colors, pink for children, yellow for athletes, dark gray for old men.

She found the opening and pulled the hood over her head. It had some sort of give to the material, a little Lycra or jersey, but once it was on, it fit snugly. There was a lighter material, gauzelike, over the eyes and mouth that enabled her to see somewhat and breathe and she supposed to talk, but not be seen. It was a little claustrophobic inside the hood. Her peripheral vision was nonexistent; her hearing less acute. She pulled the hood off. It came off so easily that Martha felt relieved.

She put it back on, carefully tucking all her long hair inside. The same solemn calm from earlier returned; the surrendering to whatever this evening would bring.

There was a knock on the room's door. Martha stepped out of the bathroom and stood by the bed.

"Okay," called Martha, "I'm . . . okay. Come in."

The door opened. A tall man entered, wearing khaki pants and a blue shirt, socks and expensive loafers, a tie loose around his neck. He was handsome, with a thin straight nose, a solid jaw, deep-set gray eyes, but stooped and creased as if his height, his good looks, or something else pressed upon his shoulders. He carried a weight that his remote frame couldn't bear. He wasn't old, but the forty years he'd been alive had worn him down.

"I'm Dr. Hamilton." He didn't offer her his hand. "Please, sit down. There."

He gestured to one of the two chairs at the table in front of the closed peach and beige drapes. Martha started and then stopped. She hadn't noticed before the green plastic jug and two white towels on the floor in the corner behind the table. It was a large jug and after a moment she recognized it as something for a car, gasoline or water that you carried with you. That was okay then. Maybe he was having car troubles.

Martha continued to the chair and bumped into the corner of the
bed. The headboard thumped loudly, embarrassingly, against the wall.

"Sorry." Martha sat with relief.

Dr. Hamilton sat opposite her. "Are you comfortable? Can I get you
anything?" He avoided looking directly at her.

"No. I'm fine, thank you." Martha didn't know what he meant. Of
course she wasn't comfortable. And how could she drink or eat anything through this hood? Room service was out of the question.

There was a long silence. Martha could hear the waves collapsing on
the beach.

"May I, may we, open the curtains?" she finally asked.

"Yes. I suppose." He stood and pulled the drapes apart.

The ocean was very near, but Martha was more aware of her own
amorphous dark reflection; the executioners hood, the lack of herself.
She shuddered and turned away.

"Here." Dr. Hamilton stood and turned out the one burning light. "Is
that better?"

Now the ocean was visible and Martha, or whatever Martha had
become, was not. "Yes. Thank you."

She faced Dr. Hamilton across the table. She sat in a dark hotel room,
covered head to toe in shapeless navy blue and waited.

It has come to this, she thought. It has all come to this.

Dr. Hamilton looked out at the ocean. "Ms. Ward," he spoke quietly,
his voice low in his throat and warm, but hesitant, "I . . . we are here
to talk. I need—I am . . . interested in a woman's point of view. I don't
want to see you. I don't want to be confused by the form you have
taken because of your genetic background, nutrition and whatever acci-
dents of nature have befallen you. I . . . want only to know what you
think."

He paused. Martha felt she should say something, but she didn't.

Dr. Hamilton wrinkled up his face, squeezing his eyes together as if
even the shapeless form in front of him was too much to see. He swal-

lowed once and Martha watched his Adam's apple move up and down. She wondered why her own neck was the most sensitive part of her body and the place she held most private. She could hear him breathing.

He said, "We are here to talk about beauty." He paused and then whispered it again as if he loved the word itself, "Beauty."

4

UH-OH, MARTHA BEGAN TO WORRY. BEAUTY WAS
A TOPIC FILLED WITH HAZARDS, LAND MINES,
and insidious jungle vines of expectation, used as ammunition against
women. She didn't want to be the woman in this discussion, even a
woman whose own beauty, or lack of it, was completely hidden.

She looked at Dr. Hamilton filtered through the blue gauze in front
of her eyes. She knew he was unhappy. She heard it in his voice, saw it
in his face and posture, smelled it even, damp and moldy around him.
His sadness scared her. Depressed people did extreme things. What if
she said the wrong thing? What if that was the whole purpose of this
experiment?

Martha felt her chest contract. Her weight pressed down on the balls
of her feet; she was ready to run. She eyed the door, noticing that the
bed was in her way. Should she run over it? Around it?

"Ms. Ward. This is very important to me. I have been . . . no. Well.
I haven't done this before. You may not like it. We may not get on. We
shall both have to feel our way."

She tried to be conversational, "So, what kind of doctor are you?"

"I won't answer that."

"Okay. Fine."

"I've thought about this. We shouldn't know anything real about each other. I don't want to know what you look like or where you live or what you do. I only want to know what you think."

"But what I think is a product of all those things, isn't it?" Martha grimaced unseen in her blue hood. "I mean, sure, if that's what you want." She spoke with her eyes on the door, the space between them, wondering if the soles of his shoes were as slippery as her navy blue socks.

"You're right, of course," Dr. Hamilton acquiesced. "I just don't want any details."

"Fine."

He cocked his head to one side, like a dog watching a black beetle on the floor. She had surprised him. "You mean there are things you don't want to tell me?"

That wasn't what she'd meant, but it was obviously what he wanted to hear. "Yes," she said. "Of course. A woman has to have a few little secrets."

"Do you?"

What did he want her to say? She looked down at her blue body. Her gloved palms touched her hooded cheeks, then opened to him ambivalently. "Well. This makes everything a secret, doesn't it?"

Dr. Hamilton tried to smile. Martha watched him tighten his cheek muscles and pull his lips back in a stretched line. It was a very great effort and she knew he made it for her. He recognized her position, acknowledged the absurdity.

Martha's feet relaxed. Her hands opened in her lap. She smiled back at him although he couldn't see it, offering him clemency for scaring her, for making her want to run.

"Don't worry. I think I understand," she almost whispered.

"Good." He seemed relieved. "So. I wanted to start this evening's discussion with a simple question. What is the last beautiful thing that you saw?"

Martha knew it was a trick question. It was a test. How she answered would make all the difference. She didn't like tests. She never knew the answers. She was never completely certain that one answer was better than all the others.

But what else could Dr. Hamilton do? How else could he appraise her and see if they would in fact "get on"? And then she realized she could be testing him too. It was up to her as well. She might not want to continue after this evening, even though the money was so good.

So she thought briefly about what was beautiful. She didn't want to tell him what she really thought; that beauty is mostly found in minutia, that anything dissected down to its smallest parts is beautiful. She thought of the receptionist's fine bright hairs on the back of his hands. She thought of the honey-colored liquid light and shadow of the apple juice as she poured it into her glass in the morning. She thought of the warmth she felt watching a bee on her kitchen table, each of its tiny legs moving independently, daintily, through the jam. She supposed she should say the ocean at sunset; the sky after it rains; my daughter's face.

Instead she said, "But what is your definition of beauty? Is it only something you see?"

Dr. Hamilton leaned forward in his chair. "What a terrific question." His shoulders gave and seemed to shrug and roll toward her. "A great question. A great place for us to begin."

Martha was glad to make him happy. She continued in a rush, her words filling her mouth and bouncing out like popcorn from the big machine at the movies, "It can only be a combination of effects to be truly beautiful, a merging of all the senses. It must be pleasing to look at and hear and smell and feel and taste, all of that. You know, like when you see a very attractive woman and you think she's hot or whatever, or refined, and then she opens her mouth and she has one of those terrible, you know, nasal or scratchy not in a good way voices, or she smells bad, or she has stupid ideas. She's not beautiful anymore, is she?"

Dr. Hamilton had the interested but protected face of a psychiatrist.

"I mean," Martha continued, "that's a very simple example, and it's never really that simple, is it? I mean, depending on your mood, you might go for her just because she's pretty to look at. Maybe you don't care about anything else. I guess what I'm saying is, is . . ." Martha faltered, aware of Dr. Hamilton's continued silent observation. She took a deep breath and finished quietly, "Well. Even blind people have a sense of beauty. So it must be more than just visual."

Dr. Hamilton looked out at the ocean. Martha grimaced. She had talked too much, rattled on and on, and that example of the woman was such a cliché. She just didn't get to talk often and sometimes when she did she didn't stop to think. She tried to smile at him apologetically, but then realized he couldn't even tell she was embarrassed. She was suddenly angry and wanted to take off her mask and let him know her. But it wouldn't help, she told herself; he really wants someone different. She remembered suddenly the incredible woman in the bathroom at the mall and then that woman turned from the mirror and became Martha's mother, Dolly, who always knew the right thing to say. Her stomach hurt.

Dr. Hamilton turned back to her. His hands gripped the arms of his desert-colored ranch-style chair. Martha saw his knuckles go white and obvious from holding on so tight. He was going to hit her, she was sure of it. She once had a boyfriend who had hit her, but they had both been naked and she had provoked him. She knew she made some people very angry.

Dr. Hamilton stood up. Martha wondered if the hood would offer much protection, if she'd still have a visible bruise. What would the counter girl at Winchell's think? She lifted her face, proudly afraid.

To her surprise, Dr. Hamilton walked away. He went to the farthest corner of the small hotel room and leaned against it, his face to the wall.

Martha was mute. What would happen? What was happening?

Martha sat in the dark, in the yards of navy blue cotton and polyester, and waited. It reminded her of lying on the floor in her daughter's room when Jewel was only one. Jewel couldn't fall asleep without Martha in the room, so Martha would lie on the small pink rag rug next to the crib. She would concentrate every thought, every vessel in her body, on willing Jewel to go to sleep. Jewel would scream if Martha tried to leave the room too early so Martha would lie there each night for at least an hour, often more, not moving, counting the seconds. She played a game pretending she was a prisoner of war. Then, abruptly, she realized she was. The next night she let Jewel wail until Allen came home from work and went in and rescued his daughter. I'm the one who needed deliverance, Martha thought, but she didn't say anything to Allen. Jewel's face was dark purple and red and sopping with tears and snot. Martha would never forget the look of anger and betrayal Jewel turned on her and the loving way she clung to her father.

Dr. Hamilton hadn't moved.

Martha stood up. It was only ten o'clock or so, but this was obviously going nowhere. She started for the bathroom to change. Dr. Hamilton spun around.

"Don't," he said.

"I'm sorry," Martha said quietly. "I guess I'm not what you expected."

"Do you want to go?" he asked.

"Well—"

"If you're miserable, then, by all means, go. I don't want you to; I'm quite satisfied so far. I know this is very odd. You have been very brave to come here at all. I'm just having a little difficulty. It will pass."

"Maybe someone else—" Martha began, then stopped. He was obviously in such distress. "Can I do anything for you?"

"Here." Dr. Hamilton reached in his pocket and took out three hundred-dollar bills. He slapped them hard onto the dresser. "You can stay. I've paid for you to stay. Does it matter so much if we talk? What do you care what I do? If I want to stand in the corner, it's my money, isn't it?"

"Did I say something to make you angry?"

"You sound so young. How old are you?"

"Isn't that one of those details?"

"I asked you a question."

Dr. Hamilton walked up to Martha. She was tall for a woman, but he was taller. She felt at first completely hampered and restricted by not being visible as herself. There was nothing, no smile or winsome look, she could give that would change anything.

And then she found it liberating. She didn't have to be timid Martha; she could just be a tough-skinned blueberry.

"I won't tell you how old I am."

"Sit down."

"I'm not a hooker."

"You're mine for three hours."

"I thought this was a psychology experiment."

Dr. Hamilton began to laugh. It was a disturbing sound like good cloth tearing, shrieking as it ripped and then flapped in a black wind.

"Oh, Ms. Ward. How innocent you make it sound."

"Isn't it?" Martha asked.

Again her eyes caught the green plastic jug in the corner. He kept laughing. Martha felt herself trembling.

Without thinking, she shouted at him, "What is the matter with you?"

It was out. She tried to gulp the words back, but they ran headlong from her mouth and collided into the air between her and Dr. Hamilton.

He stopped laughing and looked at her.

"Another good question . . . and, what about you, Ms. Ward? What is the matter with you?"

Martha shrank back into her own body. She felt the soft folds of the sweat clothes gathered around her. She was only herself again. The blue was only a grocery bag, not a tougher skin on a new kind of fruit. She was sorry she had spoken, sorry she had come, sorry she was herself.

"I'm sorry," she said.

She stepped toward the bathroom and stumbled again over the corner of the bed. This time she fell. Dr. Hamilton reflexively reached out to catch her and then pulled his hand back before touching her as if he were afraid of being burned. His mouth was a round hole in his face that seemed to Martha to slide to one side as she fell.

She went down onto one knee on the beige carpet. She put her hands down to push herself back to standing. Letting go was a mistake. She felt the sweatpants begin to slide down her backside. She froze, unable to move, unsure what to do, terrified the sweatpants would fall and leave some horribly white part of her exposed. It was a pause, a long moment when she crouched on the floor at the foot of the bed without moving. She looked down at her own blue gloved hands and noticed how dark they looked and even elegant in the half light. Her fingers looked long and slender and encased in evening gloves, long black gloves like they wore at parties in the movies. What would evening gloves be doing on the floor, she wondered. Perhaps looking for a diamond earring that had fallen in the fervid midst of a confidential embrace. She stretched her hands against the industrial-grade carpet. When you looked closely you could see it was actually flecked with a gray and a darker brown. It really wasn't a bad carpet; it was even attractive.

"Can you get up?" Dr. Hamilton's voice was distant and professional.

"It's the pants," Martha replied. "I'm afraid I'll lose them. Just turn around, please, for a moment."

"All right then."

Martha gathered up the enormous waistband in one hand and stood. She composed herself and took another step toward the door.

"I'm sorry," she said again.

Dr. Hamilton turned to face her. "Maybe we should just call it a night."

s k i n d e e p

Martha nodded. She had been expecting this. Nothing else, but surely this.

"Unless you would rather continue?" He paused, his voice suddenly plaintive, like Jewel's asking for something she shouldn't have, more ice cream or a sip of Martha's beer. "Would you like to? Would you?"

"I don't mind," Martha said. "Okay, if you want to."

She stood there, looked at the chair, and then sat on the bed. Dr. Hamilton laughed.

"I could move the chair," he offered.

"I'm fine," Martha said to her own surprise. And she was, she really was. "Ask me a question," she said.

"Well. Yes." He pulled his chair over, across from her and sat. "You said even blind people know what beauty is. How do you think they know?"

Martha sighed. The smell of her own breath inside the blue hood was sharp and moist. She hoped she could take the hood home tonight and wash it. It was obvious there was something else Dr. Hamilton wanted to talk about, another question he would rather have asked.

"At the risk of sounding mundane," she said, "I suppose a hug from someone you loved would feel beautiful. Or the warm sun on your face. Or the smell of a flower and the softness of its petals."

"Uh-huh," agreed Dr. Hamilton.

They both sat in silence. Martha realized she had sounded like a greeting card. She knew that Dr. Hamilton thought so too. Ask me something else, she thought, ask me what you want to know.

"Was your mother, is your mother beautiful?"

Martha was so startled by the question that she gasped.

"Is that a ridiculous question?" Dr. Hamilton asked.

"Pretty is as pretty does," Martha replied. "That's what my mother used to say. She didn't believe you could be pretty unless you were nice too."

"Was she nice?"

"She was, still is, a splendid hostess. Vivacious. Charming. The life of every party. When I was a kid, she had wonderful legs and these tall, spiky, high-heeled red shoes with black buttons on the toes. She was beautiful almost all of the time."

"And the other times?"

"Then she wasn't. It was amazing how her face would change. If she was angry, or especially if she was jealous or suspicious, her face would settle, thicken. Her eyes would shrink and her cheeks flatten. Her mouth would disappear until she had no lips at all. It's like her face would just evaporate, leaving this broad, flat, white expanse—ugly— like an empty schoolyard in the snow."

"Then her saying holds true, Pretty is . . ."

"Oh, yes. She was definitely a woman who benefited from remaining content." Martha continued without thinking. "I'm afraid my daughter looks just like her, but only at those worst moments."

There was a pause.

"Sorry. Sorry, I know." Martha shook her head. "I wasn't supposed to mention her."

"How old is she? Your daughter."

"Eight."

"And you don't think she's beautiful?"

Martha stretched defiantly in her anonymous blue. "No."

"Because she looks like your mother?"

"No," Martha said emphatically. She thought of last Christmas and Jewel and Dolly conspiring over the Christmas cookies. Jewel stood, on Martha's childhood stool, in a huddle with her grandmother about gingerbread men, snickerdoodles, basic sugar cookies. Martha could see the two blonde heads that turned as one, two sets of secretive blue eyes, two giggling thin-lipped mouths that settled into straight lines when Martha joined them.

"No," she said again. "It's because she doesn't look like anything at all."

Dr. Hamilton shuddered, and shuddered again. It had been a terrible thing to say, but it was true and he had asked.

"Ms. Ward." Dr. Hamilton spoke each word with restraint, clipping the space between. "What, in your opinion, does someone need to be beautiful?"

"Interest."

"You mean, for example, if your daughter had an interest in, say, animals then she would be beautiful?"

"No. If I were interested in her. Then I would see more than just her separate pieces."

"Don't you love your daughter?"

"Listen, this sounds a lot like those details we're not supposed to talk about. Anyway, who cares? I mean, I'm here for you."

"You are?"

"Well. Actually, I'm here for the money. But it's your money, so we should talk about what you want."

"Okay. Good."

"Great."

"Do you love your daughter?"

Martha winced. It was her first evening here and she'd managed to show him all her worst sides: clumsy, inarticulate, cliched, thoughtless, a horrible mother.

"Of course I love her. And sometimes I think she's pretty. I just don't know what to do with her."

Martha wasn't sure any of that was true, but it sounded better. She resolved to try harder with Jewel when she came for her weekend visit. They would go shopping, to the movies, out to dinner or something. They would laugh together and Jewel wouldn't look at her with those pale piqued eyes. Jewel wouldn't leave her overnight case packed the whole time; she wouldn't be waiting by the front door when her father came to get her.

"It's hard," Dr. Hamilton said finally. "Beauty. I don't understand.

You see, that's why we're here. I don't understand what it really is. I only know it's so important. I wonder . . . how do people live without it?"

"They can't."

"No. I'm afraid they can't." Dr. Hamilton stood. "That's just what I'm afraid of."

He walked to the sliding glass doors leading out to the ocean and placed his palms against the glass. Then he put his cheek against it.

"It's cold," he said.

"It's cold in here," Martha said, suddenly realizing it was true. She was shivering. She wished she'd kept her T-shirt on.

"Do you prefer the heat?"

"I like weather. I mean, I like it to be different every day. Not like it is here. Here it is always the same."

"You mean the weather's always the same in a hotel room?"

Martha laughed out loud. "It is. It is. Anywhere in the country, Sheraton Grande or Bob's Budget Inn." She laughed again. "But, of course, I meant in L.A."

"Laugh some more," he said, turning from the glass doors.

"Oh, I can't."

"Please."

"It doesn't work that way. You laugh."

There was a pause.

"I have to leave now." Dr. Hamilton started for the door.

"Is our time up?"

He didn't stop or respond. He went out the blonde wood door and closed it behind him. Martha stood up, one hand firmly grasping the waist of her sweatpants. She waited.

She stood without moving, watching the door for his return, until finally, finally, she went into the bathroom to change.

5

DRIVING HOME IN THE CAR, SHE WONDERED IF
SHE SHOULD HAVE TAKEN THE BLUE SWEAT SUIT
with her. She had folded it neatly and put it back in the bag. She had
put the bag back on the bed where she'd found it. But it had not been
exactly clean. It had an odor, a mixture of her coconut shampoo, her
all-natural mint deodorant, and the pungent mineral smell of her sweat.
She had been chilly but nervous and had perspired under her arms and
between her breasts; even some between her legs, a moist, feral feeling,
not sexual but territorial.

She didn't like to think of him dumping her clothes into his washing
machine and being aware of her smell. She had given him enough of
herself, her unattractive moments. She thought of stumbling, of falling,
of spilling too many words and shook her head. She rolled down the
window and let the wind take her long hair. She didn't care what it
looked like anymore.

As she turned off Route 1 onto the number 10 freeway eastbound,
she passed an old tan and white pickup with a camper parked on the
shoulder. She glanced over and noticed two young children sitting
alone in the cab. Even at fifty-five miles an hour she could see they
were Mexican, big dark eyes so sleepy, staring at each face that drove

by. Why were they out so late? Where was the driver of the truck? Should she stop to help? But it was too late; she had passed them and there was no way to turn around.

Could their father have left them alone in the truck while he walked to the nearest gas station? She was sure they were with their father, or an uncle or a much older brother. No female would have left them isolated on the side of the highway, obvious prey to any lunatic that happened by. She knew a mother would have bundled them up and made them trudge along with her, taking turns being carried.

Or maybe they were decoys planted to stop someone just like her. She would want to help and she would be murdered instead, while the kids, older than they looked, hid their heads beneath the dashboard. Then they would take her little blue car on a joy ride and leave it over by the Los Angeles River stripped of its wheels, seats, engine parts, and her.

Poor kids, she thought, anything can happen at any time.

The September she was seven her grandmother, Dolly's mother, had come to live with them for two months after her husband, Martha's grandfather, had died. She was a large Missouri farm woman and she was awkward, out of place and anxious in their small house on the edge of Washington, D.C. She was uncomfortable on their furniture, the picnic benches they used at the kitchen table, even the huge green easy chair, so she often just stood, staring out the kitchen window at the tiny backyard, nothing like her Missouri expanse, only a patch of worn and threadbare grass, a spindly dogwood tree, and a rusty swing set.

Martha had been starting off to second grade. Audrey was in fifth. Martha's father, who was not Audrey's father but their mother's second husband, had already departed from their everyday life. They didn't know their grandmother well and when she arrived Martha had been stunned. Audrey was the very image of her. They had the same wide cheekbones and sharp chin, the same clear blue eyes that were made to look long distances across the fields. Fair and plump, Audrey was an easy favorite. Her straight blonde hair was familiar to Grandmother; she looked like she belonged. Grandmother called Audrey "that Pruitt girl," Pruitt being her own maiden name.

She called Martha "Firethorn," after the pyracantha branch she dusted and put on her front hall table every Thanksgiving. Martha knew it was fitting. She was small, quiet, skinny, with an inferno of kinky red hair. Even at seven, she didn't cuddle well or giggle. Grandmother was barrel shaped with an enormous farm wife's bosom, a single dropped shelf of breast. Her arms and legs were long and bony as if all the fat had rolled to the middle. Audrey could cozy up to their vat of grandmother and find a lap, while Martha would only hover at her grandmother's pointed elbow. Too often, reading a story or watching TV, Grandmother would sneeze and that keen elbow would jab Martha in her little ribs.

Each school-day morning for the two months she was there, Grandmother stood both the girls up together and took their photos before they left for school.

"Just in case," she said, her old voice dry like a stack of yellowed newspapers and flat with southern Missouri. "Just in case you get kidnapped. We'll remember exactly what you looked like."

The first day Martha burst into tears, thinking it meant they wouldn't pay the ransom to get her back.

Dolly laughed, trying not to, in that way grown-ups did when they didn't take you seriously. She explained, "No, no. It's just so we can tell the police what you were wearing. It's ridiculous, really. Humor your grandmother, darling, she's from a tiny town."

Martha obediently stopped crying, but she wasn't convinced. She knew they couldn't afford to pay a ransom. She didn't even have any new clothes for school, only Audrey's hand-me-downs. She accepted and continued to accept for the next two months that her mother and grandmother just wanted one last photo of their absent and forsaken girls.

Her mother still had those pictures. Two months, Monday through Friday, two sisters side by side. Audrey looking sweet, then bored, and finally annoyed. Martha always looking a little alarmed. It was interesting to see the passage of time from long ago in such small increments. She could watch the progress of the scrapes on her knees and the growth of her hair until one day suddenly it was all cut off. It had been summer when they started and it was winter when they stopped. Her grandmother was never sure if the cold weather photos should be with coats on or off, so some days it was one, some days the other.

Martha saw a short Mexican man walking along the shoulder of the road carrying a green plastic jug. That's him, she thought and was relieved.

"Hurry," she said to him out loud. "Hurry."

In the rearview mirror, she saw the lights from a car behind her brighten the man's legs and the green plastic jug. Just like Dr. Hamilton's only not new, old and dirty. Was it gasoline in there? Was it gasoline at the hotel? If Dr. Hamilton was having car trouble, why was the jug in the hotel room? Why did it have two brand-new clean white towels folded next to it on the floor?

She watched the man in her rearview mirror as long as she could. She had to believe he would reach the children in time, the car would be running again, they would soon be home with the mother yelling at him and bustling about getting their children milk and snacks and putting them to bed. Later, after the kids were asleep, she would give her husband a beer and punch him softly with her plump brown fist and then they would laugh a little together in relief and gladness that they were all home safe.

What an odd evening it had been, she thought. She yearned toward her little house, her wooden floor, her soft creamy bed. She felt her eyes puddle up with tears. She was tired. Perhaps tomorrow morning, sitting in her customary booth at Winchell's, she would put aside the blind and think about beauty. She would like to be better prepared.

It had been about the time that her grandmother had left that things had started going weird at home. Grandmother needed to get on with her life, she said, and no one protested much when she made her plane reservations.

"All alone. All alone," Grandmother said at the airport. "Well."

It was a special Pruitt "well"—large and square.

"Well," Grandmother said again, "I never expected much more."

She kissed them each, gave Audrey an extra pat, and exited. The next time Martha saw her, she was dying of cancer.

Two days later, Audrey and Martha missed the bus to school. Dolly had to drive them, but she didn't seem to mind. Suddenly, in the middle of the Capital Beltway, she made an abrupt U-turn over the median. Martha was young enough to trust her mother whatever she did, but the morning rush-hour traffic and the deep green gully of the median strip scared her.

"We're not going to make it!" Audrey screamed like the stagecoach driver in an old western movie.

But they did, the sea green Ford station wagon galumped through the long grass and tired landscaping and spun its tires on the dirt on the other side.

"Where are we going?" Audrey asked. Martha was too startled to say anything.

"Home," her mother said.

"You could've just gotten off at the next exit." In the face of insanity, Audrey was always pragmatic.

"Home to Missouri," her mother replied. "I never should have left."

They never made it all the way to Missouri. Somewhere just past the sign welcoming them to Ohio their mother pulled over on the shoulder and began to cry. She cried for an hour straight. Martha remembered clearly the field outside her window, stretching on and on, its harvested plants gone for another year, leaving only the dried stems. The field was the sandy brown that made her think of cowboys and the West. She remembered the way the car shuddered gently when a truck passed them going sixty and the way the darkening light turned her mother's hair from blonde to gray.

And then her mother stopped crying and started up the car. They got off at the next rest stop. Martha was so glad to see the big square sign announcing Howard Johnson's Restaurant. The garish orange and turquoise adornments; the glass of HoJo Cola; the smell of fried food and cigarette smoke was comforting and normal. She and Audrey were ravenous and they ordered cheeseburgers and French fries and onion rings and milk shakes and ate it all taking enormous bites and giggling at each other. Dolly crossed her legs out the side of the booth, smoked cigarettes and drank black coffee and looked so beautiful and fatal, her blue eyes liquid from all that crying, that the truckers all slowed down as they passed the table.

When they were back in the car they got on the turnpike toward home. They never said a word about it, to each other or anyone.

Martha turned on her radio. A pop song with a singer of indiscernible gender wafted from the small, tinny speakers. She passed the green sign labeling the freeway "The Christopher Columbus Transcontinental Expressway." She had never heard anyone call it that. She wasn't aware that it crossed the continent; she had supposed it ended somewhere in the suburbs. This freeway had cement barricades separating east- and westbound traffic. Martha could never cross those barriers; to turn around she would have to use an exit and not all the exits were easy on, easy off.

Where would she go anyway? Allen and Jewel were here. Her mother had retired to Florida. Audrey lived in Salt Lake City. Only her father was left in Washington, D.C., and he had his own life. So did she.

Her house was dark when she pulled up. She wished she had remembered to leave a light on.

The palm tree in the front yard rattled and knocked like bones on a cannibal's necklace. She fit her key in the lock and pushed the door open. She was happy to be home.

She closed the door behind her and locked it and suddenly, to her own distant wonder, sank, folding to the floor. She was exhausted and it didn't matter. She hugged her knees in the dark room and breathed deeply the smell of refuge; the lentil soup she'd had for dinner, the lemon oil she used on the hardwood, and the creaking odor of the house itself.

Across the room, she noticed the answering machine blinking.

She tensed in terror. She couldn't breathe. Something had happened to Jewel and Allen hadn't been able to find her. She knew it was bad news. She had always been a little psychic that way and now she knew.

She forced herself to get up and walk to the answering machine and push the button. It was a short message, it rewound very quickly.

"Thank you," Dr. Hamilton's precise voice said. "See you tomorrow night."

Martha felt the tears begin again. She had to go to bed. She hurried to her bedroom, her bed, her nightgown, and the graced escape of sleep.

6

SHE SLEPT SO HARD THAT WHEN SHE WOKE UP
HER FACE FELT BRUISED. THE STAB OF
bleached sunlight through her bedroom window made her wince. she
pushed herself out of bed. She couldn't find her slippers. Her bathrobe
was tangled on its hook. In the bathroom mirror her features looked
uneven, swollen to distortion. She had overslept. She couldn't eat. The
bloodless sun was already too bright in her kitchen. She decided not to
go to Winchell's. She didn't often break her routine, but today she
would. She would go to the club and pick up her last paycheck. She
could call, but she didn't know if the accountant, herself an ex-topless
waitress, would remember her or even after speaking to her remember
to put the check in the mail.

She dressed cautiously, hating everything that had to touch her skin.
Even her oldest T-shirt, washed until it was barely cloth, with holes in
the hem and under one arm, irritated her neck and her back between
her shoulder blades. It was as if sometime during the night her entire
body had been scoured with fine-grade sandpaper. Rubbed up and
down, each nerve was brought two layers closer to the surface. She
pulled her long hair up into an knitting ball knot, just to get it off her
neck. She found a forgotten gauzelike skirt that hung loose around her

waist. It slid to her hips and reminded her of the blue sweatpants of the night before—and the night to come.

It was already ninety degrees. Her car offered her a little belch of baked air when she opened the door. The hot vinyl seat seared her legs even through her skirt. She leaned forward, pulling herself tight to the steering wheel, not wanting to rest her back against the seat. It made it peculiar to drive, but then everything felt odd this morning.

The sweat began on her temples and upper lip. She should have bought a car with air-conditioning, but usually she didn't feel the heat. She stopped at the stop sign at the bottom of her hill.

A young girl, a teenager, stood on the corner with her boyfriend. She had long dark hair, smooth like a gush of oil down her back, and pure skin. She wore jeans and a tight ribbed tank top. She looked cool and knowledgeable. He was cute and skinny, his chest and belly scooped out like a melon slice, curved toward his girl, ripe and inviting. She laughed up at him, then buried her head in his open flannel shirt.

Martha ached. What had happened to her? Why had she never been like this girl? Not once, not with Allen. Never. And now it was too late.

She watched them cross in front of her, the girl pulling the boy by the front of his jeans. Martha could see the white and red waistband of his underwear clean against his adolescent skin. On the opposite corner they stopped, noticing her. They frowned at her. Martha couldn't look away. Suddenly, with a smile, the girl lifted her little shirt and flashed Martha a glimpse of her sweet plump breasts. Then she stuck her tongue out like a five-year-old, turned and skipped away. The boy jogged after her, delighting in her. Martha felt herself widen and grow years older.

At the Sweet Spot, she tried to pull into the parking lot, but an enormous red and white Coca-Cola truck was blocking the driveway. Martha started to back out, then changed her mind and bravely honked her horn. She honked again before realizing the truck was parked, the delivery person probably inside. She was breathing rapidly. She had been ready for a fight, or at least a rude comment. She backed out onto

the street and parked at a meter, knowing she had not a single quarter.
She knew she'd get a ticket on a day like today, and on a day like today k
she didn't care.   i

She opened the back door to the club and was grateful for the air-   n
conditioning, the dark, even the stale smells of makeup, men, and
liquor. She stood still for a minute, letting her eyes get accustomed to d
the false night, enjoying being there. She had liked her job. She had not e
made any friends, but she had not felt alone either.   e

She had to pass the Coke machine on her way to the office. The   p
waitresses had complained that the bar Cokes were expensive, with too
much water and not enough syrup, so the owner, Mr. Sugar, had put in
a machine near the dressing room.   5

The delivery guy was there stacking the cans of Coke and Diet Coke   1
with an accomplished rhythm. He knelt on the rug in front of her with
his back to her, the blue-and-white striped uniform shirt stretched
across his straight back and tucked in tight to the navy blue pants. His
arms were muscular and smooth, the lightest brown of Central America.
His hair was thick and black and stood up short like the bristles on her
father's oval hairbrush. His head bowed over his work and Martha saw
the beginnings of a tattoo on the back of his neck that ended somewhere beneath his collar.

She took a breath. She never complained, she never said anything to
anyone, but first she had honked and now she spoke.

"Your truck is blocking the driveway," Martha said. Although she
meant to be strong, her voice was soft and difficult to hear over the
clanking cadence of the soda cans. "I said," she began again, louder.

"I heard you." The delivery guy stopped and looked up at her.

Martha swallowed. He was beautiful. It stopped her hard like a slap,
an affront of pleasure.

"I don't have a quarter," she said softly.

It was what she had wanted to say, but now she didn't know what it
meant.

"That's okay. Here." He handed her a Coke. "So . . . you work here?"

His eyes were green, the green of summer fields and new peas; his lashes were thick and black like a ring of secret forest.

He smiled at her. The corners of his mouth lifted, revealing straight teeth so white they were a field of snow against his desert-colored skin.

"I haven't seen you here before," he said. "I would've remembered."

He was speaking to her. She shook her head and a strand of her long red hair fell from her messy bun and across her bare arm. The skin that had been so painfully sensitive at home was now quivering, straining toward this man. The feel of her own soft curl against her upper arm made her shiver.

"You don't work here?" He had a deep hollow at the base of his neck between his collarbones, just the size of her thumb.

She had to say something. "Your truck," she managed, resorting to the lines she had rehearsed. "I had to park on the street."

He stopped smiling and turned away from her, back to the dependability of his red and silver cans. "I'll be done in a shake," he said.

Martha sighed. He took that wrong too.

"I'll move it in a minute." He sounded annoyed, put out, worse— disappointed.

"I'm sorry," Martha said. "It doesn't matter. I'm just here to pick up my last paycheck. I used to work here, but I don't anymore. My husband, he's my ex-husband really, but anyway, he doesn't like it."

He turned back to her, narrowed his cool, springtime eyes to look her up and down. "I wouldn't like it either," he said.

She handed him back the can of Coke.

"Diet?" he asked.

"I don't drink soda," she said apologetically.

"Me neither," he said and laughed. Martha laughed too.

"I worked at night," she said. "That's why you never saw me."

"What do you like to drink?" he asked.

"Apple juice," she said, then winced. What a stupid thing to say. It should've been champagne, sloe gin, an adult beverage at least.

"I know the place with the best apple juice in the whole world. I'm not kidding. I do. It has . . . phenomenal apple juice. I mean it."

"That's nice," she said.

"That's nice." He laughed again. "It's not nice. It's fantastic. I'll take you there."

"Oh . . . oh, oh, well . . . oh." The ohs jumped out of her mouth and danced in a circle around her head. She wasn't doing very well. If he just wouldn't look at her.

"What do you think?" His hand brushed back and forth through his hair. She noticed another tattoo on one of his fingers. She wished she could look closer. She thought of really seeing the tattoo on the back of his neck. The sweat began again on her temples, between her breasts.

"You wanna go with me or not?"

"Oh, oh." She clapped her hand over her mouth, cleared her throat, her head. "I mean, my paycheck."

"You get your check, I'll finish my load, then we'll go—you can ride in my truck."

"Well, okay. Okay, I will." She smiled.

He grinned. He seemed truly pleased. She started to step past him, and he put his hand out and touched the back of her arm, just above the elbow.

"See you in a minute," he said.

"Okay. Okay."

The spot on her arm was scorched. She retreated gratefully down the hall and into the office.

In the office, the accountant, Belle, didn't remember her. "When did you work here?" she asked, looking at Martha over her half glasses. Belle had been a waitress at the club a long time ago. She didn't like the younger girls; Martha saw the way Belle's false eyelashes fluttered over her, took in the hole in her T-shirt and the old skirt. Belle's mouth, upper lip shaped like two tall bright-red mountains, flattened into a plateau.

She shouldn't do that, Martha thought; the lines that show up around her mouth make her look old.

"I don't know if I have a time card for you." It was obvious that Belle didn't want to have her time card.

"It was just a week ago, I mean . . . I just quit."

Belle nodded and began sifting through the employment records on her desk.

Martha looked at the photos taped to the dingy shrimp pink wall. They were pictures of children: a fat baby girl in a blow up swimming pool wearing a green bathing suit over her soggy diaper; a little boy in his store-bought superhero Halloween costume.

"Your kids?" Martha asked.

Belle looked at the photos. She frowned as if the pictures shouldn't have been there, as if they'd given her away. "They're my sister's. I have a career, she has kids."

Martha couldn't say anything else. She stood there, shifting from foot to foot, listening to the noises from the Coke machine in the hall. She fingered the hole in her T-shirt and wished she'd worn something prettier. It made her wonder why he wanted to take her for apple juice in the first place. She wasn't having a good day, her hair was frizzy, her face was puffy. She knew men had this idea about topless waitresses, that because they were uninhibited about their breasts they were easy to sleep with. It was not the case. Not at all.

Well, Martha thought, he can buy me apple juice and I can ask him about his tattoos.

"You ready?" His voice from the doorway warmed the back of her neck. She turned to him, then back at once to Belle. "Almost." She looked at Belle. "I'm just waiting . . ."

Belle pushed her lips together, creating an earthquake for her mountains, making the fault lines around her mouth even deeper. She looked past Martha at the Coca-Cola guy standing large in the doorway. She looked back at Martha and then at him again as if they were a conspiracy of some kind, plotting the takeover of the Sweet Spot Topless Club.

Belle used a tiny gold key to open her center desk drawer. She took out Martha's check, already in an envelope with Martha's name on the front. She handed it to Martha.

"Good-bye," she said.

"Thank you," Martha replied.

As they pulled out of the parking lot in his truck, Martha looked down at her tiny blue car. A pink ticket fluttered on the windshield and she laughed. He laughed with her, not knowing why. Martha smiled at him, thanking him for helping her with this terrible day.

7

SHE LIKED SITTING IN HIS COCA-COLA TRUCK.
SHE LIKED BEING UP HIGH. THE WARM DARK-
blue vinyl seats were smooth without decorative lines or piping. The
cab smelled of him; a light blend of citrus aftershave and musky deodorant. It was tidy and a silver crucifix on a black leather thong hung
from the mirror. He saw her looking at it.

"Are you Catholic?" he asked.

"No," she said. "Are you?"

"Yes."

He said no more. Martha loved religion even though she didn't have
one of her own. She had always been drawn to the extremes of spiritual-
ity. High mass in Latin with incense and incantations; Orthodox Jews
in prayer shawls and curly long sideburns and wives who kept their
hair hidden. As a child she had gotten up extra early to watch *Mass for
Shut-Ins* on TV. The organ music over the credits could make her cry.
And, when she was sixteen, she had followed with great interest the
man who somersaulted the entire route of Paul Revere's ride through
Boston in homage to the Maharishi.

She touched his crucifix. "I had one," she said, "when I was little. I
kept it under my pillow to chase away vampires."

"I guess it worked." He smiled at her.

"So far," she said. "But I don't have it anymore."

"You can use mine."

"Thanks."

She watched him drive out of the corner of her eye. She watched the muscles in his thigh flex when he stepped on the brake. She tried to read the tattoo on his finger when he flipped up the turn signal.

"My name is Reuben Rodriguez."

"Martha," she replied. "Martha Ward."

"Hi, Martha."

"Hi."

He made a left turn and Martha let herself lean toward him. She was suddenly reminded of riding in her mother's station wagon, the back-seat wide and boiled potato beige, the sticky vinyl of her adolescence leaving its impression on her freckled summer legs. She had leaned toward a man in the backseat in just this way. Who was he? Why was he in the back with her? Where had they been going? Her mother had been driving. Audrey riding up front.

Then she remembered. It was Lars. He was on a date with her mother. At that time, they thought it was just another date. No one knew—except maybe Martha's mother, who knew everything before it happened—no one else knew that he would become the next phase in their lives.

Martha was eleven and wearing her first pair of panty hose. She was practicing at being sophisticated, crossing and uncrossing her legs until Audrey turned around and told her to cut it out, she was being ridiculous. It was Lars who smiled at her and told her something new.

"You've blossomed," he said.

"What?" Martha wasn't even sure he was talking to her.

"In the short time I've known you, Martha, you have really blossomed."

Martha filled with warm, syrupy pleasure. He had sandy blonde hair and tiny bright-blue eyes. He was big and Nordic, at that time a harm-less polar bear of a man. It was the first time an adult had complimented her appearance in a grown-up sort of way, not the usual "isn't she pretty," from aunts and grandparents. Her father didn't find her attrac-tive and her mother never noticed. This man had paid attention. Martha smiled at him and on the next right turn leaned toward him, not even aware that she was flirting.

"Here we are," said Reuben.

He pulled into a parking lot at the Hollywood Holiday Spa. It was a massive structure, a bench press of a building, painted irreconcilably pink.

"Where?" she said. "Where are we?"

"This is my club," he said. "They have the best juice bar in the whole United States. Probably the whole world."

"Have you been to many juice bars?"

Reuben laughed. "To tell the truth, which I absolutely always do, I've never been out of California. But I've been to every health club in L.A. and this is the best."

Martha felt her throat tighten. She tried to swallow and couldn't. She and this exceptionally handsome man, who obviously worked out a lot, were going into the premier Hollywood health club. She knew what was inside: scantily clad starlets with perfect butts and matching socks and wristbands; even their sweat smelled good. She was overdressed, overnourished, underpumped.

"You must work out," Reuben was saying. "Don't you?"

"I take aerobics twice a week," Martha said. "At the Y."

"Oh."

It wasn't enough; Martha pretended not to notice as Reuben gave her the once-over, eyeing her stomach, her arms, her thighs hidden in the loose gauze skirt.

Reuben pulled his truck into a parking spot right in front. A sign at the end said, "Reserved."

"It's okay," Reuben said before she asked. "They know me."

He sprang from his truck, a young man's move that made Martha think of oiled thighs and the gluteus maximus, and came around the front to help her down. Martha fumbled for a moment with her skirt, gathered it around her, and slid to the black asphalt.

"Good job," he said. "It's not made for skirts."

Then Martha caught the toe of her sandal on the curb of the parking lot and stumbled. She wasn't really a klutz, but when she got nervous she stiffened and her arms and legs didn't work as well.

"You okay?"

"Fine. Thanks. Sorry."

He held open one of the big glass doors. Even from outside she could smell that peppery health club air: a mixture of air-conditioning, air freshener, industrial cleaners, deodorant, and sweat. She could hear the slamming beat of the canned pseudomusic.

She tried to smile at him as she went in.

Inside it was worse than she had imagined; there were intersecting lines of turquoise and lavender neon and rosy industrial carpeting. The music was loud, pervasive, and everywhere there were beautiful bodies. It was hard to notice anyone's face. And they all seemed to know Reuben.

"Hey, Reuben."

"Hi, Reuben."

"Reuben, how ya doin'?"

He smiled and answered everyone by name. Even in his delivery uniform, he fit right in.

The juice bar was in the very center of the club. You could sit and watch people working out all around you. The row of Stairmasters were along one side; the stationary bikes along another. You could see into the aerobics room. Martha figured it was designed that way to keep you from eating very much. She looked around and was sorry for every doughnut she'd ever eaten, every time she'd skipped aerobics, every night she'd sat on her blue couch and finished off a bag of popcorn watching cable TV.

Reuben steered her to two stools at the corner. The counter guy, a dark-skinned African American, wore a pink sleeveless muscle shirt. His biceps were the reason people called them muscle shirts. He smiled at Reuben.

"Reuben, Reuben." His white teeth were like piano keys in his ebony face. "Just the man I wanted to see."

His voice had a lilting cadence from Jamaica or the Bahamas. He put his two hands on the counter. His shoulders were shiny, oiled. Martha wondered what moisturizer he used. But his hands were dry. She could see the pattern of the skin on the back; fine, tiny diamonds of wrinkles. It made her think of the rhinoceros at the zoo, only in miniature.

"I brought Martha here for some apple juice. I promised her the best apple juice in the world."

"How you doin', Martha?"

"Fine, thank you."

"Martha, this is Quakoo. Quakoo, this is Martha."

They shook and Quakoo's palms felt as dry as they looked, soft and baby powdered.

"You came to the right place for apple juice," he said. "Make it myself, while you wait."

They watched Quakoo open the dormitory-sized refrigerator and take out a bag of apples.

"Organic," he said, without looking back at them.

"Of course," said Reuben.

"How'd that audition go?"

"Ahh, shitty. I'm too ethnic."

"Guess I won't bother calling." Quakoo laughed.

"You're an actor?" Martha asked.

"This is a million-dollar face." Reuben didn't have to convince her. "Or it will be, when I find a producer smart enough to figure that out. Quakoo too."

"What about you, Martha?" Quakoo smiled at her.

"Oh, no. No, no, no."

"Writer?" Quakoo asked. "Director? Producer?"

"I'm not in film, movies, you know. I like to watch them."

"Smart girl." Reuben nodded at her. "It's a terrible business."

Martha watched Reuben and Quakoo laugh together. She could tell they didn't really think it was awful. She'd been in L.A. long enough and met enough wishful actors to know that they all believed in their own special futures. She had envied it at times, the confidence and optimism, the desire.

And, looking at beautiful Reuben next to her, she thought he was probably right; that big Hollywood opportunity really would come along for someone so appealing. He even had nice ears. Ears were important. Lars had terrible ears, ears without lobes; they just grew into his neck like fins.

She remembered the first time she'd had someone's tongue in her ear. Her sister, Audrey, heard about it from a girlfriend and wanted to try it out before making a fool of herself with some guy. She pushed Martha face down on the rough brown carpet in the den, straddled her back and poked her tongue in Martha's left ear.

"How does it feel?"

"Gross!" Martha screamed. "Get off of me!"

Audrey got up, disappointed. "You're too young," she said.

Martha actually thought it was sort of disgusting and wonderful at the same time, but she said nothing.

"I know," said Audrey. "You do it to me."

"Are you nuts?"

"Come on, come on, you've got to."

"Yuk! Why?"

"You have to, that's all. I have to know. I'm dying to know. Do it. Or I'll tell Mom what you said."

"What?"

"You know, about her hair."

Their mom had just dyed her hair bright yellow blonde for her Nordic boyfriend with fins for ears. The dye had made her soft hair dry and scratchy. Martha had told Audrey their mother's head looked like a hayride.

"Okay," said Martha. "Okay." She closed her eyes and tentatively licked Audrey's ear, once, quickly.

"Keep it in there," Audrey commanded. "Move it around."

Martha did as she was told.

"Gives me shivers," Audrey said, pleased. "It's a definite shiver giver. Can't wait to try it on someone who counts."

Martha had looked forward to some boy doing it to her, but only one guy ever had and there had been other problems with him. Allen had loved it when she'd done it to him. Were they called "wet willies"? She'd never stuck her tongue in his ear again after Jewel was born; she couldn't seem to get interested in putting her tongue into anything. It was all just a waste of time.

The juicer gnashed and bit at the apples, then growled as it ground them up. Quakoo stretched his dark body to the music. His skin changed color as it moved under the juice bar lights, first purple, then blue, then a flat dark gunmetal gray. It was dangerous skin.

A stunning woman, younger than Martha, long blonde hair, with a bare midriff and breasts like twin nose cones on the space shuttle walked up to the counter on the other side of Reuben.

She looked familiar to Martha; an actress probably.

"Hi, Reuben."

The health club goddess had a surprisingly low, deep voice. Maybe because her neck was so long.

"Hey, Jennifer."

Jennifer did the hair toss: her head went down over one shoulder and then snapped back making her hair fall in a cascade of blonde streaks down her back. Martha had never been able to do the hair toss.

"Where've you been? I've missed you," she said.

"I've been around." Reuben sounded uncomfortable. "Uh . . . Jennifer, this is Martha."

Jennifer leaned over the counter past Reuben and smiled sweetly at Martha. Her breasts were squished against the Formica, deepening her chasm of cleavage.

Martha nodded hello. It was obvious she wasn't enough of a threat to Jennifer to even require a dirty look. Why did women like Jennifer, five years younger, childless, never married, make her feel ten years old? They had years of knowledge she would never have.

Then Martha recognized her. Jennifer was one of the models in the Victoria's Secret catalog. Martha sighed.

"I tried that new thing you showed me," Jennifer was saying to Reuben. "With the weights, remember?"

"Sure."

"I really felt it. I did. Just like you said. Right here." She lifted one sculpted arm and touched her bare side with a long glazed fingernail. Reuben wasn't looking.

Martha suddenly realized that Jennifer was old news to Reuben. He didn't want to talk to her. He didn't care how she looked.

"That's great, Jen—I'm glad it worked."

There was a pause. Jennifer nodded. "Yeah. Well. Thanks." She started to walk away, then turned back and tapped Martha's forearm. "Nice meeting you."

She dissolved back into the club and Quakoo turned from the juicer and laughed.

"Very scary," he said. "Very scary, boys and girls."

"Isn't she in the Victoria's Secret catalog?" Martha asked, willing her voice to sound conversational and nothing more.

"Yeah," said Reuben.

"She's loony tunes," said Quakoo. "She is here twenty-four hours a day. If the club is open, she is here."

Reuben nodded. "I like to work out too, but sometimes there's more to life."

Quakoo lowered his voice. "I hear she never stops exercising. I mean never."

"You're right, man. You think she's enjoying herself, know what I mean? Then, come to find out, you're just a new way of working on those abdominals."

Quakoo and Reuben laughed, then Reuben looked over at Martha, sitting quietly on her stool. "Oh," he said, "I'm sorry."

"That's okay."

"It was nothing, really."

"Sounds that way."

Reuben and Quakoo laughed again.

"I'm glad you came," Reuben said to Martha.

"Why?" It was an honest question, Martha meant it honestly.

But Reuben laughed. "You crack me up."

He drummed on the edge of the counter in rhythm to the music. Martha tried to see his tattoo. Finally she took his right hand and pushed it flat. She read the gracefully looped blue writing around his ring finger.

"*Por Vida*," she read.

"For Life," said Reuben. "Only it didn't work out that way."

Quakoo put two tall soda glasses filled with a dark mahogany liquid in front of them. The top was frothy. Martha had never seen apple juice like it.

"No straws," Quakoo said. "Bad for the environment."

"Waste of plastic," Reuben agreed.

"And paper," Quakoo said.

Martha put her hand on the old-fashioned glass, out of context in this place. She stroked the ridges tapering to the round base. She wanted to like this apple juice. She wanted to think it was the best juice she'd ever tasted. She wanted to turn to Reuben and smile enthusiasti-

cally, giggle flirtatiously, all those things that other women did. She
wanted to make Reuben and his friend happy. She always wanted to
make people happy. Maybe that was why she avoided most people.
Usually you had no choice, usually you couldn't do a thing for anyone.

She took a sip. The juice was not cold. It was lukewarm, body tem-
perature. She rolled it around in her mouth. It tasted not like one
apple's nectar, but like an entire orchard; the dirt, the sun, the wind,
even the bad apples rotting at her feet.

"Wow," she said.

Reuben grinned. "What I tell you? Now you know, Reuben Rodriguez always tells the truth."

Martha giggled and flushed happily at her giggle. She was here and
it was okay. He was handsome and he was glad she was with him. He
touched his glass to hers.

"You're going to be a famous actor," Martha said. She couldn't look
away from his eyes. "I can tell."

Later, when she got home, she sat right down at her little wooden desk
to pay the parking ticket. She always paid her bills right away. This
ticket was worth it, she thought, I love this ticket. She looked forward
with relaxed anticipation to her job that night with Dr. Hamilton. She
could talk to him. She had time. She would be prepared.

8

DRIVING TO MALIBU SHE REHEARSED SOME IDEAS ABOUT BEAUTY. IT HAD BEEN AN EASY ASSIGN ment this afternoon, researching beauty. She'd already been thinking of it incessantly, all afternoon, all evening, thinking of Reuben.

She wasn't sure she liked him, but she liked looking at him. It was like being at the movies; he had the same unnatural and yet seductive perfection. Talking to him she had the identical feeling of surrender to the manufactured magic. Reuben couldn't be real. Sitting across from him at the juice bar she had waited for the curtain to close and the show to be over.

At the Belle Noche, the same desk clerk, in the same vest, remembered her and gave her the key without asking. Martha was pleased.

In the room she found the brown paper bag on the bed as before. She took it into the bathroom and opened it. Inside was her blue costume and a new typed note, "I have included a belt to correct the pants problem. A. Hamilton."

The clothes were freshly laundered and Martha felt a twisting of guilt. Tonight she would take them home and wash them herself. She wondered if he had done this laundry, or if it had been his wife, his maid, his nurse.

The belt was stretchy red and blue striped elastic with the sort of plastic clasp found on a backpack. It was a child's belt but made for an adult, adjustable, one size fits all.

It held the enormous waistband firmly in place. Martha felt more secure. She felt a calm gratefulness, a maternal appreciation of Dr. Hamilton. She came out of the bathroom, noticed without concern the green plastic jug and the two white towels neatly placed underneath the table. She composed herself in the sand-colored chair and waited, looking forward to his knock.

But when Dr. Hamilton came in, he was agitated. He almost slammed the door but caught it at the last moment and let it thud shut. She could see he wasn't about to sit across from her and listen to her practiced thoughts.

"I have had a difficult day," he said. His mouth barely opened; only his lip curled back over clenched teeth. He still wore his suit jacket and his tie, tightly harnessing his neck.

"Difficult is hardly the word," he continued, "but that's what they say, isn't it? A difficult day, a hard day. 'Poor Dad, he's had a bad day.' What does that mean? That I found it impossible to take each step, to move one foot after the other, to open my mouth, to speak, to eat, to be part of the living world? Or simply that I spilled coffee on my favorite tie, they were out of the grilled chicken for lunch, traffic was bad, and I was late getting home. It's ridiculous, really, the limits of the human language. It is an absurdity that any of us believe we can communicate with one another. Not man to woman or parent to child, but any of us."

Martha tried to look sympathetic, understanding, then remembered he couldn't see her.

He fished in his pants pocket for something. She heard the jingle of change and keys before he found it and took it out. It was a lighter, a cheap plastic cylinder, the color of an ugly marigold. The wick made a long dark stain inside. He tossed it from hand to hand, twisted it around in his fingers. She hadn't thought he was a smoker. She looked for the cigarettes in his pocket, the yellow fingers; she knew his teeth were even and white.

Suddenly, he threw it, hard, against the wall.

Martha jumped.

"I'll go," she said, "I'll go."

"Why are you always leaving?"

"I don't know what you want."

"Why did you come back?"

"Didn't you think I would?"

"I didn't expect you."

"You bought me a belt," she said and paused. "Thank you."

There was another pause. A longer moment of working silence. She could hear his effort.

"Ms. Ward," he began. His voice was quiet, a measured control. "Sit down. Please."

Martha sat. "Do you want to tell me about your day?"

"Oh God, no. Tell me about yours."

Martha thought of her crabby morning, about her paycheck, meeting Reuben and drinking apple juice.

Instead she said, "I've been thinking about beauty." She took a deep breath and recited,

"'Beauty is truth, truth beauty—that is all
Ye know on earth and all ye need to know.' "

Dr. Hamilton folded heavily into the chair opposite her. "Ah, Keats, 'Ode on a Grecian Urn.' And did you find 'A thing of beauty is a joy forever'?"

"Yes. That's pretty, isn't it?"

"Why? Tastes change. People change. Even what is true can change. Keats is making an enormous assumption, don't you think?"

"Well . . . I don't know."

"You've been studying," he said. "Please don't. I've read the books, looked it up in my *Bartlett's Quotations* too."

"But they say it so much better than I can."

"I don't believe that. Besides, that's not why I want you here. I need the experience of someone who's lived in this world, a woman who knows what it is like now, right now. Not a man who thinks of beauty romantically or even philosophically, but a woman who lives with or without her own personal beauty every day."

Martha felt a tightening of inadequacy. He knew what she looked like. He had chosen her because she wasn't beautiful. She thought of Reuben sitting next to her, his oblique look at Jennifer fresh from the pages of Victoria's Secret. She shook her head to erase herself from the scene.

"Why are you shaking your head?" Dr. Hamilton asked.

She paused. She couldn't forget following Reuben through the health club, the way people leaned toward him. She spoke quietly, "You know? Beautiful people have friends. It's true. People like them."

"Just because of the way they look?" Dr. Hamilton sat forward on his chair, rested his long arms on his longer thighs.

"It starts that way. People give them things, do things for them because they're attractive. They get what they want. They do what they want. They're not afraid to go, to try, to be seen. It allows them protection."

"Protection?"

"From loneliness. From rejection. To be ugly is to be lonely, to hide, knowing the response from others is reserved."

"Deserved. You mean, deserved."

"No. Reserved. You have to get to know a person who's not attractive, learn to appreciate their personality. You know, you've probably had dates with the fat cousin with the wonderful personality. How many dates does it take, are you willing to have, to discover her special quality? You reserve your opinion until you see if there is something else that makes an unattractive person appealing. For a beautiful person, their appearance is almost always enough."

"You sound angry."

Martha was embarrassed. She was afraid of seeming defensive.

He continued, "It seems so important. It is so important. I have no idea if you are beautiful or not. I don't know if you are plump or thin, blue eyed or brown, the condition of your teeth, skin, hair. And yet I respond to you as if you were attractive. If you weren't, I wonder if your opinion would be as valid, as interesting." He paused. "Are you lonely?"

"You're trying to find out how I look. I won't give it away." But Martha thought about it. She didn't think she was lonely. But she was alone most of the time.

"Tell me one thing." Dr. Hamilton sounded like a six-year-old boy the day before Christmas.

"Why?"

"I want to know."

"Why? Why should I tell you? If you want to know—I can simply take off this suit, these clothes I'm wearing. I can show you."

"No! No! Please. Don't do that!"

Dr. Hamilton stood and backed away from her. Martha was silent, surprised at his sudden passion. He stood behind his chair. Martha noticed that the cigarette lighter had broken. It was leaving a dark kerosene blotch on the perfect carpet.

"The lighter," she said. "It's going to stain the carpet."

"What? Oh." He stooped and picked up the lighter. He threw it into the plastic trash can, then stood there smelling his fingers.

"Are you lonely?" Martha asked.

"No," he said, then added, "Yes. I have too many people in my life. Sometimes that's worse."

"No one you can talk to about this."

"No. No one."

"So. See? Even attractive people can be lonely."

He looked at her. Martha wasn't flirting with him. She sat completely still so he would know that. She wanted him to sit down again. He made her nervous standing there with his hands on his face.

She nodded, "You're right. I practiced. I did some reading. It's an interesting topic, beauty."

"Yes." He stood where he was.

"I liked what Bertrand Russell said—"

"You did do some research."

"I have a philosophy book. I kept it from college."

"And he said?"

"He said—he thought that when we see a beautiful person we are naturally reminded of God. Or the Gods. Whatever it was. And therefore he thought beauty was a good thing, because it led people to loftier thoughts." She paused, but Dr. Hamilton was silent. "Am I right?"

"I think that's basically what he said. Do you think he's right?"

"I don't know much about God, but I know—" She thought of Reuben. "I know that looking at something beautiful makes me happy. I feel lucky. I feel that there are good things in the world."

"Does it follow then that ugliness makes us think of—the devil, despair, what's terrible about the world?"

"I guess so. Sure. I drove through downtown the other day, way downtown near the jewelry stores. I was coming home from the dentist. I saw a man going to the bathroom in a phone booth. He wasn't just peeing. Four o'clock in the afternoon."

"But. Yes, that's ugly. But what about personally? There will always be ugly things in the world. Baby mice eaten by snakes. Crazy men doing disgusting things. But for you—personally—what does it mean?"

Martha paused. She knew about ugly. She knew what it felt like to be ugly. "I'm not . . ." She took a deep breath, started again. "I look so different from the rest of my family. More like my father—who is not my older sister's father—but not exactly. I'm a combination. And in my mother's family I'm a different ethnic background. My grandmother searched through my hair looking for horns."

"How old were you?"

"Seven. She laughed about it. It was kind of a joke."

"That's terrible."

"I've never felt beautiful, but—" Martha didn't want to say more about herself.

"But?"

But she did. "I have gotten things because of the way I look." Martha surrendered. "And I have not been pretty enough for some things."

"Like what?" Dr. Hamilton smiled at her and finally sat down.

"There were boys I wanted to date." Dr. Hamilton nodded, unimpressed. "I wanted to be a cheerleader, but it rained and my hair frizzed." None of this was what he wanted to hear. "I . . ." Martha paused and sighed, then continued, safe in the anonymity of her dark blue skin, "I didn't make much money in tips—not as much as the other waitresses—at the club."

"What club?"

"I worked at the Sweet Spot."

Dr. Hamilton shrugged, so?

"The . . . it's a . . . topless club." Martha cringed inside her sack. She had never been embarrassed about her job before. She hadn't minded telling him over the phone. She had told her neighbor, an older Catholic woman with seven kids, without blushing. She couldn't even remember how her neighbor had reacted. But she watched the frown on Dr. Hamilton's face. The way his eyes looked up and down her shapeless blue form, focusing finally on her feet in the blue men's socks. "I'm sure I told you that when I spoke to you about the job. I thought that was why you hired me."

"I don't remember much about our conversation," he said without looking up. "You were the only applicant."

"Oh, brother." Martha couldn't help herself. She had thought there would be lots of women who wanted this job. Three hundred dollars a night just to talk to a man. Most women couldn't pay their boyfriends to say two words to them, much less have a discussion.

But Dr. Hamilton laughed. It was a chuckle really. He sounded truly pleased. "You're perfect," he said. "A topless club. Beauty in society, incarnate."

"I guess."

He chuckled again. "What else could I expect?" he said to himself. "What else?"

Martha was annoyed and insulted. "You try walking around without your shirt on in front of a bunch of strange men and try to sell them overpriced, watered-down drinks, keep their hands off you, and get tipped for it. It's not as easy as it sounds."

Dr. Hamilton only laughed some more. "That's a picture," he said. "Ms. Ward, thank you. You have made my day."

Martha fumed. She had told him a secret, something she had been reluctant to say, a truth that was difficult for her to admit, and he was ignoring her.

"I think it's a pretty strange request," she said, "to ask a woman to come here, alone. I don't think you have any right to laugh at me."

Dr. Hamilton sobered immediately. She continued, "If I'm not what you want, all you have to do is say so."

"Oh, no, please." Dr. Hamilton's face was used up when he stopped laughing. The wrinkles around his eyes and mouth appeared deeper, dug into his face. "I think you're the perfect person for this job. I wasn't laughing at you, only at myself. Can you see me as a topless waiter?"

Martha smiled inside her hood. She liked the way Dr. Hamilton looked; even well worn he was attractive, but she didn't think she'd want him prancing by without his shirt.

"Do you have any hair on your chest?" she asked.

"Hardly any," he replied.

"Oh, then, well—"

She paused and he interrupted, "Ms. Ward, you were telling me something personal. That you didn't make as much money as the other women, you thought because of your appearance."

He had been listening. Martha felt a warm pull toward him, a desire to protect his hairless chest.

"I have never been to one of those clubs," he said. "I don't have a moral objection to them—I appreciate their function—but in my line of work . . ." He stopped, obviously not wanting to make a revelation. "Anyway," he continued, "I don't think beauty has much to do with the tips. It's attitude, isn't it? Like any other service person. If they do their job well, if they have the snappy patter down, if they seem to like me, think I'm special, even though obviously I'm just another customer, then they get the tips."

Martha had never thought of that before. She felt better.

"How did it make you feel, working there?"

"I'm not a good waitress," she said. "I'd get the drink orders wrong. I spilled things. I got flustered with too many tables. That made me feel stupid. How hard can waitressing be?"

"You just told me how difficult it is. You challenged me to do it and I don't think I could. But what about being topless?"

Martha didn't want to tell him she was proud of her breasts. She didn't want him looking for them through the blue. "I didn't think about it," she said. "That's true. I didn't feel like they were my breasts. It was all just part of the uniform for work . . . just like this is." She indicated the bag of blue surrounding her.

Dr. Hamilton stared at Martha for a long moment.

"Too many clothes, or not enough. Are you saying neither of them is really you?"

"I have revealed more of myself here," Martha said, "than I ever did at the Sweet Spot. I can't speak for the other women, but I have places more secret than my own body."

Dr. Hamilton groaned. He leaned back in his chair and stretched his arms to the ceiling. He folded the long, muscular fingers of his hands together in the air and brought them down over his head, separating them and covering his eyes. He sat for the longest moment. Then he stood.

"Thank you," he said. "I'd like to leave with that thought."

"But it's only been—"

"That's all right." He put three hundred-dollar bills on the bureau next to the television.

"I wish," Martha began, then stopped.

"Yes?"

"I wish I could make your day better."

"Do you?"

"You seem so sad."

"I'll see you tomorrow. Tomorrow night."

"Okay."

"Is the belt all right?"

"Perfect."

Dr. Hamilton left, closing the door behind him.

Martha leaned after him, wanting him to stay.

Outside, in the hallway, Dr. Hamilton turned and placed both palms against the blonde door. He seemed to be listening for something from within.

Inside, Martha placed both gloved palms flat on the pale wood tabletop. She leaned forward and listened too but heard only the shrouded quiet of a well-carpeted motel room. She turned her face to the door.

In the hallway, Dr. Hamilton pushed the button for the elevator and stepped in and away.

9

THE NEXT MORNING, THURSDAY MORNING, MARTHA WALKED CALMLY UP THE HILL FROM Winchell's. At home, she washed her face and packed her aerobics clothes. She saw women who wore their exercise clothes all day, to the market, the library, the movies. But Martha didn't. She liked wearing the right clothes at the right times. She hated to think she might be inappropriate. She would sometimes see a woman in exercise leggings, usually a small child or two with her, and notice the way the bottom curve of her rear end wiggled, the flesh on the side of her thighs, the saddlebags, accentuated. The woman would always be wearing a big T-shirt, usually with some company name or sports product logo, "Just Do It," long and loose, but not enough to cover the round bump of postchildbirth stomach.

Martha loved women's bodies, but not at the grocery store. So Martha was careful to wear her exercise clothes only for exercising.

The phone rang. Martha ran to pick it up. Perhaps Dr. Hamilton was firing her. It was Reuben. His voice was bright, brighter than the gray summer haze outside, brighter than the green numbers on her digital alarm clock, brighter than anything.

"Hey," he said, "how are you?"

She was terrified by the crunch in her chest. "Fine, oh, fine. Just getting ready to go to aerobics."

"Oh. I'll let you go."

She had said the wrong thing again. "It's okay. I have time." Reuben didn't know she left too much time to do everything.

"I was wondering—how about a movie?"

"You and me?"

"What do you think?" She could hear him smiling.

"When?"

"Tomorrow night?"

"Sure." Then Martha remembered. "Oh. I can't. My daughter's coming."

Reuben gave a loud exhale. "You didn't tell me you had a kid. Where's she been?"

"She lives with her dad. I have her every other weekend. She's eight."

"Wow."

Martha didn't reply. She waited.

"Well, shoot, what am I talking about? I have a son," Reuben said. "He lives with his grandmother. He's twelve, no, excuse me, thirteen."

"You were only—"

"Seventeen. Two years older than his mother was. I was a kid. It was the thing to do. Anyway, I help him out now. I send money every month. I almost never see him . . . that's too bad."

"Where's his mother?"

"She died."

"I'm sorry. I'm so sorry." Martha had never known anyone whose wife had died.

"She had it coming. Don't get me wrong—I'm sorry she's dead, for our son. We were never married or anything. She was bad, *loco*, couldn't get out of it."

"And you did?"

"I did. I did." His voice didn't sound bright anymore; he sounded dusty, packed away in a closet and forgotten.

Martha thought of Reuben and this girl together. She saw them standing in the barrio, young, looking at each other across the street. The girl was golden brown and sweet like a caramel. She saw the girl beckon to him, pull him up to some small, hot apartment, her parents' bed, the crucifix hanging on the wall. The image shimmered like heat waves from black asphalt. The girl was hot. Reuben was hot for her. Martha was jealous.

"How'd we get talking about this stuff?" he said. "What about Monday night?"

"That'd be fine."

"Okay." He sounded relieved, glad to be back in the present tense. "Okay. Where do you live?"

"Why don't I meet you?"

"Why?"

"It's hard to find. My street is narrow, winding—"

"I won't be driving the truck."

"Oh." For a moment, Martha was disappointed. She wondered what he would be driving. A man's car was important to her.

"Trust me," he said. "I'll find it."

She gave him her address, said good-bye, and hung up. She hated giving her house away. He would bring her home. He would want to come in. She would hate that.

And now it was a real date. She didn't want to go on a date. She didn't like dates. Her mother used to work hard to set her up with dates. There was the electrician, young and dirty, who came to rewire the fuse box after Lars had tried to burn the house down. There was the cook, a Rastafarian, in the little restaurant where they had plotted her mother's subsequent divorce. There was the architect, four feet eleven inches and missing both of his index fingers, who came to give an estimate on enlarging the kitchen in the new boyfriend's house. And Martha had dutifully gone out with all of them.

Her mother had been her pimp, Audrey called it, since Martha was fourteen, starting with Tuna.

They were in Missouri waiting for her grandmother to die. Dolly, Audrey, and Martha sat in Grandma's clean little house for the whole summer and waited. Her grandmother had cancer. Her grandmother who had been large and terrifying was now barely a whisper in a white bed. She didn't eat anymore or sit up or open her eyes. They took turns sitting with her, reading aloud, feeding her half a teaspoon of ice shavings every hour.

Tuna had dropped by the house with flowers and a covered dish from someone. He was distantly related, as were most of the people in this small town. He looked Audrey over. Martha watched his ears go back and the bob of his Adam's apple as he swallowed hard. Smart guy, Martha thought, to realize Audrey was more than he could handle. Then, to her horror, he turned and gave her a smirky smile. It was her mother who smiled back, gave him her best smile, her smile for men.

Everybody called him Tuna, although his real name was Frank or Fred or something normal. Martha knew why. He had fish lips, wet and loose in his face, always slightly open, the round *O* of a goldfish breathing in a bowl.

When he called later that evening, Martha didn't want to come to the phone.

"He's nice," her mother whispered furiously, holding one hand over the mouthpiece. "You need to get out. Why not go? Why not have a good time?"

It was too hot. She was fourteen. She'd never been on a date before. She didn't have a matching shorts outfit. Her hair frizzed wildly in the humidity. But she couldn't say no to her mother, so she went.

He picked her up in his father's big car and took her to a family picnic. After they ate, he left her on the redwood bench at the picnic table and went to drink a beer and play Frisbee with his brothers. Occasionally, they looked over at her and then grinned at each other.

The potato chips left a gray grease-stain map on her paper plate. She pretended the blotch of ketchup was a sea of blood-drenched waters. Left alone at the table, she surveyed the remains of dinner. The bees hovered over watermelon rinds and soda cans; the potato salad congealed in the pink Tupperware bowl, the mayonnaise turning as yellow as the mustard. The table seemed to sag with expiration.

She turned on the uncomfortable picnic bench and lifted her hair off the back of her neck. There was no breeze. The relentless Missouri summer was like a piece of hot damp fabric surrounding her, a stifling shawl of heat.

Two older women, identical with moon gray hair permed tight and flowered blouses over green, jelly-bean bright polyester pants, came to clear the table and noticed her.

One spoke to the other, "Well." There was that Pruitt "well," as drawn out and flat as a cowpie, "We—ll, we—ll. You know who this is? Sure you do. Ella Pruitt's granddaughter. Her mother is Louise Elaine, Dolly they always called her—you know, the one that lives back east now and that's been divorced. No, this ain't Ted's child. Can't you tell by that hair? That's Audrey, the older girl. This un's from the other one, the next one." She dropped her voice to a whisper as if Martha wasn't sitting right there. "The one that's Jewish."

Martha was used to it. She'd been hearing it all summer. Most people were perfectly nice about it, more fascinated than anything else, and open and talkative in a midwestern way.

She didn't tell them that Dolly was no longer married to "the Jew." There had never been a discussion about it, but Martha knew her mother was keeping the divorce and Lars, the new man she was practically living with, a secret.

"How's your grandmother, child?" The one who hadn't been talking spoke to Martha.

Martha didn't know what to say. When her grandmother died, she could go home. But then her grandmother would be dead. The night before, on Martha's watch, her grandmother suddenly groaned out loud. Martha jumped up from the blue vinyl chair and then just stood there, chanting to herself, "Please don't let her die when I'm here. Please don't let her die when I'm here."

But then the nurse came in and changed the IV bottle and nothing had really happened after all. Martha sat back down. Her mother and sister would sit holding Grandma's hand, but Martha couldn't touch her. Her skin was a green so pale it was almost white. Her arms were thin enough to see all the bones in her elbow and the slow blue pulse of blood at her wrist. Once Martha pressed one finger tentatively against her grandmother's forearm and then quickly took it away. A dark bruise immediately blossomed and the indentation remained.

"Poor thing. You give her our best."

"I will, I'll do that, thank you." Martha smiled. She had no idea of this woman's name.

"She sure did love to play bingo, your grandmother."

"Really?" Martha smiled politely.

"She went here and there, all the way to Hannibal if there was a game with a good pot. Oh Lord, yes. She used to make some money."

Martha was surprised. Her grandmother used to make the girls wear dresses on Sundays; she disapproved of any sort of wildness or excess. Certainly she didn't sanction gambling.

The woman laughed. "I never seen anything like her—she played bingo just like a Catholic."

She patted Martha's hot hand and smiled at her. "You tell her I said hi. You just tell her we all miss her. Now, you go on. Here comes Tuna."

Martha turned gratefully to the tall boy with the mouth of a flounder. He was safe and easy to dislike.

He sat on the bench next to her and looked at her.

"How old are you?" he asked.

"Fourteen," she said. "How old are you?"

"Eighteen."

"Are you going to college?"

"Hell no. I got a job already. Over to the farm store." He paused and looked over at his brothers, who were watching him. One of them was spinning the Frisbee on his finger. Martha watched him and wondered how he did it. The letters on the Frisbee made a white stripe as it went around.

"I've never seen anybody with hair like yours."

Martha had to close her eyes to stop watching the Frisbee. "You mean, red?"

"I've seen red hair. But wide, that wide. It's the widest hair I ever saw."

Martha knew what he meant. She'd asked Audrey to cut her hair, bob it just above her shoulders, hoping that shorter it would be more manageable. Instead it just frizzed and curled straight out from both sides of her head. She looked like a hedge that needed trimming.

"Can't you wet it down or something?" He grinned and his brother with the Frisbee snickered.

When he brought her home that night he turned to her and slid his right arm along the back of the seat. Maybe he wanted to kiss her, she wasn't sure, but she saw his wet, ocean-dwelling lips coming toward her and she leapt from the car and ran into the house.

"Didn't you even say thank you?" Her mother was shocked. Martha realized she must have been watching from the dark living room.

"Oh, Mom," she said. "He's too old for me." She couldn't admit her failure, not to her mother, not to the Homecoming Queen. Her mother had been the life of the party, the party girl, the good time gal, with a different date every night of the week. Martha knew her own lack of social life was a big disappointment.

She ducked past her mom and into the bathroom. She shut the door and stared into the mirror. She didn't even look as good as a shrubbery; she was a clown, Bozo, her hot, pointed face a shiny crimson moment in the mass of hair.

Her mother slammed the bathroom door open and stood there, her hands on her hips.

"Don't tell me you embarrassed me."

Martha wanted to shake her mother. Look at me. I'm an embarrassment just standing here. Look at me. But she said nothing.

"What did you do?" her mother asked. "What did you do?"

"Nothing." Martha was beginning to cry. "I didn't do anything. He took me to the picnic. I met his mom and dad. I sat on the bench."

"Honestly, Martha."

Her mother was exasperated. Martha didn't know what she was supposed to have done.

Her mother sighed. "I tried to do something nice for you. I tried to get you out of this goddamn depressing house for a night. Have some fun. I don't know why I bother."

Now her mother's lip was trembling. Her wide, Dolly blue eyes were shining, liquid, exquisite. She shook her head and her straight, thick dark blonde hair brushed over her shoulders like a child's.

"I'm sorry, Mom." Martha touched her mother's graceful white elbow. "I'm sorry. I'm sorry. I had fun. I did."

Her mother gave her a brave, trembling smile. "You did, honey? I'm glad. That's what I wanted. That's all I wanted." She stroked her daughter's glazed cheek. "You've let yourself get all hot."

"It's my hair," Martha said in a small, tentative voice. "Why is my hair like this? I hate it."

"Nonsense," her mother said as she left the bathroom. "Men love red hair. Wash your face and come in the kitchen for something cool to drink."

From then on, Martha went out with every guy her mother ever suggested. She slept with some of them. She always told her mother she had a wonderful time. She never went out with any of them twice.

Jesus, it was hot. She came home from aerobics, a sweaty trip in her car, and found no respite in her house. The air was still and clogged. The rectangle of sunlight on her carpet was unbearable to walk on.

Martha took a shower. The second shower of the day.

The six hundred-dollar bills from Dr. Hamilton saluted her when she opened her underwear drawer. She could smell them. Her underpants smelled like money too. It was a distinctive, papery, not quite clean smell. It made her smile to think she had such richly odored panties. She couldn't help but think of Reuben and if—if he ever got to take her underwear off—if he would notice how they smelled.

She decided to go to the bank and make a deposit. The bank would be air-conditioned. She liked the black and tan tiled floor, the high ceiling and red velvet ropes outlining where to wait in line. She liked going to the bank. She could see herself on the security camera and imagine being a thief. But she didn't really want to go. She wanted to have the money in her drawer. She liked having it there. Allen paid for almost everything, the mortgage payment, the taxes, the water bill. He didn't even know she was working. He was giving her extra to tide her over. She decided she'd go to the movies instead.

When she emerged into the warm evening light, she felt removed. She saw herself as in a movie, a visual, immune from the heat and the noise. Music played under her as she waited for the elevator in the parking garage, as she walked to her car, as she took out her keys.

"Oh, oh, oh, oh."

She turned. A homeless man was walking through the garage, barefoot, talking to himself. She knew him. She saw him everywhere. He was tall and lanky, dirty blonde hair. He had no face. He had been burned. A group of teenagers attacked him one night, woke him where he was sleeping in an old sleeping bag, soft flannel duck print inside, broken zipper.

"Hey. You piss your pants?"

"You smell like shit."

"Wha'chou got, man? Nothin'? You got nothin'?"

"He's a crazy man. Fuck him."

They taunted him. Surrounded him under the freeway overpass. It was late. They were high on something, maybe just themselves. They moved around him, a sadistic dance bending toward him, circling him, a roundelay of danger. One of them, not the leader, just the flunky, carried a plastic liter Coke bottle full of gasoline.

"Go on, go on, go on," the others chanted.

"Do it!"

"Do it!"

The flunky, the youngest one, fluttered to the center of the circle and poured the gas on the crouching man. He poured and he giggled, his voice as high as the telephone wires, as high as the cars passing overhead in oblivion.

The homeless man felt the thick liquid trickle down his neck. He tasted it, bitter in his mouth, and his nose filled up with the acrid, road trip smell of it. He felt it slide inside his ear. It made him think of the swimming pool when he was a child. He would get water in his ear and his mother, curved and round in a brown bathing suit, would rub his ears with his soft white towel.

"Do it!"

But it wasn't the youngest who threw the match. At the last moment, he turned away. Then they all ran, scared of the screams, knowing they would hear those screams forever.

She knew the story. But the burned man scared her just the same. He passed her, averting his face. She got in her car and locked the door behind her. She wasn't in the movies anymore.

"When you look in the mirror, how do you feel about what you see?" Dr. Hamilton seemed very calm, but distant. He had moved his chair away from Martha, back from the table, across the oatmeal-colored carpet.

"I don't have a mirror," Martha replied. "Not a full-length one."

"I can't believe that." Dr. Hamilton sounded truly surprised.

"My ex-husband took it when he moved out. It was his mother's. It was lovely, you know, one of those freestanding old-fashioned mirrors. It had a dark cherry bentwood frame. But the glass had a bulge in it, just under my chin. My neck looked enormous. It was hard to look anywhere else."

"When did he leave?"

"It'll be five years in January."

"Don't you want to buy another one?"

"I think about it sometimes when I see them at the drugstore. Jewel, my daughter, stands on the toilet seat and looks at herself in the medicine chest mirror."

"But you look at your face."

"I like to watch myself brush my teeth." Martha paused and shrugged, embarrassed. "I guess that comes from being alone so much."

"You must be remarkably secure about your appearance."

Martha laughed inside her blue camouflage.

"Why is that funny?" Dr. Hamilton asked.

"I don't know. I don't know why it's funny."

"Are you secure? Do you like the way you look?"

"I try not to think about it. I guess I just don't know exactly what I look like. I mean, I could describe you the particulars; color of hair, eyes, height, weight. But I'm not sure how they all go together. I don't really want to know. Whenever I see myself in a store window or something, I'm always surprised."

"Pleasantly?"

"Not always."

"And yet you worked at a job in which your appearance was paramount."

"The Sweet Spot? It was breasts they cared about. Some of the women had terrible, tragic faces."

"Tell me more about working there. Why did you do it?"

"I thought the money would be good."

"You had no misgivings about . . . being half naked?"

"I told you. It was just a costume. I was a nude model for a figure drawing class my first year in college. There was a moment, when I first came into the room and I was still wearing my plaid flannel bathrobe, when I felt self-conscious. I had to keep from looking at the students. That's when I felt they judged me. They looked at my robe, my hair, my feet. Once I was naked and in position, I was fine. I was practically not there at all."

"Being naked makes you invisible?"

"Doesn't it? In a way? I slept with the art teacher. I guess most models do." As Martha spoke, she remembered his condo of white leather furniture by the beach. She'd been expecting a skylit loft and more. "He wasn't a very nice guy, but if I was naked he left me alone. I could do what I wanted, make myself at home." There hadn't really been any home to make.

Dr. Hamilton was silent, looking at his khaki-covered legs. Martha worried she'd said too much once again. She listened to the ocean moving rhythmically through the drawn curtains. She watched a piece of dust jump and fall back, jump and fall back, caught in the air-conditioning vent.

"I saw a man today," she said. Her blue-gloved fingers rubbed the arm of the chair. "He was just a homeless man. But he was terribly disfigured."

"How?" Dr. Hamilton asked. He smiled, a twist of professional compassion on his face.

"He was burned. Horribly. His face was just gone." Like mine, she thought, when I'm here.

Dr. Hamilton's smile fell into a slack, crooked line. He closed his eyes and dropped his head.

"He was attacked," Martha continued. "What hospital would have taken him? Doesn't it take a long time to heal from burns? Where would he have gone? Do you know? What would have happened to him?"

"I don't know," Dr. Hamilton spoke precisely, angrily, without looking up. "County hospital. After that, I don't know."

"I'm sorry," Martha said. "I just thought—"

"He's screwed now, isn't he?" Dr. Hamilton's anger was growing. "Before, maybe he could have found a job, been rehabilitated somehow. Not anymore. No one wants him around."

"Well—" Martha felt like she had betrayed the burned man. He was part of her neighborhood. Someone she saw two or three times every week. Like a friend.

"Why did you want to talk about him?" Dr. Hamilton asked.

"I think sometimes he's Jesus," Martha said.

"Excuse me?"

"He's Jesus. He walks barefoot all over my neighborhood and wherever I go, I see him."

"That makes him Jesus?"

"He seems so sad," she said. "He's disappointed."

"Are you religious?"

"No. Not at all. But I do believe that a savior might try to come here. I'm afraid that's how he would be treated."

"A bleak prospect."

"Yes."

"No one wanting to be saved."

"No one knowing they need saving."

"And you, Ms. Ward?" Dr. Hamilton looked up. "Do you need saving?"

"I don't know. See? I don't know either."

Dr. Hamilton sighed. "Tell me. When you see him, do you look at his face?"

"No." Martha didn't have to think. "His nose is missing, his lips. I'm afraid."

"It's not contagious."

"No. I'm afraid he'll be angry at me."

"Why?"

"Because I have a face. Anyway, he looks away from me too."

"Maybe you are hideously ugly to him."

"I feel guilty."

"Oh yes. Spare me from the guilt. I know about guilt. I know about people who wish they could act normally, who feel guilty that they're disgusted, sickened by what they see."

"I made a friend, in college, who had terrible acne." Martha remembered Carl. He might have been handsome, but his face was covered with pimples and boils, abscesses. His eyes were startling, white, clear and Bic pen blue, in the middle of his erupting face.

"I liked him," Martha continued, "but I couldn't go out with him. I didn't want to touch him. It's awful of me, but he scared me too. Once he hugged me and kissed my cheek hello, but I couldn't kiss him back. He knew it."

"Do you believe that those who are maimed or disfigured or crippled are closer to God?"

"I . . ." Martha was suddenly desperate to say what Dr. Hamilton wanted to hear. "I guess so. Sure."

"Bullshit." Dr. Hamilton laughed his wretched laugh. "They are just the people they were before whatever happened to them happened. It's *People* magazine that makes them heroes. They're not. They're scum like the rest of us."

"But—"

"Oh yes, adversity makes us strong, isn't that what they say? But it's not true. It's easier to be strong when you're smart, rich, successful, and have all your arms and legs."

He stood abruptly and crossed to Martha.

"Put your hand on the table," he said.

Martha hesitated.

"Do it. Do it!"

Martha placed one blue hand on the polished tabletop. The glove was too big for her and lying flat like this the tips of each finger were empty, collapsed on themselves.

Dr. Hamilton reached in his pant's pocket and took out a Swiss army knife. He opened the largest blade.

Martha trembled. Inside her mask, her nose was hot, her eyes watered. She was going to cry, but she couldn't take her eyes off the knife, the white cross on the shiny red plastic. She couldn't move her hand.

"If," Dr. Hamilton said, "if I cut off your finger, would that make you a better person? Would it? Would you rise to the challenge, learn to play the piano with the remaining nine? If the pinkie made you strong, would the thumb make you stronger? What if I cut off two fingers? Your whole hand?"

Martha's whole body was shaking now. But Dr. Hamilton continued.

"Let me tell you what it would make you. Obsessed. Angry. Ugly. Would you ever be able to think of anything else? No. No. No. Your entire existence would be centered around those missing parts."

He threw the knife down into the table. It landed and stuck between Martha's outstretched fingers. She stared at the knife. Then she got up. She started for the door.

Dr. Hamilton reached out and grabbed her arm. Martha tried to pull away from him. He held on tight. His fingers were strong. He was hurting her. She shook herself wildly, but he wouldn't let go.

He made a strange, growling sound, and Martha looked at him and saw that he was crying. He let go of her arm and stood there, great horse-sized tears galloping down his pale face, leaping off his chin.

"Your arm," he said, "your arm. It's so little."

And he cried harder. "I'm sorry," he sobbed without moving. "I'm sorry."

Martha took a step back to him. She reached out her baggy blue arms to take him in. He was like a child, crying with his mouth open, his hands reaching for the ground, unable to comfort himself.

But before she could touch him, Dr. Hamilton took a great gulp and ran from the room. He left the door open. She heard him skidding down the hall and the slam of the stairway door behind him.

10

ALLEN STOOD NEXT TO HIS CAR. IT WAS NEW.
IT WAS A NEW COLOR; ''PEARL,'' ALLEN HAD
said. Not white, not gray, not beige, but the product of a mixed marriage of all three.

Jewel stood next to him, her small Barbie suitcase in her plump
chalky hand. Martha tried to smile at her, tried not to notice the pastel
aqua Minnie Mouse shirt, the flowered shorts, the way Jewel wouldn't
look at her.

"Okay, Opie, see you Sunday." Opie was Allen's nickname for Jewel,
short for Opal, because of her milky white skin. He gave his daughter
a big hug and kiss. "I'll miss you."

"We'll have fun," Martha said.

Allen looked at her for the first time. "You okay?" he asked. "You
look tired."

"I'm fine," Martha said, pleased that he'd noticed.

"What have you been doing?"

Martha recognized the suspicious tone. She pulled the sleeve of her
T-shirt down, over her upper arm. Dr. Hamilton's fingers had left three
oval bruises, almost the same navy color as her costume.

"Nothing," she said. "I went to the movies last night, with a girl-friend."

"Oh, good." He was already halfway back in his car. Martha saw the golf clubs in the back seat.

She and Jewel stood out on the sidewalk until he drove out of sight. Jewel's lips were moving silently.

"What?" Martha asked. "What are you saying?"

"I'm counting," Jewel replied, then spoke louder. "One million, two hundred and seventy-two thousand, four hundred and fifty-six. One million, two hundred and seventy-two thousand, four hundred and fifty-seven. One million, two hundred—"

"Why?" Martha interrupted.

Jewel gritted her teeth. "I'm going to be in the *Guinness' Book of World Records*. I'm going to count higher than anybody. Daddy thought it was a wonderful idea. See? I'm keeping a book, so I don't lose my place when I'm interrupted."

She pulled a small notebook out of her back pocket.

"One million, two hundred and seventy-two thousand, four hundred and fifty-eight. One million—"

"You're already up to one million? I just saw you two weeks ago."

"It goes fast when I'm left alone."

Martha nodded, chagrined. She walked into the house and Jewel followed her, still counting.

Martha tried not to think how long the weekend was going to be. She wished Jewel was still a toddler, still three years old, just the promise of a girl. They could sit on the couch. Martha could put her arm around her, read her a book, ask her what the cow says, the duck, the sheep.

Jewel walked down the stairs to her room carrying her suitcase. Martha waited, not sure whether to follow. When Jewel didn't come back up, she went down.

Jewel's bedroom was still exactly as Jewel had wanted it, two years ago. True, Allen had paid for everything, but Martha had painted the walls pale pink and sewed the curtains with the kitty cat fabric and made matching pillows for the bed. She had stenciled roses on the knobs of the white dresser, but all the drawers were empty except for one pair of Jewel's pajamas and a bathing suit, two sizes too small.

Jewel's suitcase stood ready and waiting by the door as always. Jewel lay on the white sleigh bed and stared at the ceiling. She was counting.

Martha sat down on the floor next to the bed. This room was like a different world. When Jewel wasn't there, Martha kept the door shut.

"One million, two hundred and seventy-two thousand, four hundred and ninety-six."

"Want to go out to dinner? Your choice."

"McDonald's?"

"Tony's Pizza?"

"You said my choice."

"Okay. Okay. McDonald's it is. In a half hour or so, okay?"

Jewel nodded and her lips kept moving, saying numbers.

"How was your day?" Martha asked. "How's your friend Lily?"

Jewel rolled her eyes. "Mother, if I'm going to break a world record before I'm nine, I have to keep counting."

"Okay." Martha stood up. "I'll come down in half an hour.

She walked slowly up the stairs and into her clean, silent kitchen. She was at a loss. Jewel was only here for two and a half days, every other week. They should be doing something together, talking. Martha had prepared herself for that. Now that Jewel was busy counting, Martha didn't know what else to do. She sat at the kitchen table and watched the clock. She tried to figure in her mind how Jewel had counted so high in just two weeks. Twenty-four hours in a day, sixty minutes in an hour, sixty seconds in a minute. If she counted one number every two seconds or three seconds—she couldn't do the figuring without a piece of paper. Still, there was school and homework and sleep. Say she counted five hours a day. That was three hundred and fifty minutes, times sixty—never mind, Jewel had done it and if Allen thought it was a good idea, then she would keep doing it until she succeeded. Martha pressed the bruises on her arm and wondered how long that would be.

When she went downstairs in exactly thirty minutes, Jewel was asleep. Martha sat on the bed next to her. Sleeping, Jewel still looked like a baby. Her white-blonde hair was tucked under her head, making her look almost bald; her mouth was open, moist and pink; her arms were up and her hands curled on either side of her head. Even her breath, warm and steady, smelled sweet.

The morning of Martha's fifteenth birthday she remembered sleeping just like this in her bottom bunk bed in her little girl room. Her room was green and rust and gold, earth colors. She wore her favorite night-gown. It looked like a T-shirt and had a sun on the front and a crescent moon on the back.

It was her birthday. She was fifteen. She and her mom had bought her first real bra, white cotton and lace with a pink rose in the middle, only the week before.

This morning she was dreaming of birds, a flock of pigeons, taking off one by one. She heard their wings flutter, flutter in a rush and their soft coo as they called to one another, "Watch me, I'm going. Good-bye, I'm going." She smelled the sour city smell of their beaks and claws.

She was pulled from her dream by her mother, who had tiptoed into her room and crouched on the side of her bed, ducking her head beneath the top bunk and stroking Martha's face.

"Martha." Her mother's voice was soft and gentle like the pigeons. Martha loved her voice, loved to hear her mother speak. "Martha, wake up."

Martha kept her eyes shut. Her mother continued to stroke Martha's cheek and smooth her bangs back off her forehead. Her hands were too cool; it felt good, but shocking at the same time.

"Martha, sweetheart, wake up. It's your birthday. Your birthday. Wake up. You're five years old today."

Martha's eyes opened. Her mother smiled at her, but there was something funny about her round blue eyes.

"Mom?"

"Good morning, sweetheart. Happy birthday."

"Thanks."

Martha had sat up on her elbows, too tall already to fit under the bunk. Her mother frowned at her, backed away from the bed.

"Get up. I have to make your lunch, get you to school."

"I take the bus. Remember? I take the bus."

"Nonsense. You're five years old. You don't take the bus to kindergarten. I would never let you take the bus. You're a baby."

Martha was afraid to speak. She got out of bed and stood in her very favorite nightgown on the braided rug. She shivered.

"Want to wear your pink dress?" her mother asked as she opened the closet door. "I know we usually save it for best, but today is a special day. Your pink dress, I love your pink dress. I bought it for you. With my own money. I brought it home in a box. A box! With a bow. And a sticker from Lord & Taylor. Where is it? Martha? I can't find it!"

Martha ducked past her mother at the closet and ran into the living room. The living room was empty. The house was empty. Lars hadn't come home again last night. The chairs didn't look as sturdy as they had the day before.

Martha hurried into the kitchen. The coffee pot was full; her mother had a cigarette burning in the ashtray Audrey had made her in third grade.

She dialed Audrey on the phone.

"Audrey?"

"You woke me up."

"Audrey. Come home. Mom's . . . Mom's . . . she thinks I'm five years old."

"Oh Jesus."

Audrey was eighteen and angry. She'd moved out of the house into her boyfriend's studio apartment two months earlier, but she was still home a lot at dinnertime, eating and fighting. And she was still making it to her senior year of high school, just enough to graduate.

"Come home," Martha whispered and begged.

"Soon as I can." Audrey paused. "I've been waiting for this."

She hung up. Martha wondered how her sister knew that this would happen. Martha hadn't known. As her mother so often told her, she was self-centered and selfish. Her mother was in trouble and she hadn't even noticed.

Her mother screamed from the bedroom. She ran into the living room, her arms filled with Martha's clothes.

"Look at this mess!" she said. She flung clothes across the room. "How am I supposed to find anything in this mess? Where did you get these clothes? Did you give all your things away?"

"Those are my clothes. Mom. We gave the pink dress away."

"Never! I love that pink dress. I love you in that pink dress. I'll never forget how beautiful you look. Like the frosting on a cupcake. Just like frosting!"

Her mother collapsed on the floor surrounded by mud- and grass-colored clothing.

"What is this shit?" she whimpered. "What happened to your dress?"

"We gave it away, Mommy. A long time ago."

Audrey arrived and then Lars, the stepfather. Lars put two dollars into Martha's hand and told her to buy lunch at school. Then Lars, with Audrey, took Dolly to the hospital.

They left and the house was empty again. Martha stood in her spot, in her nightgown, in the living room for a long time. She watched the sunlight falling through the pane of glass in the front door move across the floor until it touched her toes. Then she fled.

When she got home that afternoon her mother was in the kitchen making her a birthday cake. It was pink angel food, decorated with fresh flowers, not frosting.

"I was afraid you'd say you're too old for birthday cake." Her mother smiled anxiously. "You're not too old, are you? Fifteen's not too old, is it?"

Lars threw his log-sized arm around Martha's shoulder. "Of course not!" His voice was loud and perfectly modulated; he had been a radio announcer briefly. "Of course she's not too old. What a ridiculous thought."

Martha gave Jewel a pat, then a gentle shake. "Jewel," she said, "Jewel, time for dinner."

Jewel woke, groggy, unsure where she was. She looked at her mother without recognizing her.

"McDonald's, remember?" Martha smiled.

Jewel's hand reached for the little notebook on her chest. She clutched it and then began to cry.

"What?" Martha was terrified. Jewel never cried.

"I lost it," Jewel sobbed.

"What?"

"My place! I fell asleep and lost my place." Her nose was running, and her small shoulders rose and fell with each sob.

"Oh. Well." Martha was desperate to comfort her. "Guess what? I was listening. I know just where you fell asleep."

"You do?"

"Sure." Martha was lying. She couldn't help it. "Let me see—one million—um, what was it?"

"You don't remember!"

"Yes. I do. The last number was twenty-nine. I don't remember the rest, but—"

"One million, two hundred and seventy-two thousand, five hundred and twenty-nine! That's it. You're right!"

Jewel gave her a sudden damp hug. Martha took a deep breath of her daughter's smell, sweaty and tart and delicious. Jewel pulled away. She wrote the number on her pad and smiled at her mother.

Martha felt her fingers lengthen, stretching across the pink bed-spread toward her little unbeautiful child. But she pulled them back into her lap, held her own hands tight together.

At McDonald's they played a game together. They made up stories about all the other people who were there; where they had just been; where they were going. Martha often played it by herself. She never thought Jewel would enjoy it, but she had suggested it and now Jewel was gig-gling and hiccuping into her orange soda and trying not to stare. An older woman in a dark red dress smiled at them as she walked by with her tray. Martha knew she was smiling at the picture, the picture of mother and daughter laughing together. She smiled back. Then she and Jewel made up a story about that lady too.

This is going to be a good weekend, Martha thought. Jewel and I will have fun.

Saturday they went shopping. Jewel had made a face at Martha's blue jeans and faded T-shirt.

"You should wear things that match, like Susan does," Jewel said and then clapped a hand over her mouth. "I'm sorry. I didn't mean—"

"It's okay. Maybe I should buy some new clothes," Martha said. "Maybe we should both get something new."

She fingered Jewel's polyester shorts set. It was lavender and had a fake Indian motif complete with fringe at the shoulders. Jewel twirled in it, so Martha could get the full effect.

"Very nice," Martha said. "Let's go see what we see."

Martha avoided the mall, taking Jewel to a trendy westside shop instead. A pregnant woman with a protruding belly button ring and maroon hair shopped for black baby clothes. Jewel stared until Martha pulled her away. They found Jewel a little dress in olive green rayon and a black vest. Jewel's eyes were shining. And Martha was surprised at how pretty her daughter looked.

The male cashier flirted with Martha and asked Jewel if she was her sister. Jewel proudly answered, "She's my mom. Really."

They went to a movie and out to dinner again, this time for pizza.

In the car on the way home, Jewel resumed counting.

"One million, two hundred and seventy-two thousand, five hundred and sixty-three. One million, two hundred and seventy-two thousand, five hundred and sixty-four. One million, two hundred and seventy-two thousand, five hundred and sixty-five."

Martha joined her, first in her mind and then out loud.

"One million, two hundred and seventy-two thousand, five hundred and sixty-eight. One million, two hundred and seventy-two thousand, five hundred and sixty-nine."

They laughed. Martha reached across the emergency brake and smoothed her daughter's wispy hair back from her cheek. Her fingers couldn't believe how smooth Jewel felt.

But on Sunday, when Allen came to pick Jewel up, Martha wasn't sorry to see her go. She was exhausted. It was too hard to be what Jewel wanted her to be. When Jewel was there, Martha was a mom. She ate differently, she slept badly, she worried. She took two-minute showers, not wanting to leave Jewel alone with a bowl of cereal and Saturday morning cartoons. She tried to do whatever Jewel wanted her to do, even though Jewel rarely said anything. How did Susan do it? Maybe it was easier for full-time mothers; maybe they got used to it.

After Jewel left, Martha changed the sheets on her bed and then closed the door to her room.

11

MONDAY MORNING AT WINCHELL'S. MARTHA
TRIED TO THINK ABOUT THE BLIND. SHE
tried to think about beauty. But she could only think about Reuben and
their looming date. She and her father, Marvin, used to date. After he
and her mother separated he would call her on the phone and ask her
out on Friday nights. It was a standard thing, but he called anyway.

Each week, Martha would get all dressed up and wait on the orange
couch by the front door. She was always ready a half hour early. And
he was always at least a half hour late.

"Hello, Dolly. Oh, hello, Dolly," Marve would say to Martha's mother.
He never got tired of that old joke or any old joke.

"You're late," her mother always replied.

"Better late than never." Her father loved clichés. He often spoke in
whole sentences composed of trite phrases and overused aphorisms. He
was a round-faced man with dark dots for eyes and a surprising button
nose. Martha thought of him as a Jewish Charlie Brown with added
tufts of kinky, curly red hair. The hair was just like hers.

"Time to hit the trail, get this show on the road, shuffle off to Buf-
falo," he said to Martha.

Dolly stood on her tiptoes to see over his shoulder to his car. She was looking to see if he'd brought a woman. Even after she married Lars, she still wanted to know about Marvin's dates.

Sure enough, he had a woman waiting in the car. Her name was Betsy. She was young, bleached blonde, and wore purposefully ripped T-shirts that fell off one shoulder. Her blue jeans had little rhinestones in them. Martha didn't like Betsy very much. She wasn't very smart, even a nine-year-old could tell that. Betsy had been with them for the last two Fridays. Martha hoped her father would dump her soon.

"Her again?" her mother asked.

"A bird in the hand—" her father replied cheerfully as he got in his car. "Bye-bye blackbird!"

They went to the movies. They'd been to the movies with Betsy every time and they weren't really movies for children, but Martha never said anything. She tried hard to laugh at Marvin's jokes, smile at his girl-friend, be the perfect date.

First, they stopped at the People's drugstore next door to the theater to buy Martha an enormous bar of chocolate. She knew she'd have to hide it when they went into the theater. She loved chocolate, but she wished sometimes they would just buy the popcorn.

While she was deciding on her candy, Marvin and Betsy went down another aisle and began to giggle together like kids being naughty. Martha chose her chocolate and her father hurried over and took the candy from her.

"Wait right here," he said. She could see he had a box of something; she could see a picture of a man and a woman and a sunset. She could read the word "ribbed" but nothing more. She didn't ask.

Then they went to the ticket booth.

"One adult and two children," he said, just like he did the last time and the time before that.

"Two children?" The ticket person peered through her window at the three of them.

"I'm in my second childhood," her father replied and waited for the laugh.

Betsy giggled accordingly and the ticket person smiled indulgently. Her father sighed with smug satisfaction as he bought the tickets.

Betsy sat on one side of Marvin, Martha on the other. Last week, Betsy and Marvin had held hands. This week things had progressed. The moment the lights went down, they started kissing.

Martha pulled her candy out from under her sweater as quietly as possible. She opened it gingerly, slowly, tearing the red outer paper bit by bit, not wanting to make any noise. She kept her face up watching the screen so the usher wouldn't think she had anything in her lap. She was always afraid the usher would come, find her contraband candy, and kick her out. Her father would be furious with her.

After about fifteen minutes, her father leaned over to her.

"We'll be right back," he whispered. "You stay and watch the movie. Don't go anywhere."

"Okay."

"You have your candy?"

"Yes."

"Good. We'll be right back."

He and Betsy slid out of the row and up the aisle. Martha hoped they were going for popcorn. If they bought popcorn, maybe the usher wouldn't mind about her candy.

She watched the movie. It was interesting. It was about a group of men who robbed a bank and then went to Mexico where another man made them work for him. Even though they'd robbed the bank, they weren't bad guys. There was some gruesome violence and a scene where two men took turns doing something to a woman. It seemed to Martha that women were usually useless in the movies.

The credits rolled, the curtains closed, the lights came on, and still her father and Betsy hadn't returned. Martha waited in her seat. Everyone else left. Then the ushers came through with their brooms and dustpans on long handles.

"You'll have to leave," a tall usher with a shiny face said to her. Martha jumped; she knew she'd get caught. "I'm sorry," she began. "If you want to watch it again, you'll have to buy another ticket."

Martha nodded, relieved, held the remains of her candy bar smashed under her sweater, and left the theater. It was dark outside and the lobby was crowded with people buying popcorn for the next show. She didn't see her dad or Betsy anywhere.

The next show began and the lobby emptied. Martha stood inside the glass doors, looking out. The ushers swept the red patterned carpet, made popcorn, talked to one another. No one said anything to her.

In a while, her father's car pulled up out front. Betsy was gone. He motioned to her to come on, come get in the car.

Martha slid into the front seat. Her father was disheveled. He wasn't wearing his jacket. There was a funny smell in the car, Betsy's perfume and something sour too. Now that Betsy was gone, maybe she and her Dad could spend some time together.

"Sorry, Chickadee." Marve patted her thigh. "I guess it's true—time flies when you're having fun."

"Baskin-Robbins?" Martha asked. They always went for ice cream after the movies.

"Not tonight, Josephine." Her father didn't look at her. "I have to get back to Betsy. She's waiting, anticipating."

He drove her home, turning corners with screeching tires and accelerating through yellow lights and yield signs. As she started to get out of the car, he took her hand, pulled her back.

"Don't say anything to your mother, okay?"

He sounded so serious, Martha just stared at him.

"I mean, about the movies, and you waiting and all."

"Sure, Dad."

He smiled and let go of her hand. "You're a sport, you know it?" He patted her face. "And we love ya for it!"

Martha flushed with pleasure. She got out of the car and stood on the curb.

"Until next week. Same time, same channel! Don't touch that dial."

He drove off without waiting for her to go up the steps and inside her house.

When she took off her clothes for bed that evening, the chocolate had melted and stained her best white blouse and her undershirt. Her mother was livid, but Martha didn't mind. She held her father's praise and his secret.

She stared into her closet and worried about what to wear with Reuben. It had been so long since she'd been on a date. Now she wished she had that full-length mirror. She tried standing on the toilet seat like Jewel, but she was too tall. All she could see was her stomach.

She tried blue jeans and a T-shirt, a long skirt, a big top, but nothing felt right. Finally, she decided on a sleeveless summer dress. It was blue with small white flowers and almost new. She had bought it at the beginning of the summer for a lunch with Jewel and her piano teacher that had never happened. It was loose fitting and not too motherly. Anyway it was too hot to wear anything else.

Reuben rang the doorbell right on time. Martha was pleased. Since Marvin she couldn't bear for men to be late. She opened the door and Reuben smiled when he saw her. He looked her up and down and told her to turn around once.

"Nice dress," he said, but his eyes narrowed like he was thinking something else.

He looked great. He had perfectly worn-in blue jeans, hip black shoes, and a dark green T-shirt that made his eyes look as lush as her imagined rain forest.

She couldn't get her key out of the lock when she locked her door as they left. Reuben leaned forward to help her and his hand brushed her bare arm. He looked at her, and she blushed.

He had a 1968 four-door Dodge. It was a cool car and Martha felt relief.

They saw a movie. It was the same movie she had seen by herself the previous Thursday, but she didn't say anything. He ate popcorn, but she didn't. He groaned in the movie, disgusted with the male star's acting, nudged her when the one Hispanic character actor had his line, shook his head at the end. Martha had liked it, but she didn't say so.

Afterward they went for a beer, but she was too nervous to drink. She didn't say much, just listened to him talk about the crazy people he met at his auditions, about how hard it was to be a Latino actor, about his family, about his life. She wondered why she wasn't listening to anything he said. She already knew she liked him. Was it just because of the way he looked? His succulent green eyes, his smoothly turned arms, the way the snap on his pants lay flat against his belly. He was nice. She didn't really care what he said. She couldn't help but think of Dr. Hamilton. She wanted to tell him about Reuben. About this. She looked forward to his reaction.

And then they came home in his car. He pulled up in front of her little house, turned the car off, and turned to her.

He was going to kiss her. He wasn't smiling. He looked concerned, almost angry. There was a straight line between his eyebrows she hadn't seen before. He was concentrating. She had thought this kiss would happen tonight—she would have been disappointed if it hadn't—but now she wasn't sure she was ready. It had been a long time since she'd kissed someone, anyone.

Martha became very aware of her mouth. She ran her tongue over her teeth, both sides. She was glad she had exemplary oral hygiene and kept regular six-month dental appointments. Dr. Rachel, her dentist, was tall with long, skinny fingers and fresh, scrubbed skin. She was a lesbian and wore her hair dyed black and lacquered straight up. Martha lay in the chair and counted the hairs sticking out around Dr. Rachel's head in silhouette against the white tile ceiling. They were stiff and straight like the hairs in her nose. She wore a mask and rubber surgical gloves, and she had made Martha fill out a signed declaration that to the best of her knowledge she didn't have AIDS. Martha had never been tested, but it had been so long since she'd had sex that she thought she was safe.

There had been only that one time, since Allen had left, that one time with Simon. Simon was a regular at the club, and he always sat in Martha's section.

He was short. Even when he was sitting on the stool, when Martha walked up his eyes were just the height of her nipples.

"This is what I call keeping abreast of the situation," he said.

Martha laughed. "What would you like to drink?" It was what she always asked; it was direct and left no room for innuendo.

"A Brandy Alexander," he said. "Did you know this drink was named for Alexander the Great?"

He didn't drink, not really. A man who ordered a Brandy Alexander couldn't be a drinker. It was like chocolate milk. Simon sat on his stool and took tiny, delicate sips of the one drink for more than an hour. Martha liked to watch him. He pursed his lips, squeezed them flat and barely let any of the milky liquid through. Then he would pause, swallow, smack his thin lips and shudder.

He was in his fifties and had lots of hair, on his head, sticking out of the front of his polo shirt, even on the joints of his thumb. He wasn't as tall as Martha, but he was intensely vigorous. He came into the Sweet Spot night after night and sat in Martha's section.

One night he asked Martha out.

"Let's go take a bite out of somethin'," he said.

The something had been her. Martha knew that was what he meant and she didn't mind. She had been divorced for a year and thought no one would ever want to sleep with her again.

His small house was dark, no lights in the windows or out front. It was in a U-shaped configuration of similar houses: pseudo-Tudor, with patches of stucco purposely missing and fake brick showing through.

He said it had been part of the Disney offices, long ago, when the Disney Studio lot had surrounded Los Feliz.

Inside, it was overly quaint, just like the Seven Dwarves. There were useless nooks, indentations, and corner openings too small for televisions, stereos, even a bookshelf. The doorways were arched and there were candle-sized niches carved into every wall.

The carpeting was an incongruous sixties avocado green. The drapes were floor length over the small, many paned casement windows. And there was a smell, not unpleasant but pungent and male, of laundry, bananas, Lipton tea, and paperback books. Her father's apartments had always smelled like this.

He asked her to parade in front of him in her costume from work. He asked her to serve him a glass of milk from his own kitchen and his hand trembled when she handed it to him. He kissed her lips and his breath was coated with milk like a toddler's. He was determined, passionate, oral, and afterward ashamed. She felt okay. She thought she'd done a pretty good job, after so long.

Simon had come into the club once more, a week later. He ordered a beer but didn't drink it. Then she never saw him again.

Now, she couldn't remember how to do it. She thought of movie kisses, made a list of things to remember: tilt your head to one side to keep your nose out of the way, close your eyes, open your mouth, but not too much. What about her tongue? Did you French kiss the first time? If you didn't, what did you do with it?

Reuben was moving toward her. She wished he'd open his eyes. Without his eyes she felt adrift; his face was a blank coffee-colored ocean. Why was she going to kiss him?

Then she did. Instinct took over; she tilted, closed, opened to him, and they kissed. She remembered what to do with her tongue. He tasted green like his eyes, fresh and summery. He made her think of organic vegetables; it was healthy, it was good for her to kiss him. He liked kissing her too.

Her hand smoothed up his back and into his graze of hair. It surprised her palm, soft instead of bristly, not lacquered, but clean and polished. When he pulled away her body went with him. She didn't want to stop now that she'd begun.

He smiled. She plunged into him again. Her hip hit the gearshift knob, recalling her first kiss. A loose chain link in her girlfriend's backyard fence had pressed into her back, leaving a bruise she would finger proudly for days. She had loved kissing that boy, had spent subsequent hours kissing him, and never done anything else. That wasn't possible anymore. Once you'd done more, you could never go back.

"May I kiss you?" Allen had asked on their second date. It should have been a red flag of warning. She should never have said yes. She should have waited. She wanted a man to grab her, pull her head back, and kiss her because he had too. If he had the time to ask, then he didn't really need that kiss. And foolishly she had gone on and made love to him that night too.

"Wow," Reuben said into her hair. "I've been thinking about this."

"Me too," Martha said.

Then there was a pause without any more kissing. Martha sat up and looked out the open car window at her little house. The porch light was on. A light in the living room glowed yellow through the front windows into the star jasmine. They were kissing in the car, making out as if they were teenagers afraid of her mother. But it wasn't her mother, it was just her house. And she didn't want him to come in. Maybe she did. No, she didn't. It was just a good night kiss.

Martha opened her door. "Well," she said, "I had a lovely evening. Thank you." She got out of the car.

Reuben laughed. He opened his door and got out. Martha walked up to her front door. She reached into her bag for her keys and Reuben kissed the back of her neck. His lips were a cool brand on her hot skin and she turned to him and kissed him again. He was the right size, her head fit into the hollow between his neck and his shoulder; he didn't have to bend, she wasn't on tiptoe. Her tongue went out and ran in a circle around the inside of his mouth. Reuben sighed and slid his mouth across her cheek and down her neck.

He was going to come in. She knew that now. She pulled away from him and opened her front door. He followed her in, a step behind.

Automatically she put her keys and purse down on the little table where she always put them. She turned to Reuben.

"Would you like something? A drink of something?"

Reuben only grinned and took her hand and led her to her blue couch. He sat down and pulled her down in his lap. His arms went around her and he kissed her again.

And she kissed his mouth and his neck and his ear and his cheek and even his eyelids. Reuben's hand slid across the flimsy rayon dress and across her breast. He stopped, looked at her.

"You're not wearing a bra."

"No," she said, "I can't with this dress. It shows."

"Wow." He shook his head appreciatively. "You have great tits."

"Thanks," Martha said. It was a compliment, but it sort of spoiled the moment. She pulled away from him and sat up.

"Sure I can't get you anything?" she asked. "I need a glass of water."

"Okay," Reuben said.

He stood and followed her into her kitchen.

"You got any cookies?" he asked.

Martha laughed. She did and she was glad. She had bought chocolate chip cookies with sprinkles for Jewel. After Jewel left she put them in the freezer.

"They're cold," he said. "And hard."

He was laughing too. There were crumbs on his lips, crumbs the color of his skin. She put her palms flat on his chest and kissed him. He tasted sweet. Now there were crumbs on her lips.

He ate cookies for breakfast too. He brought them to her bed and ate with one hand and traced figure eights around her nipples with the other.

She stared at the tattoo that spanned his shoulders. It was an eagle, the head just at the base of his neck, the wings stretched shoulder to shoulder. In its sharp talons was a mouse, eyes wide open in fright. She could almost see its tail whipping back and forth.

"It's old," Reuben told her. "I was young, and stupid."

Then he kissed her, matter of factly, like a handshake.

"I gotta get to work, you know?" he said. "I don't want to leave. Boy, I don't want to leave."

"Okay," Martha said, "I should get up too."

"I never even asked you—where do you work?"

"I work at night. For a doctor."

"At night? What do you do? Are you a word processor?"

"I'm . . . I'm his office assistant."

Martha was sad about lying, but she didn't want to tell him anything about Dr. Hamilton. "It's just three nights a week," she said. "You know, whatever needs doing."

"Hmm." Reuben looked thoughtful. Then he kissed her again and smacked her thigh. "Aerobics is great, but free weights—that'll really make a difference. I'll take you to the club. I'll show you. You won't be able to walk the next day."

Was he going to ask her out again? Was he asking her? Martha knew it was easy to sleep with somebody once, but not twice. The second time was the key, the tough one. Would he come back?

"I'll call you," Reuben said and slipped into his shoes.

Martha got up and put on her pink robe. She walked him upstairs to the front door. And then, Reuben did an amazing thing. He turned back to her and took her face in his hands, one on either side. He held her like a bowl of soup, looked into her eyes, and smiled at her.

"We're going to be friends," he said quietly. "Reuben Rodriguez always tells the truth."

He didn't even kiss her, just left.

Martha showered, dressed, went to Winchell's. She savored her plain cake doughnut. Her mouth was tender. She was sore other places too. She shifted her bottom on the molded red plastic bench and winced, but happily. It had been so long.

She thought of the rest of her day stretching out before her. She sighed. She didn't want to spend it waiting for her phone to ring. She didn't want to walk up the hill this morning, hurry into her house, and look for the green blinking light on the answering machine. But she knew she would.

Then she thought about Dr. Hamilton. A ripple of fear slid through her. Suddenly, she felt anxious to stay alive and whole. She worried about what she was doing and what might happen in that hotel room. The bruise on her arm was almost gone. She remembered how his knife had shuddered when it hit the table top, the shiny blade wavering in the lamp light.

"No," she said out loud.

Embarrassed she looked around, but the morning regulars at Winchell's hadn't heard her. The balding, overweight security guard sat with his back to the window and the parking lot and mumbled into his coffee. The woman and her husband who were there every morning, both in their seventies, sat without speaking, their doughnuts untouched in front of them. The woman wore too much makeup and her hair was dyed a bright glittery brass. Her husband always wore the same brown pants with a small variety of short-sleeved plaid shirts. They sat all morning and never said a word.

Martha wanted to leave. She wanted to go on to the grocery store and get home. She frowned. Her schedule was getting all messed up. This job wasn't good for her. She should look for something more normal, something other women did, something where Reuben could send her flowers. Her coworkers would giggle, laugh with her, tell her to marry him. And when Reuben left her, they would be sympathetic, angry at him for her.

And then, just as suddenly, she felt herself looking forward to tonight, the dark hotel room, Dr. Hamilton, his blue button-down shirts, his somber neckties. She had been his only applicant. He wouldn't really hurt her. She was all he had.

She went grocery shopping. She changed the sheets on her bed. She picked up her book and sat down in her big chair. She was trying to read in alphabetical order all the major works she'd missed in high school and as an urban studies major in college. She was up to the Ks so she was reading Keats. She hadn't found all those quotes about beauty in a book of quotations. She should have told Dr. Hamilton that. She had really read those poems. She was reading more than just the ones Keats was famous for. Dr. Hamilton thought she was an idiot. She pushed the book off the arm of the chair. It hit the hardwood floor with a satisfying smack. Romantic poetry wasn't helping. She baked a cake. It was a recipe she'd copied from a magazine at her dentist's office. Canned peaches and curry. She knew she'd never eat it. Usually she was so happy alone, but today she felt trapped and restless, as if she were standing outside of her own skin, but not able to go and leave it behind.

She played a game. If Reuben calls, I'll go see Dr. Hamilton. If he doesn't, I'll quit. I need to find a real job, an ordinary job, something with a future.

By the time she was sitting with Dr. Hamilton that evening, she was edgy and irritable. Reuben hadn't called.

"I slept with someone last night," she said, bluntly, belligerently.

Encased in blue, she knew Dr. Hamilton couldn't tell if she was smiling or not. But she could see that she had made him uncomfortable. He scratched his ear and sat up straighter.

"I'm not married," Martha continued. She knew this wasn't what he wanted to know or hear or talk about, but she was feeling perverse. "I'm divorced. I haven't slept with anyone in a very long time."

There was a pause.

"So?" Dr. Hamilton felt compelled to finally say something.

"So, I guess I slept with him because he's so handsome."

"Oh." Pause. "Ms. Ward—"

"Would you call me Martha, please? It really bugs me when you call me Ms. Ward."

"Martha—I have attempted to keep this on a professional level."

"Oh, yeah, right." Martha tilted her head and crossed her arms in front of her chest.

"I agree," he began, "I agree it's all somewhat irregular. But—"

He stopped. She had bothered him, she could tell. He was frowning, the muscles in his jaw were tight, and his chin came forward.

"Frankly, Martha, I'm surprised you came back."

"Because I slept with someone?"

"Because I scared you so last Thursday."

"You didn't scare me."

"Didn't I?"

"No."

"Your . . . costume, that suit, had a different smell when I washed it. It was a smell I recognized from my research work—the smell of a frightened animal."

Martha was mortified. She opened her mouth to speak, then said nothing.

"I didn't mind." Dr. Hamilton shook his head. He seemed sorry he'd mentioned it. "Really. I'm not . . . I mean, of course you were frightened. I'm afraid I frightened myself."

"It's all right, I'm fine." Martha felt empty, tired of being angry.

"Thank you."

"I'm sorry."

"What are you sorry about?"

"I wasn't in a very good mood when I got here." She sighed. "I wanted you to know about Reuben. That I'd slept with him."

"Why?"

"I just wanted to tell somebody."

"Was there no one else?"

Martha thought about her day. She had been bursting with words, thoughts to shout out. She had needed a friend. She had wanted to go to lunch with another woman and talk about Reuben. But there wasn't anyone she could call. She had a friend, Tracy, who had a boy Jewel's age and a younger girl. She had been Martha's baby friend, through the nights without sleeping, the teething. But then there had been the divorce and they'd grown apart. Maybe if Martha made the effort. She sighed again, a resolution; she would call Tracy tomorrow.

"I should have called a friend," Martha said, "but . . . it's hard."

"Your friends are married." Dr. Hamilton nodded. "They don't really understand, do they? It's been so long for them. They just want to see you married, settled down, as finished with the whole process as they are."

Martha laughed. "You're right."

"I like to hear you laugh. It's a cliché, I suppose. But it's something pleasing to me. A form of audible beauty."

Martha smiled inside her hood, pleased, only a little embarrassed. Dr. Hamilton wasn't flirting with her. He was just telling her the truth. It was a good feeling.

"You said you slept with this man because he was so handsome. Is that really why?"

"Yes."

"If he had been unattractive, then you wouldn't have?"

She thought of Simon with his gray hairy chest and his milk mustache. "Well," she said, "maybe. If he seemed nice and if he really wanted to."

"That sounds more like you, Martha," Dr. Hamilton smiled at her.

"It does?"

"It does to me."

"Do you think I'm easy?" How many men had she mentioned?

"I think you want to make people happy."

"That's true," Martha agreed. "That's not a bad thing."

Dr. Hamilton shrugged. "But what about you?"

"Believe me. I was happy to sleep with Reuben." She blushed and then felt safe inside her blue hiding place. "Even if I didn't have an orgasm. It was really nice that he was so good looking. I was flattered, no, astounded that he found me desirable.

"But," she continued, "it's not hard to get a man to sleep with you once. It's the second time—" She paused, wondering if her answering machine would be blinking when she got home. She closed her eyes and willed the green light to be flashing, signaling rescue as she walked in the door. "He didn't call today," she finished quietly.

"It's only been a day," Dr. Hamilton said. "Give the guy a chance."

Martha laughed again and Dr. Hamilton smiled.

"I've been reading Keats," she said.

"Not a good idea when you're struggling with romance."

"No," Martha agreed. "But great when you're thinking about beauty."

"Yes." Dr. Hamilton nodded, paused. "So. It's not just the famous quotes. You actually have read him. I'm sorry again."

"That's okay." Martha felt a warm flowering of gratefulness. He had listened and remembered. "I've read a lot of his poetry. He had such a reverence for beauty. He worshiped it, really."

"But it seems to me that all that exploration of the beautiful only made him melancholy."

Martha nodded emphatically. "I find him sad too. And so nostalgic."

She relaxed in her chair. Dr. Hamilton slouched in his. He ran his hand through his lanky light brown hair. Martha forgot about her disobedient answering machine and settled in to enjoy their conversation.

"I understand him. Beauty makes me sad," she said.

"Why?"

"It's almost painful, I see it and I want it so badly. And it's unattainable. I'll never have it. It's not a matter of finding the right wishing well, or the genie in the bottle. I'll never stop traffic unless I'm run over by a truck. That's what my father used to say."

Dr. Hamilton grimaced.

Martha continued, vehemently, "Sometimes I come out of the movies and I'm so angry at those women actresses. So angry and sad, it makes me depressed that they're so perfect. I know some of it is special effects and makeup, but I'm the one who has to go to the pizza place afterward, sit in that lime green fluorescent light and smile at my date when he's got a movie star in his mind. It really makes me unhappy and uncomfortable. It's not fair. It shouldn't be so important. It's a freak act of nature, the right combination of genes."

"But this beautiful man just slept with you. He must have seen something there."

"I don't know. I'm not talking about me. I mean, in general."

"You are my generality. You're all I have to go on."

"Haven't you ever felt inadequate?"

Dr. Hamilton paused. He exhaled, his face tensed. Martha saw a curtain close, the end of an act. She was sorry; he was suddenly his usual self. "All the time," he said. "I feel completely inadequate at every particular moment of every single day."

"I'm sorry. I'm sorry."

"It's not because of my appearance."

"I didn't mean to—"

"It's different for men," he interrupted. "In most cases, that is."

"Let's talk about me." She didn't really want to, but she didn't want him looking at his hands, the arms of his chair, his lap. "That's what I'm here for."

"Did you enjoy the sex? Did you leave the light on?"

Martha didn't want to answer him. She didn't want to tell him she'd enjoyed it. She didn't know what this had to do with beauty. But she wanted him to smile. "It's never so great the first time. We both really wanted to, but then it got so awkward. And no, I turned the light off. But I don't have any curtains in my bedroom and the moon was pretty bright."

"Where was your daughter?"

"She doesn't live with me."

"Martha." He stopped, didn't go on.

Martha waited. And waited.

"I'm not a voyeur."

"I know."

"I was just curious, that's all. Sex is very much a part of beauty—attraction."

"We kept bumping into each other." She could tell Dr. Hamilton was confused. "That's what I meant about it being awkward. I tried to take my dress off and knocked him in the chin with my elbow. He wanted to kiss me, but his hand slipped on the bed and he bit my lip."

Dr. Hamilton smiled.

"In the middle of everything I bumped my head on the wall. Hard. It kind of spoiled the moment."

Dr. Hamilton laughed, he actually closed his eyes and laughed. Martha watched his hands relax.

"I'm not sure it's usually this bad for everyone. It's been a long time. I'm out of practice." Martha laughed with him. What had seemed tragic this morning seemed funny now, even a little sweet. "I really like him. I'd like a second chance."

"If you get one, I hope you live through it." Dr. Hamilton was happier again.

Martha chuckled, nodded. She took a deep breath and exhaled looking at the ceiling. She was glad she was here. She wasn't frightened anymore. We're through the worst of it, she thought. He's better. And so am I.

1
2

WHEN SHE ARRIVED HOME THAT NIGHT, REUBEN WAS SITTING ON HER DOORSTEP. SHE HAD remembered to leave her porch light on and she smiled at his halo of amber light. She was glad to see him, but sorry she'd changed the sheets. A small part of her wished he had just called. She was tired from her lack of sleep the night before and from her work with Dr. Hamilton.

He skipped around the car and opened her door, hugged her as she stood up. Martha was taken again with his smell, a musky deodorant clean scent, and his smooth skin. She allowed herself to be happy to see him. She was happy to see him. She kissed him and led him into her house.

In the warm living room light he turned to her, looked her jeans and old T-shirt up and down. Her hair was flattened by the three hours in the hood.

"You go to work like that?" he asked.

"I . . . I have to wear a uniform." She stuck out her tongue as if she didn't like it. "And a hat."

"Oh." Reuben nodded. "What size are you?"

"Eight?" Martha shrugged. She wasn't sure.

"Leave it to me." Reuben circled her with his vigorous arms. "Three months, if you work hard, you'll be a size six."

Martha wasn't sure what to say. Was she supposed to thank him? Was he so unhappy with the way she looked now? Was he threatening her with all that hard work? She didn't know, so she just smiled and pushed uncomfortably at her long hair. He made her aware of her blue jeans, snug in the hips; her skinny arms protruding from her T-shirt sleeves. She took him downstairs to bed, but kept the light turned off.

After that, Reuben spent the night two, sometimes three times a week. She joined his gym and gave up her Armenian aerobics class. She bought matching exercise clothes and tried hard to smile without envy at the supermodels. After all, as Reuben said, they were all just working toward the same goal. She only had coffee at Winchell's now, never a doughnut.

The counter girl said to her, "Hey, Martha. You're wastin' away."

Martha was pleased. Reuben wanted her to drop six pounds.

Weeks passed. The rhythm of her days returned, different but comforting in their new regularity. Reuben bought her clothes; skimpy, tight things she would never have worn before, but he wanted her to show off her changing body. He liked them and she wore them. It was just another uniform, the one she wore with Reuben. It seemed to her she had always worn costumes for men. Party dresses for her dates with Dad; shapeless grunge for her stepfather, Lars; preppie suburban mom for Allen.

And Tuesday, Wednesday, and Thursday nights she ran to Dr. Hamilton. She would get into her aging blue car, fasten her seat belt, and zoom away from her little house. Sometimes she left Reuben there, sitting on her couch, watching her TV. She felt like she was escaping, but from what she wasn't sure. She felt wicked with Dr. Hamilton. Surrounded by yards of baggy blue she let her stomach hang out, her thighs spread, her hair droop and flatten in the hood's safety.

And, occasionally, she'd stop at the lobby candy machine and buy forbidden chocolate for the ride home. She'd never been a candy eater before, but now she craved it. Probably her metabolism was higher, or her magnesium level had dropped. She meant to ask Reuben about it, but she always forgot when she saw him.

She was glad Reuben liked her. She couldn't quite understand it, but he seemed to take a Svengali sort of interest in her. He was warm and sexy and sweet. He called when he said he would. He showed up at her house with flowers and carrot juice. He talked to her about his hopes, his work. She liked doing what he said.

At the celebratory dinner following her high school graduation her father had taken her aside.

"Congrats," he said and patted her back.

"Thanks." Martha tried not to sound grateful.

"You know what I always say." He didn't wait for her reply. "Poets are born, not made. You're obviously not a poet. So, what you gonna do, Chickeepoo? At least you're not fat."

"Yes?" she said, confused.

"I'm saying," he replied, frowning, and shook his head at her, "you've gotta strike while your iron is hot, or as hot as it's ever gonna get."

Martha was lost. She could see the disappointment on her father's face. She wanted to say the right thing. She had an idea and her face lit up.

"Well," she said bravely, "I don't want to put all my eggs in one basket."

"You've only got one basket that I can see," he replied.

He looked at her sadly. She had failed, let him down.

"What? What?" she asked.

"Get married," he said, "to the richest guy who'll take you. It's as easy to fall in love with a rich man as it is a pauper."

Martha was stunned. "I'm going to college."

"I know," he said. "Frankly, big deal. You're no brain surgeon. Remember. Make hay while the sun shines."

He walked away from her. She knew he thought she wasn't beautiful.
He'd made that clear several times. But he'd never said anything about
her intelligence before. It was true he often confused her. She couldn't
keep up.

She had always fallen short for him. He wanted her to be a ballerina.
He had arranged for her to take classes with one of the most prestigious
ballet schools in Washington. Martha was ten, late to get started in
ballet, but excited. Her mother took her shopping for the required pale
pink tights, black leotard, and beautiful pink ballet slippers. Martha
loved those shoes. The leather was so soft; they were so specific. The
first day she and her mother worked for thirty minutes to control Martha's red frizzy curls into a proper bun.

Her father picked her up and chuckled when he saw her.

"There once was an ugly duckling," he sang to Dolly.

"Shut up, Marvin," Dolly said.

But Martha had heard him. Without thinking, she started to run her
hand through her hair.

"No," her mother cried.

Too late. Martha had pulled one side of curls free.

"Mom," she cried, dismayed.

"You'll be late," her mother said. "It looks fine. Really."

The fourteen other little girls were already at the bar when Martha
and her father arrived. They turned as one and looked at Martha without smiling. They were perfect, every one of them. Martha turned away
but everywhere she looked, there she was. Mirrors bounced her lop-
sided messy reflection back to her. Martha stared at the floor and her
beautiful pink shoes.

She realized quickly that the teacher, Lydia, was her father's girl-
friend. Martha recognized the way her father leaned toward Lydia and
the way she giggled in return. She was dark, strong with a surprising
protruding bust.

For two months, Marvin took Martha to dance class and hung
around the piano, making eyes at limber, lovely Lydia. Martha, mean-

while, danced like a fish. She flopped and contorted. She bit her lip, concentrating too hard, and drew blood more than once. She was so skinny the pink tights bagged and wrinkled. By the end of class they were in puddles around her ankles. She was tall and awkward and couldn't hide in a room of graceful swans. Her father would roll his eyes at her and then laugh with Lydia.

After he and Lydia broke up, he found her lack of grace less amusing. He seemed to blame her for Lydia dumping him. But he made her keep going. He kept signing her up for a new session and paying for the lessons. She would hold back the tears as she pulled on her uncomfortable tights and wriggled into the long-sleeved leotard.

"Just call him up," her mother said. "Tell him you're not going."

"No, no," Martha lied, "I'm liking it so much better."

Lydia singled Martha out in class. "If Martha can do it, so can the rest of you."

And Marvin picked her up later and later every time. Martha brought a book with her. She would sit on the steps leading up to the studio door and read and wait. In the winter, she would hop from foot to foot, run to the corner and back to stay warm. Her father didn't like to come in anymore. He never came to her recitals. But Martha kept at it and years went by and she kept telling him how much she loved it.

His only reply was, "Nothing comes of nothing."

Reuben was taking her to meet his family. He had an enormous family and on the nights he wasn't with her he was usually having dinner with his mother or one of his aunts or visiting a cousin.

At first Martha didn't believe he was really so busy with family obligations. Her parents were both only children. Her grandparents were dead. Audrey lived a plane ride away in Utah. She couldn't remember the last time there had been a family event. Not that they weren't close. She talked to her mother every other Sunday no matter what and Audrey called on her office WATS line about once a month. Her father even came to visit every year or so for four days. But it wasn't anything like Reuben and his family.

She showered and made sure to condition her hair carefully. She was better with her hair now. She could control the frizz if not the curl. Women who went for permanents always astounded her. Why would anybody want this hair? She cleaned the steamy bathroom mirror and put on her makeup, thick black mascara, a little liner, blush, and lipstick.

She put on the dress Reuben had selected for her. It was a straight white sheath, sleeveless and high necked. There were tiny gold flecks in the material. Martha never wore white. Her arms and legs were so pale. And the flecks in the dress reminded her of her own pale freckles. She pulled her hair up and back the way Reuben liked it. She put on high-heeled white pumps.

Reuben had bought her a full-length mirror. He hung it on the back of her bedroom door, but she usually forgot it was there. Today, she used it. She stood for a long time just staring at herself. She was white, the plastic virgin with the dress of hard white frosting on top of the wedding cake. When Reuben knocked at her door, his special three knock rhythm, she didn't want to move. The image in the mirror looked as if it would break.

Walking cautiously, hesitantly, she climbed her stairs and crossed the hardwood floor to the door. It was like her mother had moved after her heart surgery. Stunned and stiff, quiet, fragile with care.

Reuben knocked again, impatiently, just as Martha opened the door. He looked her over critically and then shook his head.

"Wow," he said. "Wow."

"I look so white," Martha said.

"You are white, girl." Reuben laughed. "You're my white, honky, gringo girlfriend."

He put out his arms to hug her, but Martha stepped back.

"You won't break."

"I might," she said, smiling. "I might."

The party was in his aunt's backyard in Echo Park. They drove down a pretty street. The houses were well kept and there were signs of children. They pulled up in front of a beige stucco house with a fenced yard and a pot of geraniums on the flat, concrete stoop.

There were lots of cars parked up and down the street and Reuben had to squeeze in. They walked together down the sidewalk.

"I should have brought flowers or something," Martha suddenly said.

"Why? You're a girl," Reuben said, as if that was enough.

They opened the gate and walked up to the open front door. A kid, sixteen or seventeen, shaved head, tattoos, baggy pants, and sleeveless undershirt, scooted out the door.

"Hey," Reuben said.

"Hey," the kid said and continued on. Then he saw Martha and stopped. "Hey," he said, "what's this?"

"This is my girl," Reuben said. "What's this?"

He pointed to the tattoo just barely showing on the kid's chest. The kid looked down and Reuben lifted his finger and flipped the kid's nose.

"Aw, Reuben. Cut it out."

"You cut it out. When you gonna wise up?"

"Fuck you."

"Watch your mouth." Reuben popped his cousin on the head.

The kid shrugged and ran off, hopping over the fence. Reuben watched him go.

"He looks tough," Reuben said. "Ah, shit. *Jose tiene un corazon mui dulce.*"

"What does that mean?"

"It means he's gonna get himself killed." Reuben sighed. "I said he has too sweet a heart."

"Spanish is so beautiful," Martha said.

"I'm glad you think so."

Reuben kissed her. Martha kissed back.

"Stop that," a woman shouted at them from the doorway.

Martha gasped and turned to the voice, but Reuben laughed. A large woman with beautiful dark eyes and short, fanciful red hair stood in the doorway, hands on her substantial hips.

"*Perdon, tia Esmerelda.*" Reuben bowed. "I can't help myself." He turned to Martha. "Martha, this is my aunt, Esmerelda Cordona. *Tia Esmerelda*, this is Martha Ward."

Martha smiled. The woman didn't smile back, but gestured with one of her heavy arms for them to come in, come in.

The living room was black and gold. The carpet was gold, the lamp shades were black, and the black coffee table was decorated with gold glitter. On the wall above the gold sofa, mirrored tiles alternated with black squares depicting religious scenes. A black crucifix, with a golden Jesus, hung alone on one wall. There was a warm, spicy smell of cilantro and cooked chili peppers, and Martha could hear women talking and laughing in the kitchen.

On the black recliner a man was sleeping. He was fat and mustached; he wore a black T-shirt and his two front teeth were gold. He fit right in.

Reuben leaned over to Martha and whispered, "He's a cliché, isn't he? Fat Mexican sleepin' it off."

Martha giggled nervously. *Tia Esmerelda* turned around.

"Come on, you love birds. The family's out back."

The yard was green and well cared for. Plastic colored lanterns surrounding Christmas lights were strung from side to side. Three picnic tables were squeezed together. There were dark-haired men and women and teenagers and children and babies everywhere. As they walked down the three steps from the back door it seemed to Martha that each and every one of them turned to look at her. Martha swallowed hard and crossed her white arms behind her trying to hide them.

"Told you you wouldn't be overdressed," Reuben whispered into her ear.

It was true. The women, the young women, all dressed for this backyard barbecue as if they were going to a club. They wore makeup, hair spray, tight dresses, dark stockings, and high heels. Martha looked again and she knew why. It was for the young men with tan, bare, muscular arms, tight white T-shirts, and baggy gray or khaki trousers. There was a dance of sorts going on here. The young men clustered near the barbecue grill in one corner. The young women posed under the tree opposite. They looked back and forth at each other and away. One of the men, hair slicked back and shiny, threw a fake punch at one of the other guys and danced away avoiding the return hit. All the time, he had one eye on the gaggle of girls.

Reuben walked her over to the tree. Martha knew he was going to deposit her and head over to his friends at the barbecue grill. The women looked at her, smiling grudgingly—they liked Reuben, but they weren't sure about her.

"Ladies," Reuben said, "this is my friend, Martha."

"Hi." A tall busty girl with dark sleepy eyes spoke for the group.

"Hi," Martha said. The tall girl had rhinestones on her long red fingernails.

"That's Sharon." Reuben pointed to the tall girl. "And Jessica and Anna and Marie and Raymona. They are all, in one way or another, related to me. Some more distantly than others, right, Sharon?"

Sharon put one incredible fingernail in her mouth and pretended to flick something from her teeth at Reuben. He laughed.

"His cousin was goin' out with my sister," Sharon explained, "but he dumped her, bad. Somehow, I just keep comin' around."

"Must be the good food," Reuben said.

"It's certainly not the company." Sharon turned away from him.

Reuben laughed again.

"Martha, stay right here, okay?" he said. "You want something to drink?"

"Sure," Martha said. She wasn't thirsty, but she wanted something to do with her hands.

"I'll see what they got."

He walked off, not toward the table with the sodas but toward the other men. Martha was left with the women. She knew they were all younger than she, but they had a worldly weariness that made them seem older.

"So, Martha," one of the women, Anna, said, "you're a natural red-head, aren't you?"

"Yes," Martha said brightly. "And you're a natural brunet?"

The women laughed. Martha sighed.

"Sorry," she said. "That was a stupid thing to say. I mean, nobody dyes their hair just brown, do they?"

There was a silence. Martha blurted on, making it worse. Some part of her brain was screaming, why don't you just shut up?

"I mean, your hair is beautiful, a beautiful brown, but it's—I mean, the kind of women who dye their hair, well, brown's not the color they choose, is it?"

She stopped, finally. The group of women just looked at her, five pairs of dark brown eyes, five heads of dark brown hair. Finally, one of them, a little plump and not quite as pretty as the rest, laughed.

"I know what you mean," she said. "I always wanted to be a blonde, myself."

"Me too," Martha said with relief. "Any color but red."

"Even brown?" Anna asked.

"Oh yes. I was teased so badly as a child."

"How long you been seein' Reuben?" Sharon broke in abruptly.

"About a month and a half," Martha replied.

"Where'd you meet?"

"At my club," Martha replied truthfully and without thinking, then cringed.

"You belong to the same health club as Reuben?" the plump girl asked.

For the second time the girl had saved her from an embarrassing moment. Martha smiled at her gratefully. She didn't think she could tell Reuben's Catholic family that she used to be a topless waitress.

"Yes, I do," Martha replied, "I do. It's very nice. Do you?"

One of the other girls snickered and poked the plump one in the ribs. "Does it look like she belongs to a health club?"

Martha was shocked, but the plump girl just laughed. "I'm built for comfort, not for speed," she said proudly.

The others laughed affectionately.

Martha looked around for Reuben. He was standing with the guys across the way. Martha watched them. They were elegant together, comfortable with each other, like a pride of young lions, stretching, moving, brown and beautiful. One of them had long hair, very long, pulled back in a pony tail. It was like a tail undulating back and forth as he talked. As Martha watched he took it out of the rubber band and shook it free. Martha saw his handsome face in profile and imagined him curled next to her, licking her neck, her face, her ear.

"You got one already," Sharon said beside her. "Don't go lookin' at Raymona's *chico*."

Martha was startled. "I wasn't, I'm sorry, it's just . . ."

"I know, I know. Give up Reuben, white girl, and maybe Jorge will go for you. You never know."

Martha looked at the four other girls, talking together. Sharon read her mind.

"Yeah," she said, nodding toward the plump one, "that's Raymona. She's his *ruca*. Hot and heavy for years. That baby, on that old lady's lap, *y el nino*, that boy, by the swing set, those are hers—and his." She paused. "But you wanna break up this happy home, you not happy with what you got, you can go for it, see what happens."

"Oh no," Martha said, "I just thought . . . they all looked like lions to me."

Sharon looked at Martha. "Watch out they don't bite you," she said and laughed.

Finally, Reuben returned and led her over to meet his mother. She was a short, gray-haired older woman who spoke very little English. Reuben translated the standard pleasantries, but Martha felt she wasn't making a good impression. A little girl, three or four, snuck up behind Martha and touched the back of her arm. Martha turned and smiled at her, but the girl ran away terrified.

They sat down to eat and Martha watched the girls split up and sit with their men and children. All the women, except Sharon, had at least one child. And all the women, except Sharon, had a boyfriend or husband. Martha watched them with their kids. They were tough and loving and casual.

"What are you cryin' for," Raymona said to her four-year-old son. "You've got nothin' to complain about, stupid! Look at this food. Here." She speared him a barbecued sparerib. "Stick this in your mouth and shut up."

Then she hugged him hard and kissed the top of his head.

Martha was amazed. No one in her family spoke that way, to any one, even in private. They weren't allowed to say "shut up" or call each other "stupid." They weren't allowed to get angry with one another. If her mother was angry with her, she told Audrey and Audrey told Martha. If Martha was angry with Audrey, she told her mother. Audrey and Martha were never angry with Dolly. They couldn't imagine it; their mother was too fragile.

After the trip to the hospital on Martha's fifteenth birthday, things changed. Audrey moved back home. Lars was around more, at least at first, and their mother was cheerful all the time. Now, Martha could suppose she was medicated. But at the time, it seemed that whatever had happened to her had happened for the best. But there were odd things too.

Martha came into the kitchen one morning dressed for school in a plaid skirt and a black turtleneck. Martha loved that black T-neck; it was cool. Her mother turned from the coffee pot and froze. Her eyes went hard and flat and her lips pressed together, Missouri style, Audrey called it, just like their grandmother's.

"What are you wearing?" she asked. Her voice was tight. Her words clipped at the ends.

"What's wrong?"

"No child of mine wears black," Dolly said. "I won't have it."

"Why not?"

"It's unseemly. Pruitt girls don't wear black."

"Mom," Martha began the familiar preteen whine, "Mom, but everybody wears black."

"Not Pruitt girls."

"I'm not a Pruitt girl. I've been wearing black for ages."

"You will stay home."

"What?"

"Until you change that shirt and apologize to me, you will stay home. In your room. Now!"

Audrey had entered just at that moment, followed by Lars, looking sleepy and fat in his beige pajamas.

"What's goin' on?" Audrey asked.

"Mom won't let me wear this," Martha answered, "because it's black."

"Young lady," her mother said, "I told you to go to your room."

Martha left and Audrey followed her.

"Whatever she wants," Audrey said, "just agree. Put the turtleneck in your backpack and change in the forsythia bushes. That's what I always do."

"But why? I've worn this shirt lots of times. She never said anything before."

"Just do it," Audrey said. "Mom's nuts. She's really nuts. Just do what she says."

"But—"

"Fine." Audrey was angry now too. "And if Mom goes to the hospital again, it'll be your fault. Go ahead, wear the stupid shirt."

Martha had changed and apologized. Her mother had kissed her and hugged her and told her she was the best girl in the world.

There were words they couldn't say. Nice words, not swear words or anything, but words like "butter," and "slick" and "pie pan." "Butter" would make her cry, but most of the words just made her angry.

There were places they couldn't go, movies, department stores, most restaurants.

And her mother gave up eating. She had crackers crumbled into milk, or milk shakes, or coffee, but almost nothing else. She wore the same clothes day after day and kept them completely clean.

Their grandmother came again to visit, just after she was diagnosed with the cancer. Martha wanted to go to a slumber party and her mother wouldn't let her. Martha got angry and stomped her feet and slammed her bedroom door. Her grandmother walked right into her room without knocking and stood at the side of her bed.

"Get up," Grandmother said.

Martha sat up and swung her legs over the edge of her bed, but the scowl was still on her face.

"Let me tell you something." Grandmother's voice was as sharp as her elbows. "Your mother is going to be dead. And I am going to be dead. And you will be alone. And no one will care if you went to that sleepover party or not. Now straighten up and help your mother in the time she has left."

Martha didn't know her mother was going to die. She didn't know being crazy was a terminal disease. She stared at the imposing force of her grandmother and began to cry.

"Stop it," came the voice like splinters. "Stop it. You can't help your mother like this. If she dies now, won't you be sorry."

Her mother was still alive. Grandmother had died a long time ago. But looking around the table at Reuben's family, Martha had never felt so alone. It was easier to be alone when you had nothing to compare it with. She wasn't so happy anymore.

"I'm going to learn Spanish," she told Reuben that night in bed.

"Why?"

"So I can talk to your mother."

"So you can eavesdrop on my conversations," Reuben said.

"That too." Martha curled her body next to Reuben's. She cupped her hands around his strong biceps.

"Everyone told me how beautiful you are. Like an ice queen, my grandmother said."

"Really? Is an ice queen good?"

"You need to talk more. Stop watching. Staring at people. It makes them uncomfortable."

"Okay," Martha whispered, "I will. I promise."

"Lighten up. You're such a thinker. It's too much."

"Okay," Martha said and held him tighter. "Okay. Okay. Okay."

13

JEWEL PHONED.

"HI . . . MOM." JEWEL'S LITTLE CHILD voice was quiet, hesitant.

"Hi, Jewel." Jewel never called.

"This weekend," Jewel began.

It was Martha's weekend with Jewel. She knew Jewel didn't want to come.

"Are you busy?" Martha let her daughter off the hook. "That's okay. I understand. We'll make it up next time."

"Thanks, Mom." Jewel's relief was obvious. "My friend, Sonya, is having a huge Halloween party—actually it's her whole family's party—there's gonna be a moon bounce and food and a magician. Everybody's going. Grown-ups, kids."

"Sounds great," Martha said. "Of course you can't miss it."

Martha remembered her mother warning her that this would happen. With such infrequent visits, Dolly had cautioned, eventually Jewel's main life would interfere. "I suffered with you and your sister and no husband," sniffed Dolly. "It's no picnic, but you can do it too."

"Thanks, Mom. Thanks." Jewel paused. "Do you want to come? You can."

Martha knew that Jewel was just asking her to make her feel better. Martha knew Jewel expected her to say no.

But Martha said, "Yes. Yes, I'd love to."

Halloween, the actual day, was on a Tuesday, so Martha would miss seeing Jewel in her costume. This Saturday night party was her only chance.

"You really, I mean, you really wanna come?"

"Sure."

There was a pause. Martha knew Jewel wasn't thrilled, but Martha wanted to go, to assert herself. She was her mother after all.

"Okay. Okay," Jewel said as if making up her mind, "I'll tell Dad he can't come."

"Okay. Great. I'll pick you up. What time?"

"Seven o'clock. You sure you want to? You have to wear a costume—at least a mask, or a funny hat or something."

"What are you going to be?"

"Raggedy Ann, remember? I told you that last time. Susan made me the coolest costume."

"Oh, right. Great. Well, I'll think of something."

She would think of something. She didn't sew, but she could glue and staple. She could always rent something. It was only Wednesday.

By Saturday morning she still hadn't thought of anything. Reuben was no help. He thought she should be a hooker and wear the fishnets and tiny skirt from the Sweet Spot.

"On second thought," he said and put his arms around her, "I don't want any of those horny dads making moves on you."

She ran to the costume store, but everything she liked—Little Red Riding Hood, Queen Guinevere, Alice in Wonderland—was already rented. The salesgirl suggested wearing her bathrobe and slippers, putting her hair in curlers, and carrying a frying pan.

"What would I be?" asked Martha.

"A housewife," the twenty-year-old girl replied and laughed as if there was really no such thing.

As Martha headed up the stairs from the bargain basement she spotted a dusty pumpkin costume hanging in the back. She pulled out the huge spherical body, orange material stretched over an umbrella spoke frame that gave when she pushed on it and then sprang back into shape. There was also a hat, green felt pasted over chicken wire squished and bent to look like a stem.

Martha looked at her watch. Looked at the costume.

"With your hair, it'll be perfect," the salesgirl said.

"I'll take it."

Reuben couldn't stop laughing at her. She wore the orange orb over a black T-shirt and green tights she had just bought. She tried to tuck her hair up under the green hat, but then the hat wouldn't sit straight, so she left it hanging long and curly. She was dismayed to see how the color of her hair just matched the pumpkin.

"What are your legs supposed to be?" he asked when he could control himself.

"I don't know," Martha said. "Roots."

"Pumpkins don't have roots." He laughed again. "Just don't come to any of my parties looking like that."

Then she couldn't get into her car wearing the costume. She tried flattening the sides with her arms, but they were too springy. She tried scrunching the pumpkin up behind her, but it was too stiff. Finally she had to take the costume off altogether. She drove on the freeway to the west side of town feeling naked in just her black T-shirt and green tights. Her little stem hat kept bumping and scraping on the ceiling.

She pulled up in front of Allen's big, traditional California ranch house and stopped. She didn't drive up the circular drive. She didn't want to get out of the car without her pumpkin on. She didn't want to just honk for Jewel. Why hadn't she thought of this before? She could have brought a skirt to throw on, or a pair of jeans.

Instead, she opened the car door and got out, crouching down behind the car. She didn't close her door; she didn't want to make any noise. She opened the back door and tugged on the pumpkin. She couldn't get a grip on it, and the pumpkin was too round to fit through the door easily. She couldn't get it out without standing up.

"Shit!" she said and yanked. It sprang from the car, knocking her backward and onto her bottom on the street.

Allen's front door opened. Allen stood there, casual in autumn corduroy and cashmere even though it was still eighty degrees outside. He squinted into the darkness.

"Martha?"

Martha threw the pumpkin on. She got it backward, the face on her backside, but she didn't care. She slammed her car doors closed and walked up to the house.

"Look at you," Allen said.

Susan came to the door and stood next to him. She was wearing a lovely rust and olive patterned dress and enameled pumpkin earrings. She was plump with thick dark hair and big brown eyes. She had a round, inviting bosom. Martha thought it looked like she'd put on weight. Martha tried to touch her own flat stomach but patted the orb of pumpkin instead.

"We didn't think you'd be in costume," Susan said.

"Oh. Well." Martha shrugged. The pumpkin skin lurched up and down.

Jewel appeared. She looked wonderful. Red and white striped stockings. A gingham dress with a white pinafore. And a remarkable red yarn wig. Her face was made up too.

"You look terrific!" Martha hoped she didn't sound surprised.

"Thanks. Susan made it. She did my makeup too."

Martha smiled at the triangle nose, the big black drawn lashes. "It's wonderful, Susan. Really it is."

Allen put a proprietary arm around Susan. He smiled with smug self-satisfaction. Martha hated that, men who took personal pride in what their women accomplished as if they were somehow responsible.

"You look good too," Jewel said.

"I've got it on backward," Martha said, turning around. "See?"

"Oh."

She had scraped one of the triangular eyes loose when she pulled the costume from the car.

"Oops."

"I have a needle and thread," Susan said, "or some glue."

"No. Don't bother."

"Really, it's no trouble."

So Martha stood in the large, clean, color-coordinated living room of her ex-husband's new house and let Susan kneel at her side and sew the eye back on. Jewel waited quietly, shifting from foot to foot, careful not to touch the makeup on her face.

"How do you drive in that thing?" Allen asked.

"I can't," Martha said. "I have to put it in the backseat."

Allen nodded. He tried not to laugh, but couldn't help himself and snorted loudly, once, twice.

"Sorry, Martha," he said, "but . . . a pumpkin?"

"It's all they had," she replied.

"It's very festive," Susan said brightly. "And appropriate."

The party was enormous, the house more of a mansion than a home. There was valet parking by attendants in Three Musketeers costumes. Martha didn't want someone to park her car. She needed it to hide behind when she put on her orb.

She sat for a moment while the Hispanic musketeer in lace and knickers waited. She took a deep breath and opened her car door. She got out bravely as if she didn't care that her underwear showed through the thin tights. Jewel came around the car to help.

"You're so skinny," Jewel said. "Susan and I are dieting together."

Martha was dismayed to hear the edge of unhappy envy in her daughter's voice. Jewel shouldn't, couldn't, be jealous of her. Martha had always been resentful of Dolly's beauty, her ease with men, her popularity. It was a terrible feeling, tragic, to be jealous of your own mother.

"You look beautiful," Martha said as she pulled on the pumpkin. "You do. You don't need to diet."

"Thanks," she said grudgingly, not believing.

"I mean it." Martha nodded emphatically. "Looks like you've lost five pounds already. That's enough."

"Really?" Jewel's smile was worth the lie.

Inside, the entire place had been turned into a haunted house. Waiters in vampire gear served special Halloween treats on trays. Bats and cobwebs hung from the ceilings; a suit of armor in the front hall was motorized to drop its spear as you went by. Jewel immediately saw three girls she knew and was surrounded by them; they squealed over each other's outfits.

Martha was the only parent in a costume. Some of the adults wore hats or a silly necktie, but no costumes. Martha smiled at the other grown-ups, but no one approached her.

"Who are our hosts?" She interrupted Jewel.

"My parents," said a girl dressed like Shirley Temple. She tossed her blonde corkscrew curls. "Harvey and Roberta Gold. You can't miss 'em—they're the ones looking completely crazed."

The group of girls giggled. Martha smiled politely.

"I'll see if I can find them," she said.

Jewel barely looked up as Martha walked off.

The house was huge. Martha felt invisible and conspicuous at the same time. Everyone looked at her giant orange body, but nobody looked at her. Martha wandered from room to room, pretending to admire the decorations, wondering how long Jewel would want to stay.

A woman, in her early fifties and dressed for a cocktail party, put out a jeweled, manicured hand and stopped Martha.

"Dear," she said, "my husband wants some more of those little sandwiches. The ones shaped like bats."

"Oh," Martha said, smiling, "I don't work here. I'm a parent."

"Well," said the woman, frowning, "sorry. It wasn't apparent to me."

Martha laughed, but the woman wasn't joking. She strutted off in search of a vampire.

Martha turned a corner and found herself in the kitchen, where, despite the catering crew that was trying to continue the flow of canapés, a large group had congregated. One of the men, short and bald with a smooth open face, looked over at her. He looked her up and down, then laughed. He gestured her over to the group.

Martha came up next to him.

"Nice pumpkin," he said. "Very nice."

"Thank you," said Martha. "I feel ridiculous."

"Don't. You look great. The rest of us are just chickens."

Martha smiled at this guy. He was just her height. She knew his type. His type had always liked her; the slightly plump ones, insecure, in need of maternal protection. She was glad he was here.

"What's your name?" he asked.

"Martha Ward. Jewel is my little girl. She's in Sonya's class at school."

"No. You don't look old enough to have such a big daughter."

"I'm older than I look."

"Must be the pumpkin suit." He paused, putting out his hand. "I'm Jeffrey Brin. I'm the Golds' legal counsel."

"Hi."

"Wanna drink?" he asked. "I'm buying."

"Sure," Martha said. "A beer, any kind."

She didn't really like beer, but it was more adult than asking for juice. She could hold a beer all night if necessary.

Jeffrey walked out on the patio to a large ice-filled black witch's cauldron, and Martha followed him. She stopped when she saw a tall man with his back to her leaning against a Gothic-style pillar and looking out at the pool and beyond. It was Dr. Hamilton. She recognized his depressed shoulders, the layers in his light brown hair, the way he stood with his toes pointing slightly in.

Jeffrey scooped a bottle of beer out of the ice and turned to Martha. "Here you go."

At the sound of his voice, Dr. Hamilton turned toward them. He glanced at Jeffrey.

"Dr. H.," Jeffrey said, nodding hello.

Dr. Hamilton nodded back, but he was looking at Martha.

She held her breath. Under the colored patio lights, her orange pumpkin glowed. Her hat tilted toward him. But he sighed and gave her a polite smile and turned away, not recognizing her.

Martha knew she couldn't speak. He would know her voice. Instead she went back in and Jeffrey followed her.

Inside, among the noise and chatter of the others, she said quietly, "Thanks."

"Sorry I didn't introduce you, but I forgot your name. Already. I'm terrible with names."

"Martha."

"Jeffrey."

"You know him?" Martha asked.

Jeffrey nodded, shrugged. "I'm one of his lawyers." He didn't want to say more, and Martha wouldn't ask. "So? You married or what?"

"Divorced," Martha answered.

They talked about their expired marriages. Jeffrey asked her for her phone number. Martha told him she had a boyfriend. Jeffrey nodded, not surprised. And all the time Martha stood facing the doors to the patio and watching Dr. Hamilton. He didn't move. He stared out at the pool and the grassy yard beyond as if it were the most fascinating movie.

A woman came up to him. Martha took a deep breath. She was older than Martha and attractive in that way wealthy women have of being very well taken care of. She had shoulder-length, frosted blonde hair, and she was elegantly yet casually dressed in perfect-fitting Levi's and a white blouse. Martha watched Dr. Hamilton bend down to her and smile and nod. Martha watched them talk to each other. Then the woman laughed, and as they walked away together he hesitated and then put his arm gently around her shoulders.

Martha felt sick to her stomach. Her legs wobbled.

"Whoa," Jeffrey said as he took her arm. "You've hardly touched that beer."

Martha smiled at him. "I'd better find my daughter."

Martha left him but went searching for Dr. Hamilton and his friend. She saw them at the front door, saying good-bye to two people she assumed were Mr. and Mrs. Gold. A group of very young costumed children, barely more than toddlers, dressed as ballerinas, mice, cowboys, and dinosaurs, ran by. Martha saw a familiar look on Dr. Hamilton's face; of tenderness and desire so great that it was painful to him. She watched the well-known clenching and opening of his hands. She watched him turn away and lurch out the door, escaping, running from his feelings.

Martha wanted to run after him, but instead the blonde woman did. Martha heard her calling to him.

"Aaron? Aaron?"

That was what the A stood for. She had thought it was Adam. Aaron. She said it in her mind. She said it aloud. Aaron Hamilton. She liked not knowing better. She wished she hadn't seen him here tonight, but she hurried to a front window trying to see his car, his lady friend's car, to see them go off together. She did, in fact, see them. The blonde held his arms and leaned her head against his chest. The musketeer valets brought them separate cars, but Martha knew they were going home together.

And suddenly Martha had to find a bathroom. She hurried up the expansive staircase and through a dark bedroom into a rose-colored, gold-plated bathroom. She threw up and threw up and threw up. Her stem hat slipped and fell off her head, but she caught it just before it splashed into the vomit-filled toilet bowl. One ribbon slipped through her trembling fingers and dipped, only a quarter of an inch or so, into the disgusting, viscous water.

She washed the green ribbon in very hot water and pink rose-shaped soap. She rinsed out her mouth and rubbed toothpaste on her teeth. Her face was pale with a sallow, greenish tint enhanced by the felt hat.

Downstairs, she felt better. She followed a vampire looking for those little bat sandwiches herself. She should eat something. That was probably her problem. She tried not to think about Tuesday night, about seeing Dr. Hamilton again.

She ran into Jeffrey and took his arm.

"I'm starving," she said. "Catch me a vampire, will you?"

When she dropped Jewel off at home, she no longer cared about being seen without her pumpkin suit. She walked Jewel to the door in her T-shirt and tights and hugged her daughter hard.

"It was a great party," Jewel said sleepily. "Wasn't it?"

"You bet. Thanks for inviting me."

"Thanks for coming. And thanks for wearing the costume. Nobody else's parents did."

"I know." Martha kissed Jewel on her faded pink cheeks. "See you in two weeks," she said.

14

MARTHA DRUMMED HER GLOVED FINGERS ON THE
ARM REST AS DR. HAMILTON CAME IN. HE
smiled at her, as now he usually did.

"Hello, Martha," he said warmly. "How are you? How was your
weekend?"

"Fine," Martha said. "I went to a very interesting Halloween party."

"I'm glad yours was interesting. The one I went to was very dull."

"I'm sorry to hear that."

He looked at her. He heard the sharpness in her voice.

Since Halloween night she had found herself growing angry with Dr.
Hamilton. He had a life, obviously a prosperous, fortuitous life. He had
a beautiful woman who loved him. Why didn't he talk to her?

"What's in the can?" she asked.

Dr. Hamilton didn't reply. He stopped where he was and sighed.

"The can under the table. The gas can. What's it for?"

"It has nothing to do with you."

"It's been there for two months. What's in it?"

"It's not for you to worry about."

"It scares me."

"I thought we were past that. I thought we were friends."

"Then why is it there? And why won't you tell me what's in it?"

"I don't want to. And it's none of your business." Dr. Hamilton paused, then continued angrily, "It can't make you that nervous. You keep coming."

"Maybe because I'm curious."

"That the only reason?"

"Maybe."

There was a long pause. Dr. Hamilton looked sad suddenly.

"Am I so very odd?" he asked.

"Yes," Martha told him, "yes, you are. Why won't you tell me anything about yourself, your life? You know so much about me."

He sat in the chair across from her but didn't look at her. His rumpled face sagged. His shoulders drooped.

"Martha," he began softly.

"What?" Her voice was sharp.

He didn't reply. He sat perfectly still for a moment. He reminded Martha of a child being chastised—unjustly. Then he reached into his inside jacket pocket. He took out her money, three hundred-dollar bills like always, and an envelope.

He was going to fire her. That envelope looked so final, so white and finished. It might be a small bonus, or maybe a letter of recommendation for another job. Martha didn't want another job. But she knew this was it. She and Dr. Hamilton had gotten too chummy, too relaxed with each other. They talked about beauty, but they talked about other things too. They had even laughed together.

She looked forward to her evenings with him. Even tonight she had wanted to come. She didn't know why she'd been so mean and snappish. He probably carried that envelope every week and tonight, because she'd been such a bitch, he'd pulled it out.

He put the three hundred dollars on the table between them and handed her the white envelope.

"This is for you," he said.

Martha took it gingerly. She didn't want it.

"I'm sorry . . ." she began.

He waved her silent.

"Open it," he said. "It's not a letter bomb."

Inside were two tickets to the ballet, the real ballet at the Dorothy Chandler Pavilion.

"Why did you give these to me?" she asked. She was astonished, surprised at the warm moisture in her eyes.

"You said you danced as a child. I thought you'd like them. Maybe you could take your little girl."

"Thank you," Martha said. "Thank you."

"I thought about us going together," Dr. Hamilton said seriously, "but I wasn't sure about the visibility in your hood." He smiled, tried not to laugh.

"I wouldn't want to watch ballet through it, it's true," Martha said, matching his earnest tone. "On the other hand, I wouldn't have to worry about what to wear."

Dr. Hamilton couldn't help it any longer, he laughed.

"So you like them, then?" he asked.

"Yes. Yes. But, why don't you use them yourself?"

"I don't go to the ballet," he said quietly. He stopped smiling. "I can't go."

"You're allergic to tulle and Lycra?"

"No." Dr. Hamilton tried to smile at her. "It's . . . it's the beauty. I can't stand it. Those beautiful girls, their long arms and legs, their perfect profiles. The music . . ."

"They're not so beautiful," Martha said. "I danced a long time. I know a lot of ballerinas. They're emaciated. They look like concentration camp survivors. They have breast reductions so their tits won't bounce on stage. They lacquer their hair to get it in those buns. They're beautiful from a distance, but up close they look deformed."

"Really?"

Martha was exaggerating, but she felt desperate to cheer him up. "Oh yes. Maybe not modern dancers, but ballerinas for sure. You should see their feet. Gross."

"Interesting concept," Dr. Hamilton mused, "to so distort your personal beauty so you can be beautiful from a distance."

"I'm sure television people do it too. You know, TV adds ten pounds. Some of those women must be pretty funny looking in person."

Dr. Hamilton's face lifted. He sat back in his chair and looked at Martha's face—or where her face would be inside the hood—and shook his head.

"Why," he finally asked, "why were you so angry with me when I came in?"

Martha shrugged.

"Answer me. I can't imagine what I've done."

Martha didn't want to tell him. She didn't understand how she could feel jealous. But it wasn't jealousy. It was fear, fear that he didn't really need her. She watched his hand stroke the grain in the arm of the chair. She loved his fingers. They were long and strong, the joints clearly defined. He had only touched her that one time when he grabbed her arm. If she made him angry enough would he grab her again?

"You haven't done anything," she said. "It's me. I . . . I worry that I'm not enough for you."

"What do you mean?"

"I thought the white envelope—I thought you were going to fire me."

"Why would I do that? Haven't I made it clear that you've been, you continue to be, a great help to me?"

Martha felt glad and embarrassed at the same time. She didn't want him to think she'd been asking for praise. She was suddenly desperate to change the subject.

"I'm sorry. Of course, you . . . well, Reuben and I, you know, it's been a little strained lately."

She had hoped Dr. Hamilton would relax, assume his occasional role of confidant and favorite uncle. Instead, he crossed his arms in front of his chest.

"I don't want to talk about him. I'm sorry if it's not going well, but—"

"But—"

"We have talked at great length, Martha, about Reuben. How beautiful he is, what makes him beautiful, his green eyes, his white teeth, how you love looking at him and what it means to you to be able to look at him. I even know all about his goddamn tattoos!"

"I won't talk about him anymore."

"Good. Unless, of course, it has something to do with our topic at hand."

"It does. It does. The issue of beauty is very important to Reuben. I'm definitely not pretty enough for him."

"Has he said so? What a jerk."

"No. No," Martha almost whispered, "it's just that . . . I'm terrified."

"Terrified?"

"I know I'm not pretty enough for Reuben. I know it myself. But what if I'm not pretty at all? What if it's ridiculous for me to assume that I am? What if I don't know the truth, that I've lied to myself for so long? What if people laugh at me behind my back when I get dressed up and go out with him? What if they know I'm just Reuben's charity case?

"You'd think there'd be more to your relationship—"

"But what if there isn't? My mother only talked about the things I could overcome; my small breasts, my hair. My father doesn't like my type. All his girlfriends were plump and dark, the opposite of me.

"If I think about it," she continued letting her thoughts escape, "if I think about it, I panic. I know I'm not deformed, and if I sit quietly by myself, or like here when I'm with you, I begin to feel like it doesn't matter. But I know that's not true. It's just that I forget what I look like. I truly have no idea. You can't see me, so I don't see your reaction to how I look—so I don't know myself. Isn't that how we judge our appearance? By the reaction we get from others?"

"No, Martha." Dr. Hamilton had calmed down. "That shouldn't be how we see ourselves. You seem so strong in here. You know your mind. How do you think you look?"

"I don't know. I don't know. But in here it doesn't matter, does it?" Martha paused for breath and her blue-socked feet shuffled on the carpet. "You know," she said, "that's why I keep coming back. I don't have to have an appearance. My form, my grace, my comeliness, my polish, they all become abstract. They don't matter—to you."

"Is everyone else in your life so shallow?"

"Is it shallow? What else do we have to go on?"

Dr. Hamilton shuddered. "No, Martha, no. It must be more than that."

"I don't think so."

"Martha. I know you're lonely. I know you don't have a good relationship with your daughter. I know you have a boyfriend. I know you were a topless waitress. Those things contradict one another. You can't be unattractive and yet you are alone most of the time, I think against your wishes."

Martha didn't say anything. He seemed to know her so well.

"What do you look like?" he asked.

"Do you want me to take the hood off?"

"No. No. Please. But describe yourself."

"No."

"Why not?"

"I wouldn't know what to say."

"What color are your eyes?" he asked. "Your hair? How tall are you? How much do you weigh? Can you answer these questions?"

"Yes, of course."

"So—"

"No. Now I don't want you to know. In the beginning I felt I couldn't

communicate without my face, at least. Now I would hate for you to
see me."

"Why?"

Martha took a long time before answering.

"What if I disappoint you?"

"What if you're better than I expect?"

"I don't want to take that chance with you."

1
5

WHEN SHE PULLED UP AND PARKED IN FRONT
OF HER HOUSE, SHE WAS RELIEVED THAT REUBEN
wasn't there. She was tired. But once inside her house she missed him.
Driving home her mind had ricocheted off the past, going faster than
her car, filling her with memories and should've saids and wishes. But
her house was too empty and suddenly, very suddenly, she felt empty
too.

She took off her sandals and placed them by the door as always, in
case of an earthquake. She went downstairs to her bedroom, passing
the closed door to Jewel's room, opened her underwear drawer and
dropped the three hundred dollars inside. She didn't close the drawer.
The money called to her, teasing her, sticking out its green tongue at
her and laughing. She had almost seven thousand dollars in hundred-
dollar bills stashed among her bras and panties. Two months of work.
She hadn't spent any of it.

She pulled off her T-shirt, unsnapped and unzipped her jeans. They
dropped to the floor by themselves; thanks to Reuben she no longer
had to wiggle them over her hips. She stepped out of her underpants.
She stood naked in front of all that money. She gathered it in her hands
and carried it over to her bed. She wanted to bury herself in money.

She started with her feet, carefully placing the bills over her toes and
insteps and ankles. She moved up each leg. The money was cool and
tickled a little when it touched her skin. She used two bills lengthwise
for her knees. She had to layer the money over her thighs.

She felt bad when she lied to Allen that she couldn't find work. She
told him she was thinking about going back to school. His jaw tight-
ened, his hand jingled the change in his khaki pocket as it always did
when they talked about money, but he nodded as if he thought it was
a good idea. Martha could use her own money, this money lying cross-
hatched on her empty stomach, for her courses. It made her feel good
to think of how Allen's face would look when she told him she didn't
need his money for tuition.

But Martha didn't know what she wanted to study. She lay back and
placed a hundred-dollar bill over each breast. When she breathed the
paper shivered, limp seesaws on her erect nipples.

She thought maybe she would just take a trip. But there wasn't anywhere she wanted to go. She could visit her mother and her current
husband in Florida, but since Martha's divorce they always came for
Christmas and it would be Christmas soon enough. Audrey's big house
and Mormon family in Salt Lake City were not appealing. Audrey had
turned 180 degrees from free sex and drug-induced nirvana to religion
in the form of a widowed Mormon bishop and his three kids. Now they
had six between them and her only addiction was to sugar and *Family
Home Evening*.

Still the thought of going somewhere stood upright in her mind, a
pillar she couldn't get around. She would have something to tell Dr.
Hamilton. He would miss her. So would Reuben. She would come back
and Reuben would hold her in his arms and tell her how great she
looked with a tan. She was one of those rare redheads who could tan a
little. But tanning was bad for you and Reuben would only notice the
week spent without going to the gym. He was always telling her, "It
takes six weeks to get in shape and one week to lose it."

Maybe she and Reuben could go somewhere together. Club Med, a tropical island for couples where you didn't use money and every minute was taken care of. But she hated those planned events, the forced nature of every meal, swim, nap.

Lars, her first stepfather and Dolly's third husband, had met Dolly at a Parents Without Partners picnic. Martha dreaded the P.W.P. events. The men and women laughed too loud and wore clothing that made them self-conscious and uncomfortable. The children were all belligerent, suspicious, and sullen. They viewed each other as potential usurpers to their family rites and traditions—possible future stepsiblings guaranteed to make their lives even more miserable than they already were.

To Dolly's credit, she hated these events too. But she went because her best friend, Phyllis, belonged. Phyllis was the perfect P.W.P. member. She wore her dyed hair in pigtails, she drank long-necked Buds from the bottle like she was giving oral sex, and she had a high-pitched laugh, one long note of a cat in heat. She had one kid, a fifteen-year-old boy she truly called Timmy, whom Audrey dated for a while. Years later he revealed he was a transvestite and then killed himself.

Usually the P.W.P. functions were "adults only," but for the occasional picnics and baseball games Dolly dragged Martha along, and Audrey too if she could find her. Dolly always looked cool, detached, bored. The men flocked to her like ants to a fallen sweet roll. But she would only sigh and smile at them sadly, as if her personal sorrow was too much for her to share.

Lars didn't have any children. He was just passing by the picnic on his daily jog around the park, saw Dolly sitting on a peach-colored blanket under a tree, and decided to stop in. He was tall, big, Nordic with cool blue eyes and dark blonde hair. He wore clean gray sweatpants and a bright white T-shirt. His jaw was square. At first, Audrey called him Dudley Do-Right of the Canadian Mounties. But after they got to know him the girls called him Mr. Potato Skin. His skin was tough and pockmarked, not on his face, but all the other parts of his body. And the palms of his hands were always peeling. It was an allergy, their mother said.

Dolly was taken with him right off. At thirty-two, he was two years younger than she, a cab driver but well-read and informed, and he had the pure, unsullied manner of a man who had always lived with his mother. He had; in fact he still lived in the apartment over his mother's garage. He had never even had a steady girl. After the two experienced men she'd married, Lars was her Eliza Doolittle.

But he was not as malleable as she expected. He had a few hard aberrations that made him difficult to handle. Still on that sunny summer afternoon he looked like God's gift to the reluctant P.W.P. participant. Lars jogged home and showered, then returned for Dolly in his Karmen Ghia convertible. Martha and her sister went home with Phyllis.

Lars was around for a long time, most of Martha's life, from the time she was nine until after she married Allen. Before he and Dolly were married, he would come in the morning before the girls went to school and Dolly went to work at the law office and have breakfast with them. He'd come back at dinnertime, often bringing a bag of chips or a carton of ice cream. He stayed until the eleven o'clock news was over, then left to drive his cab all night or go back to his mother's garage to sleep.

Martha asked her mother one day, "Why doesn't Lars just live here?"

Dolly gasped and slapped her. Martha, at ten, hadn't thought it was a bad thing to say. It just seemed to make sense.

"How can you say that to your mother?" Dolly exclaimed. "What do you take me for? Pruitt girls don't do that sort of thing."

Dolly left the room in tears and Martha stood there, perplexed, her cheek tingling. She knew her mother was talking about sex. But Martha knew from Audrey that Lars and Dolly were already having sex. She had asked Audrey one night as they were brushing their teeth for bed why her mother was moaning and grunting in the TV room.

"Shouldn't we go help her?" Martha asked. "She sounds sick or something."

"Don't go in there," Audrey whispered emphatically. It would only be another six months before Audrey lost her own virginity. "They're screwing. It's what people do when they love each other."

From then on, Martha had this picture of Lars going round and round on top of her mother, literally screwing himself into her.

Martha hated Lars. Audrey liked him. Phyllis was crazy about him. Everybody liked Lars, except Martha. She hated the way he smelled, the way his dandruff collected on the back of his neck, the way his ears attached to his jaw directly without lobes. She hated his crewneck sweaters and perfectly pressed pants. When her father asked about him, all Martha could say was, "He's gross," but she couldn't explain why.

Lars loved Martha. She was his little pet, his own curly carrottop he called her. He liked taking her places. He'd go out of his way to drop by some of the other cabbies and show her off. He seemed, like most men, a little frightened of Audrey, but he couldn't keep his hands off Martha. Those big hands had fingers like steak fries, fat and yellow gold but squishy to touch. He would reach over in the car and squeeze Martha's knee to make her jump. For Lars she dressed down, baggy blue jeans and oversized flannel shirts. But Lars loved it.

"You look like a kid," he'd say.

"I am a kid," Martha would reply.

"I know. It's great."

He was the one person in her life who seemed to love her just the way she was, and she hated him. Her mother told her to appreciate the interest Lars was taking in her.

"God knows your father couldn't care less. When was the last time he called you? That's just the way he was with me." Any mention of Marvin and Dolly began her diatribe. "The minute he'd get some new interest, he'd forget all about me. I was sick in bed with the flu, sick as a dog, and could he bring me a bowl of soup? No. He was busy—"

Martha tuned out the familiar inventory of crimes, but it was true. Her father called less and less frequently. Their Friday night dates had become once a month instead of once a week. Martha blamed it on

Lars. No one would want to stop by the house and exchange pleasantries with him, especially Marvin, who was smarter and funnier and so much shorter.

Lars and Dolly got married eventually, pretty soon after Grandmother died. Martha cried loudly, sloppily, at the wedding.

"Shut up," Phyllis hissed at her. "Don't begrudge your mother the only happy relationship she's ever had."

"She was happy with my dad," Martha said.

"Never." Phyllis was matter of fact. "She only married him because . . ." She stopped and looked at Martha. "Never mind. This marriage is for love."

It was after the wedding that the love began to sour. Eventually it would stink, but at first there was just a slight odor of something not quite right but not yet gone.

Lars really was a potato. He was massive and quickly became lumpy. He drove his cab all night, the perfect potato job. He was in the dark most of the time, sitting in the airport lineup with an open bag of potato chips resting cannibalistically against his chunky thigh.

Dolly was a peach. She smelled of green leaves and clear skies and bright mornings on a farmer's table. She was covered in soft down, golden and blushing, even later when she grew overripe.

But peaches are delicate. They bruise easily. And she wasn't smart. When Mr. Potato Skin learned to use his steak fry fingers, Dolly sat, demure, dense, and took whatever came.

Martha thought of herself as a red apple. Generally utilitarian, not exceptional or exotic but dependable, in season.

How could a potato so terrify them both. Plodding, prosaic, dirty, best when fried in hot grease.

He had held her mother's head between his knees as she knelt on her pale green carpet.

"I'll snap it off!" Lars shouted. "Snap it like a string bean!"

16

SHE WOKE UP AT 3 A.M., DISORIENTED, TWISTED IN THE MONEY. HER PILLOW smelled of Reuben. She had bought new sheets and a new comforter cover for him in reds and browns, more masculine. He hadn't noticed. Jewel was coming tomorrow and she would meet Reuben for the first time. Martha got a glimpse, a quick image in her mind, of Reuben smiling at Jewel, but when she thought about it again, it seemed Reuben was Lars and Jewel was Martha. And Martha didn't want Reuben to be Lars. She hated Lars. And she loved Reuben.

She felt suddenly ashamed to be lying naked on her bed with hundred-dollar bills wrinkled under her butt, folded in the curve of her elbow, crunched between her toes. She pushed the money to the floor, piling it beside the bed. She didn't want to think about all that money.

She wished she could stay in her enormous blue suit. She imagined wearing it everywhere; to the grocery store and the club, to the movies, to Winchell's. She pictured everyone wearing them. She felt deliverance, a consoling safety in the idea. She gave her appearance up and loved the idea of everybody, everywhere, covered, invisible in navy blue or black or maybe brown.

Everyone that is, except Reuben. She needed to see him. His green eyes. His caramel skin. The smooth surface of his skin. She didn't think she'd like him in a sack. She wasn't sure he'd like her bagged either.

Maybe she'd try that, next time they were together; she'd cover him in a blanket and herself as well and force them to communicate. But the next time they were together Jewel would be with them. She could put Jewel under a soft, pink baby blanket. Martha smiled. Jewel could count to herself.

Martha heard a thump upstairs. And then another. She froze, held her breath and listened. Her neighbors were sometimes up at night. But all was quiet from that side of the house. Another, louder, thump upstairs.

Martha slid off her bed and tiptoed toward her bedroom door. Someone was upstairs; she knew it. She looked at the phone next to her bed, but she was afraid to make the noise of picking it up and dialing. She was afraid the lines would be cut. Silently she pulled on her jeans. Her hands were shaking. She could smell her sweat. She dropped her T-shirt over her head. She couldn't move fast enough.

She crept out of her bedroom. As a child she had practiced "Indian steps," walking without making any sound. It was a matter of putting her feet down in just the right way, putting her weight on the middle of her foot, not the heel or the toe. She knew the squeaky spots in this house as well as the house she'd grown up in.

She paused at the bottom of the stairs. There was a shuffle sound from above. A sliding, then another thump. She snuck up the stairs, one by one, stepping over the stair that squeaked and stopping just before the top.

She remembered sneaking up the stairs at her neighbor's house. She'd been invited to play with their little boy, one year younger than she, and going to the bathroom she had used her Indian trick. At the top of the stairs she could turn left to the bathroom or right to the older sister Sheryl's room. Sheryl was fifteen, really pretty but shy, and fascinating to Martha. Martha heard her in her room and walked silently to the door. Sheryl's father, Ed, was in there. His back was to the door. Sheryl stood against the wall.

"Let me see," he said.

"No," Sheryl whined.

"Now. Come on. Now. Before your mother gets done with the laundry."

Sheryl lifted her pretty yellow blouse and showed her father her breasts, swelling and ripe in her junior bra. Her father made no noise or movement; he simply stared. Martha watched stunned until Sheryl saw her over her father's sloping shoulder. Sheryl said nothing, but her eyes begged Martha, pleaded with her, but for what Martha didn't know. Martha's dad had moved out years before. Lars was not in their life yet. Martha didn't know that all dads didn't do this.

Martha went to the bathroom. Later, the father gave her a kiss good-bye when she left. Her mother asked her if she'd had a good time and Martha said yes. That night she bound her own chest in an old scarf, tying the knot as tight as she could, terrified that those offending breasts would happen to her.

Another bump. Martha took the last step on her hands and knees and she peeked around the corner. Her living room and dining room were empty. The kitchen too. She heard a thud and a clop, clop. Her windows were open. Somebody, something, was right outside. Silently, in the dark, she walked into her living room and up to the open case-ment window.

A palm tree and a jasmine bush blocked the glow from the streetlight across the way. She tried to peer beyond them. Abruptly a face rose directly across from her, separated only by the screen. A man, white, in his fifties. At first she thought it was Sheryl's father. But it wasn't. It was just a homeless man rummaging through her garbage. In his hands he held Martha's refuse; a half-eaten carton of yogurt, an empty carton of orange juice. His eyes were wide and runny in his dirty face. He and Martha were close enough to kiss.

The man left first, backing away, turning and stumbling through the jasmine, his plastic bag of soda cans clanking against his leg as he ran. She could hear him all the way down the street.

Martha closed and locked the window. She turned a light on in the living room. She went around her small house making sure every door and window was shut and locked. She sat on the couch and listened for the rest of the night.

"You should have called me," Reuben said the next day as they were waiting for Jewel to arrive. "You should have called the police."

"He didn't do anything."

"Made a mess of your garbage cans."

"He was hungry."

"You're lucky that's all he was." Reuben's eyes were hard, but his voice grew soft. "Really, *Marta*."

She loved it when he said her name with the Spanish pronunciation. She smiled at Reuben.

"I mean it. You have to be more careful. I can't believe you sleep with the windows open. Especially when I'm not here. Might as well leave the front door open."

"Okay." Martha nodded at him. "Okay."

"Next time, call the cops, and then call me. Promise?"

"Sure," Martha said, "I promise."

She wondered why she didn't feel more pleased at his concern. She was baking cookies, big gloppy chocolate chip monsters, for Jewel. Reuben sighed disapprovingly when he saw them.

"They're for Jewel," Martha said, defending herself. "She loves them."

"You said she was plump."

"Not that plump."

"You said plump. You even said chubby."

"She's only here every other weekend."

"You could set her an example."

"Like you do for your son?"

Martha couldn't help herself. It was the first time she'd ever contradicted Reuben or said anything unfavorable.

"I'm sorry," she said quickly, "I'm sorry. I didn't get any sleep last night. I guess I'm nervous about you and Jewel."

"You look like hell," Reuben said and then kissed her temple. "Early to bed tonight."

They both heard Allen's car pull up. Martha went outside first. Reuben followed. Martha turned back to look at him. He hooked his thumbs in the belt loops of his blue jeans. It pulled them down just enough so his pale green T-shirt stretched across his flat stomach. The T-shirt made his eyes an electric light for "go" in his face. His brush of black hair shone in the hot L.A. sun. Martha felt a surge of warm, syrup-over-pancakes love for him.

Allen got out of his car. He looked at Reuben unhappily.

"Hi," Martha said. Her voice sounded bouncy and false.

"Hello," Allen said stonily.

"Allen, this is Reuben Rodriguez." She put herself between the two men. "Allen, and that's Jewel."

Jewel was standing by the car holding her small suitcase crushed against her chest with both arms. She had the same suspicious, flat expression on her face as her father.

"How do you do?" Allen used his most superior lawyer voice, but Martha knew he was uncomfortable. She saw the way he sucked his soft stomach in and ran his hand through his thinning hair.

Jewel was more blatant. "Is he gonna be here all weekend?"

"No," Martha said, "just for dinner tonight. I wanted you to meet each other."

Reuben bent down to Jewel's level. "Your mom's making you some way awesome cookies."

Martha grimaced. He didn't need to sound like a teenager. Jewel's eyes were watching Reuben's hands and Martha realized she was looking at his tattoo.

"Wait till you see the eagle on his back," Martha said to her daughter.

Allen frowned and cleared his throat. "Yes, well," he said, "where did you two meet?"

"At the club," Martha said.

"What club?" Allen asked.

Martha looked at him.

"I thought you didn't work there anymore."

"I don't," Martha replied. "I was picking up my last paycheck. Reuben was making a delivery."

Allen's eyes narrowed.

"I'm an actor," Reuben said proudly. "The Coca-Cola truck is just my day gig. I wouldn't let her work there either." He gave a manly chuckle, one guy to another, but Allen wasn't smiling.

"See you Sunday," he said to Jewel.

"Okay, Daddy."

"And if you need anything," he said, "even if you just want to talk, call me or your stepmom, anytime."

"I will."

Martha's face flushed angrily. He had never said that before. "We're going to have a blast," Martha said.

"A blast?" Allen's tone was condescending.

"Enjoy your weekend," Martha said.

"Nice meeting you," Reuben called.

Allen was halfway into his car. "Oh, yeah," he said. "You too."

The timer went off, an intermittent screech from the stove inside the house.

"The cookies," Martha squealed.

She laughed and ran into her house. Reuben ran after her. Jewel stood on the sidewalk outside, a puzzled look on her face, then slowly followed them in.

The rest of the afternoon Martha felt schizophrenic. She was soft and pliant with Reuben, but then she'd feel Jewel watching her. She'd turn to her daughter and see her calculations, see her figuring how her mother changed with this man. Martha would pull away from Reuben and speak to Jewel, matter-of-fact and unemotional as always.

By dinnertime, Martha was mad at everyone. Maybe it was Jewel's obvious dislike of Reuben; maybe it was Reuben trying too hard to come down to Jewel's level; maybe it was the number of chocolate chip cookies she'd consumed, but the anger settled in her forehead, a spiky red cloud in her brain that she couldn't see around.

Jewel was counting again.

"One million, nine hundred and three thousand, six hundred and fifty-two. One million, nine hundred and three thousand, six hundred and fifty-three. One million—"

"You haven't gotten very far," Martha said.

Jewel was defensive. "I had a lot of homework."

"You'll never make it at this rate."

"Make what?" Reuben was the only one still smiling.

"The *Guinness' Book of World Records*," Jewel sniffed.

She sounded just like Allen, the same snotty preciseness. It reminded Martha of the way her life had been with Allen; every day every thing was just so, just right, just perfect. When Jewel was eighteen months old, they went to buy a new vacuum cleaner and that was the end of her marriage. It took a couple of years and Allen's finding Susan to make it final, but it was over for Martha from that day forward. She watched Allen, the giggly blonde baby on his shoulder, debate and discuss and dissect the merits of each model. Suction and velocity, Hoover vs. Kenmore. He took them apart, plugged them in, listened to their motors. Martha walked away. Jewel toddled over to a display of screwdrivers and cut her finger. Allen had been furious and Martha had felt terrible but too angry to show it.

"Her father's big idea," Martha said to Reuben. "He wants her to be a star."

"I think it's cool," Reuben said and winked stupidly at Jewel.

"You would," Martha replied.

"What's that supposed to mean?" Reuben asked. He and Jewel had the same quizzical, hurt look on their faces. They appeared to Martha like a mismatched set of salt and pepper shakers. Jewel, white and round, the salt; Reuben, brown and lean, the pepper. She could almost see the holes in their heads.

"Never mind," Martha said.

"Are we going out to dinner?" Jewel asked.

"Is that all you care about?" Martha was surprised at her own sharpness, but she couldn't stop it from coming out of her mouth. "Did you say thank you for the cookies? No. Gee, Mom, it's good to see you? No. Something pleasant? No."

"Martha, relax." Reuben was frowning.

"I am relaxed! I just think a little common courtesy is not too much to ask. You didn't say thank you for the cookies either."

"I didn't eat any."

"Thank you, Mom." Jewel's voice was small and unhappy.

Martha felt awful. Her hands shook. She wished she could put a smile on her face and leave her body there in the kitchen and let her real self fly away, up through the roof of her invaded house, above the crowds and noise of Los Angeles, and into the cool blue void above the smog. Instead she felt rooted; her soul had grown through the bottoms of her feet, through her shoes and into this mess she'd made.

"Okay," Martha said because she had to say something. "Okay. I'm sorry. I'm sorry. Let's just get out of here."

"Too much sugar," Reuben said.

"I did not have too much sugar!"

"Look at your hands. They're shaking. Sugar is bad news, changes your whole blood chemistry."

"Then if I murder you right now it won't be my fault, will it? Temporary sugar insanity."

Reuben looked at her. She could tell he didn't like what he saw. His green eyes went dull like an avocado refrigerator from the '70s. He bit his lip, twisting his mouth to one side. Martha had a sudden glimpse of him at seventy; disapproving, conservative, jealous. But then he smiled and put his cool hand on her flushed cheek.

"You crack me up," he said.

Martha turned her face and kissed his palm guiltily. She would miss him tonight, but he couldn't stay when Jewel was there.

"One million, nine hundred and three thousand, six hundred and fifty-six. One million, nine hundred and three thousand, six hundred and fifty-seven."

Jewel was counting again but whispering. Martha took a deep breath and smiled at her plump daughter.

"Of course we're going out to dinner. Don't we always?"

Martha ate a salad and drank two glasses of water to make Reuben happy. Jewel and Reuben shared a pizza. Martha wasn't angry anymore, she was depressed. She was filled with a grateful, culpable sadness in appreciation of her handsome, kind boyfriend and her sweet, pale daughter. Tears kept starting in her eyes, and she would cough and smile and blink them away. She thought of Dr. Hamilton, counting the four days until she would be with him again, and felt a reaching from her chest toward him. She knew the meaning of the word "yearn," and yet across the table were the two people most important in her life. It was the comforting nothingness of the dark Malibu hotel room she craved. She ached for the freedom of anonymity. That was all.

The rest of the weekend didn't go any better. They didn't see Reuben again and Martha felt bored without him. She didn't eat any more cookies, but she wasn't any happier. She was snappish and sensitive. By Sunday morning at eight, Jewel was sitting on the couch, dressed, suitcase at her feet, ready to go and counting out loud.

Martha stood in the arched doorway between the kitchen and the living room and watched her.

"Your father won't be here until three o'clock."

"I called him." Jewel stopped counting and spoke without looking at her mother. "He's coming early."

"When?" Martha was hurt, embarrassed. She suddenly felt under-dressed and exposed.

"He'll be here by nine."

"No. When did you call him?"

"When you were in the shower."

Martha nodded. "I would have taken you home," she said.

"That's okay."

"I . . ." Martha didn't know what to say. "I . . . I'm sorry. We'll have more fun next time."

Jewel shrugged like she didn't care. "One million, nine hundred and ninety-three thousand, one hundred and seven. One million, nine hundred and ninety-three thousand, one hundred and eight. One million, nine hundred and—"

Martha wanted to punch Allen when she saw him; he looked so smug and threw his arms around Jewel as if she was returning from a near-death experience. He looked at Martha over the top of Jewel's duckling soft head and raised his eyebrows.

"Where's Reuben?" he asked.

Martha stuttered, "He, he, he's not here. Of course. I mean, we just had dinner Friday night."

"Is this a serious relationship?"

"I . . ." Why couldn't she just say it was none of his business? "I don't know yet."

Allen gave a knowing humph. "He's young, isn't he?"

"Two years older than I am."

"Seems young. I guess it's the lack of responsibility."

"He's just in great shape. Terrific, really unbelievable shape." Martha smiled as she got one dig in. "He has a son he supports."

"Oh. Well, I don't think Jewel liked him."

"We had a fine time."

"That's why she called me this morning."

He opened Jewel's car door and she got right in.

"Jewel?" Martha said.

"Say good-bye to your mother, Opie," Allen commanded.

Jewel looked over at Martha for a fleet second. "Bye."

"See you in two weeks," Martha called.

"I guess," Allen said. He got in the car and drove away.

The rest of Sunday stretched before her. Jewel's room smelled like her as Martha changed the sheets and vacuumed. She thought of how soft her daughter was, her hairless skin as smooth as stretched silk. She picked up the vase with the pink sweetheart roses. Every time Jewel came Martha bought her flowers, but Jewel never seemed to notice. She never said a word about them.

Martha thought about calling Reuben, but she didn't want him to know that Jewel had gone home early. And she still mostly let him call her. She didn't want to appear forward. She had held his penis in her mouth, but she didn't want to call him on the phone.

She picked up the book she was reading, *Sons and Lovers* by D. H. Lawrence. She had moved on from the Ks, to the Ls in her plan to improve herself, but she found Lawrence hard going. It was too depressing. A boy in college, Jack, had told her she was just like the character Mary in the book. Her timidity and reticence drove him crazy, he said. But Martha wasn't reticent; she just didn't like Jack. She never read the book in college and now she found Mary as annoying as Jack had. She wondered where Jack was. She had slept with Jack once, to prove to him that she wasn't nervous or cowardly. He was inexperienced, rough, and left her sore and angry with herself.

She did so badly in school. She didn't know how to study. She never did her homework. She slunk around, curved away from teachers, professors, people of authority. When she started high school no one ever asked her if she'd done her homework; her mother never even looked at her report cards. Her mother was busy fighting her nervous breakdown, fighting with Lars, fighting to maintain control.

"You're an individual," Dolly would tell Martha.

Martha knew that meant she wasn't popular. It was true; she didn't fit in with any crowd.

"You have your own style," Dolly continued, meaning Martha wore funny clothes.

Lars lurked in the corners of their house. Dolly sat in the kitchen rocking chair, smoking cigarette after cigarette and staring out the window into the neglected backyard. Lars was never really doing anything. He had quit cab driving and was looking for a more meaningful profession. He leaned against the kitchen door and stared over Dolly's head. He stood in the doorway to Martha's room and watched her sit at her desk, read a book, listen to a tape. He never said anything, he was just a ubiquitous presence. Wherever Martha was, he seemed to be. Occasionally he would sigh, an almighty sigh of wonder, of longing, of the lost years of his youth. Martha refused to look at him, to acknowledge him. She walked past him to ask her mother how to spell a word or what they were having for dinner. She ignored him. And he was growing tired of it, she could tell. She looked forward to the confrontation.

The confrontation, when it came, was not what she expected. It was dinnertime, an important meal to Dolly even though she didn't eat. Dolly had become a shadow. Since her first trip to the hospital, she couldn't swallow anymore. Her throat would close and her tongue would get in the way, she said. She became aware of the mechanism of her larynx. Like the moment you become aware of your balance on a bicycle, that's the moment you fall over. So Dolly would cook big, healthy, and well-balanced meals for Lars and Martha and Audrey, and only drink herself. She had a special drink she made at dinnertime, warm milk thick with crumbled saltine crackers. The milk made the crackers soggy, slippery. It filled her up, she said. It kept her alive for almost eight years.

Martha sat at her place at the picnic table in the kitchen. It was a big kitchen, redone when Martha was two, and had room for the picnic table, the rocking chair, and her mother's sewing basket.

Lars sat at one end, on the only chair. Audrey was at a friend's house. Dolly perched on the very end of the picnic bench across the table from Martha. She was so light she didn't even tip the badly weighted seat.

"This weekend we're going to visit Lars's mother and father," Dolly announced.

"What for?" Martha asked.

"For a visit," her mother replied, eyes narrowing at Martha.

Martha said something smart. Not smart as in intelligent, but a smart remark, as in insolent, wiseass, flip. "Oh great. Racial jokes and stale cookies. There's no bigot like an old bigot."

Her mother was shocked. Martha could see the hurt on her face and the surprise; Martha was usually such a quiet, agreeable child. But Martha felt reckless, liberated. She expanded on her crack, her wise mouth, her flippancy.

"How they can sit there, snowflakes of dandruff on that black polyester sweater of his and that wicked bad breath of hers, and bitch about 'colored people'—it's disgusting."

Her mother's pain deepened. Her face grew as white as her glass of milk. But it was Lars who moved. In one instant he stood and grabbed Martha by the shoulders and lifted her off the bench. He was so large and Martha was a small-boned sixteen. Even as she went she was struck by how easily he raised her into the air and then tossed her like an empty cardboard carton right through the back screen door. Martha rolled onto the brown unwatered grass in the backyard. She stood and for a moment thought of running. But she was somehow exhilarated, fueled by her hatred for her stepfather and especially the sense that now he had justified her hatred. She waited just a moment, expecting her mother to run out, to worry about her. When she didn't, Martha charged back into the house. Her mother sat on the bench; she hadn't moved. Lars stood where he had stopped to throw her. Martha pushed past him to the table and picked up the big knife that had been used to carve her mother's famous roast chicken.

"I will kill you," she said. "Don't touch me again."

Her shoulder was beginning to hurt where she had first hit the door and then landed. She tasted blood in her mouth. She had knocked her lip against her teeth. It would be swollen later and tomorrow.

"Put that down." Lars was coming toward her.

"Get away!" she screamed.

"Don't be ridiculous," Lars said with a shake of his head, as if only he could be violent, only he was allowed to hurt and damage.

Martha waited for her mother to say something, but her mother was staring at her glass of milk. Her mother wasn't even looking.

"Don't come near me!"

But Lars came and he grabbed her wrist with the knife, twisted it so hard she dropped her threat, and then slapped her. Martha's head bounced on her neck and sprung back. He picked up her glass of milk from the table and dumped it over her head. Martha gasped. The slap hurt, but it was expected. The milk was not.

Lars laughed. Martha turned to her mother. Dolly handed her daughter a nicely folded paper napkin.

It was then that Martha ran. She ran out of the house and down the street and all the way to the Senior Citizens Center by the golf course. She walked inside, worried how she must look, and hurried to the bathroom. Her reflection surprised her. Her jaw was bright red where he had slapped her; her lip was already swelling. The milk had dried in ghost white streaks on her forehead and made her hair dark and greasy looking. She knew she smelled, or would soon, the sour smell of spilled milk. Her neck hurt and her shoulder. Her jeans were muddy, her T-shirt spattered and stained from the milk and the roll in the dirt.

An elderly woman entered, took a look at Martha and left. Martha was mortified. She ducked out of the bathroom, hunching her sore shoulders against the stares of the woman and the Center employee who were discussing her. She left the cheerful antiaging building. She had to go home. There was nowhere else to go.

When she walked in her own front door, Dolly was sitting on the couch watching TV. Lars was standing by her side with his keys in his hand. For a moment, Martha thought he was on his way out to look for her, that her mother had yelled at him, been outraged, demanded he go find her. But they both just looked at her as she came in, and Lars said nothing as he went past her and out the door.

"Mom?" Martha whispered.

"I don't want to talk about it," Dolly said. "You don't know what I've been through just now." She curled up on her side on the couch, eyes locked on the flickering television, hands tucked under her chin, feet snuggled under the cushions.

Later Lars lurked in the doorway of Martha's room as she read a book in bed.

"Sorry if I was a little rough," he finally said.

She kept her eyes on her book.

"Don't talk about my family that way." He continued, "You're a kid, just a kid. I'm the adult. Don't forget that."

Martha had a smart remark to make, but she said nothing.

17

MONDAY MORNING AT WINCHELL'S, MARTHA HAD
A DOUGHNUT. AND THEN ANOTHER, WITH SPRIN-
kles. She had cream in her coffee. She couldn't think of anything. She
was out of sorts, beside herself, literally, two Marthas sitting next to
each other on the molded red plastic bench, the inner and the outer.
Her mind watched her body eat both doughnuts and lick her fingers
for sugar crumbs. She shook her head at her own weakness and reprimanded herself, "Bad for you. Terrible. You're disgusting." But she
wasn't listening. She watched her body swell and bloat like the Chinese
brother who swallowed the sea in one of Jewel's old picture books.

She was supposed to meet Reuben at the club at noon for their workout. She didn't think she could do it. She knew she should, but her feet
were stuck to the cheerful floor at Winchell's. Her mind flew to her car,
to the freeway, in the club door. Her body contemplated a third doughnut. Finally, she pulled herself together and went out the door. She
walked up the hill to her little house, slowly, weighted with fried flour
and grease. "Lard butt," her mind said. Her body giggled.

At the club, Reuben shook his head at her.

"What's with you?" he asked. "You're movin' in slow motion."

Martha found it an effort to speak, to open her mouth. "Just tired, I guess."

"Come on, work it out."

She couldn't do her usual routine; she couldn't keep up. Reuben was disgusted with her. Her body flopped onto the exercise mat and lay there, spread-eagled, stretched flat on the floor. Her mind screamed, "Get up!"

"What are you doing?"

"I'm resting. I'm going home. I can't do this. Not today."

"You're getting sick, huh?"

"Sick and tired."

She looked up at Reuben from the floor. He was so damn good-looking, even with a disgruntled expression.

"Come over tonight?" she asked.

"Uh . . ." He looked away. "I can't. I'm going out with my cousin, my other cousin, and my uncle."

"Come later. Afterward."

"No, no. It'll be too late." He reached his hand down to her. "Get up. People are looking at you."

"If you promise you'll come over tonight."

"Come on, give me your hand."

"Promise me."

"Get up."

"Promise."

"No."

Martha sat up. She felt her mind returning to her errant body. It felt awful.

"Okay, okay." She looked around, people really were staring. Gorgeous women in matching Lycra/spandex tossed their long thick hair and watched Martha. They eyed Reuben up and down, wondering what he was doing with her. Why her? Martha could see it in their eyes. Plain, unappealing, ridiculous her. She knew she was wearing her doughnut breakfast, on her stomach, her hips, her thighs. She stood.

"Bye," she said to Reuben. "Bye."

"I'll call you later."

"Will you?" Martha turned to him. She wanted to keep the grateful desire out of her words, but she couldn't. "What time?"

"I don't know. Later."

She nodded and started for the women's locker room.

"Feel better," he called to her.

That was nice, she thought, nice of him to care.

Martha went home and went to bed. When she woke up it was five-thirty and Reuben hadn't called. She stared at her phone, her answering machine, her disappointment another pound in her stomach. She wouldn't allow herself to eat dinner. She watched television and vowed tomorrow she'd be happy.

But Tuesday morning he didn't call either. He was angry with her. She went to the club and worked out, hard, by herself. She came home sweaty and tingling with anxiety.

The phone rang.

She picked it up.

"Hello?"

"Hey. It's me. Sorry yesterday sort of got away from me."

Martha began to cry.

"You okay?"

"I . . . I think I am coming down with a cold."

"Listen. Listen. I want to talk to you. You gotta get it together."

"I will. I am."

"I mean it. I got vitamins for you. B-complex. You're too wired."

"I went to the club."

"You did?"

"I worked out. Did the whole routine, twice."

"Great." His voice changed, deepened. "You gonna be home for a while?"

"Yes."

"I'll stop by."

Sex with Reuben was pretty good. He knew a lot about the human body. He was interested in making Martha happy too. At the moment of orgasm, Martha always saw an image, a frozen frame or two, from an old black-and-white movie. She and Reuben were the stars. Reuben, dark and seductive; Martha, pale and chaste. Sometimes it was a backstage dressing room and Martha was in a satin robe with feather trim. Reuben, in a tuxedo, pushed her down on her dressing table, scattering makeup and big soft powder puffs. Sometimes it was a wet and shiny city street at night, with long, dramatic shadows and steam rising from the subway grate. Reuben wore a sinister Bogart-style overcoat as he screwed her standing up in a doorway.

They didn't go to the movies very often. Martha wasn't sure where the images came from, but it always happened. Not that she had an orgasm that often. She usually faked it, wanting Reuben to be happy, not wanting to wear him out. She had loved sex with him in the beginning. She craved it, couldn't wait to touch his smooth, cardboard-colored skin, smell his deodorant, feel his moist lips on her neck. But, the more time they spent together, the less she cared about the sex. It had been the same with Allen, and her other few boyfriends. Sex with a stranger was always preferable. She could concentrate more, lose herself, when she didn't know the man's mother. There had been a brief period, her senior year of high school, when she had slept with a lot of men, as many as she could. Only once with most of them, twice with a few. It was their taste and their desire she wanted. And her own feeling of conquest. She was surprised at how easy it was. The men seemed surprised too. The ladies' room at a bar, the backseat, front seat of his car, a stopped elevator, the conference room at his office, she didn't mind. Afterward, she was always hungry. She would go home and stand in front of the fridge, gobbling up food and licking her sticky fingers. Dolly never knew. She told Martha to eat more dinner before she went out with her friends.

Now the thought of those encounters was ugly and embarrassing.

She would never tell Reuben. She sometimes missed the suspense, but she wouldn't do it now, couldn't; she was too old and, anyway, sex could be lethal. So Reuben made her happy. Reuben was good with his hands and his mouth. He was gentle and a good size and sometimes she couldn't wait to be with him. He was quiet and that was good. Allen had been a talker and it bugged her, distracted her to have to answer his questions, "Does that feel good? Am I big enough? Do I fill you up?" Eventually, she gave up answering. He asked the same things every time, at the same moments during the event. She realized, finally, they were rhetorical questions. Her views on the subject were not required.

Afterward, Reuben sat on the edge of her bed and put his socks on. He always put his socks on first, even before his underwear.

"My feet get cold," he explained the first time she had noticed.

"Are you leaving?" Martha asked.

"Back to work."

He leaned over and kissed her. She wrapped her arms around his neck and kissed him back. Kissing was great. She loved kissing Reuben. He tasted spicy and fresh, healthy, even after dinner.

"More," she said.

"Hey, hey, let go," he said, pulling himself free. "I gotta go."

Martha sat up, letting the sheet fall to her waist, leaving her breasts uncovered. She watched him get dressed, tucking in his striped Coca-Cola shirt carefully and smoothing the pockets of his pants. He rolled the short sleeves of his shirt two times each, just so, to show off his biceps to their best advantage.

When he was dressed, he turned to Martha. He frowned at her breasts. He was done. Now he found her immodest.

"Bye," he said. "I'll call you."

She could see the distaste, a tinge of green around his mouth, a downward thrust of his chin.

"What about tomorrow?"

"I have an audition, a peanut butter commercial."

"Smooth or crunchy?"

He smiled, but in his mind he was already up the stairs, out her door, gone from her.

"Reuben?"

"What?" He stopped in the doorway.

"You're going to break up with me, aren't you? I mean, soon. This is almost it."

"Why do you say that? You're nuts. Take those vitamins. One a day, after a meal."

But she knew it was true. She had a little time left. Maybe she could make him stay.

She drove faster than she ever had to Dr. Hamilton that night. Speeding toward sanctuary. She dashed through the lobby, throwing a breathless "hi" to the night manager, now a casual acquaintance. Often they spoke about the weather or current events; tonight he handed her the key and she was gone.

Encased in the comforting hugeness of her blue suit, she waited impatiently for Dr. Hamilton. She paced. She looked out the window at the ocean, annoyed with its constancy. It was relentless and finally boring. She turned and rose onto her tiptoes when Dr. Hamilton knocked.

But when Dr. Hamilton came in he kept his body turned away from her, his face averted. He took off his jacket, hung it in the closet, loosened his tie, sat in the chair, all without looking at her.

"How are you?" he asked, staring out the double glass doors at the ocean.

"Fine, fine. And you?"

"I'm tired," he said. "I'm afraid that's my usual state these days."

"I'm glad to be here." Martha said it, meant it, wanted him to know. "I've had a hard weekend."

"Are you still seeing—that man?" he asked.

"Reuben?"

"Yes, yes. The beautiful one."

"I thought you didn't want to talk about him." Martha didn't want to talk about him. Not today.

"Is he still so beautiful?"

She thought about that afternoon in bed. "Yes."

"Is it serious? Will you marry him?"

Martha didn't want Dr. Hamilton to think of her as the kind of woman who gets dumped. "Maybe. I'm not in a rush."

"Do you love him?"

"Sure. I've been sleeping with him for months."

"Is he always attractive to you? In the morning when he wakes up? Late at night after too much beer? Sick with the flu?"

"He's never sick," Martha said. "I've never seen him sick. He takes good care of himself. He works out. He eats a lot of vegetables. Vitamins." Martha thought guiltily of the untouched bottle of vitamins sitting on the floor by her bed.

"So he works hard at being beautiful. Is that his job in life? His purpose?"

"No. He has a job."

"A job? Or a career? Something he loves to do?"

"A career. He wants to be an actor. He is an actor."

"Then appearance is his obsession."

Martha thought about how Reuben worked out for three hours every day, no matter what else was going on. How he talked about other people's clothes, hairstyles; the roll of their stomachs, size of their hips. He didn't have any friends who weren't attractive.

"He goes out with me. We work out together now."

"And are you beautiful?"

Martha thought of the aversion on Reuben's face as he left her. She remembered the taste of their last kiss and knew once more that he would leave her soon.

"You keep asking me that. I am working at it. I look better than before." She thought of her doughnuts. "Usually."

"Does he love you?" Dr. Hamilton leaned forward, put his long white-shirted arms on his pressed pant legs. The end of his tie touched the seat of the chair.

"I guess . . . I mean, yes. Reuben sees my potential. And, of course, he knows how I feel about him—the way he looks."

"Let me tell you something about beauty." Dr. Hamilton addressed her like a student, a child. "It is an obsession. But lack of it, or the fear of lacking it, is a far greater obsession. It's a million-dollar obsession. What price would you pay to be the most beautiful woman in the

world?"

Martha thought of the money from Dr. Hamilton glowing among her underpants. "Eight thousand dollars," she said. "That's all I have."

"You would give everything to be beautiful." Dr. Hamilton nodded. "You see? And it wouldn't change who you are, just how you look."

But, Martha thought without speaking, it would tell me who I am.

"And would it make you happier?" Dr. Hamilton continued. "Would I enjoy our conversations more?"

"If you could see me you would," Martha said.

"But to me, what makes you so . . . enjoyable and fascinating has nothing to do with how you look."

"That would all change if I took off this blue uniform. Suddenly you would have ideas, considerations. It would be hard to listen to me just talk and understand what I say without filtering it through the way I look. Just as I filter you through this blue gauze. I'm not sure I'd recognize you if I saw you on a street in the daylight. I'm not sure you'd recognize my thoughts if you saw me say them."

"And so you'd want the most beautiful filter you could find."

"Yes."

"You think I'd get greater enjoyment—"

"And interest."

"And have greater interest in what you say, if you said it from a pair of lovely lips, looking at me from radiant eyes, a lofty brow, the perfect, graceful turn of a long elegant neck."

"Of course," Martha said. "Anybody would. It's human nature."

"Then I am doomed." Dr. Hamilton said it lightly, but she saw a new crease in his already wrinkled forehead.

He gave an enormous sigh and with that sigh Martha heard him shutting down, ending the search for whatever he'd been waiting to hear.

"No." The word fell from her mouth without her permission.

"Martha," he said and stopped, started again, "Martha. When you began with me, I didn't know what to expect. And the more we talked, the more I believed and hoped that you could do it for me."

Martha's breath came faster; she felt a trickle of sweat under one arm. "What?" she said. "What? I can do it. Tell me what."

"I know you've done your best. I know you've been honest with me. That's all I should have hoped for. But here was my escape, here was my future, here was my sanity. And I've lost them all."

"No. No. No. I'm not well-read enough. If you've lost anything, it's only time. I'll do more research. I'll be better prepared. I'll do better."

"You can't do any better. You are perfect."

"No. Oh God, no. I'm nothing. I'm nothing. I'm no one."

"I know you. I know who you are. You are bright and shiny like a button on a child's new coat." Dr. Hamilton paused. "Never say you are no one. You are yourself. Dammit. Are you listening to me?"

"But you said I didn't help you."

"You did, for the moment. You didn't for the long haul. You can't. Imagine this. I'm driving alone across the country in a car with only three wheels. It's a hard trip, slow, exhausting, obviously bumpy. For a time you came and loaned me your extra wheel. For that I'm so grateful. You gave me a rest for a while. But I have much farther to go and you can't stay with me for the whole trip."

"Why not?"

"You have your own life. Reuben . . ."

How could he even mention Reuben; what did Reuben have to do with this? "I'm not ready for this to end. I'm not willing." Martha heard her own voice raise in desperation but couldn't stop. "I want to stay. Do you hear me?"

His calmness was remarkable. "For the first week you were always leaving. Now, I can't get you to go. I think tonight will be our last meeting."

"That's not fair. What about what I think?"

"This isn't therapy. I'm your employer."

"Is that all?"

Dr. Hamilton gripped the arms of his chair. He shook his head, not saying no but clearing it, of her.

Martha whispered, "Let me help you. Don't let me go."

"What else is there to say?"

"Tomorrow night. At least let me finish out the week. We have tomorrow night. One more hour tonight and then three hours tomorrow night." Martha seized the only power she had. "Say yes," she commanded, "or I will stand up and take off this silly blue thing right now!"

She stood. She reached for the hood, held the hand stitched hem in her blue fingers, began to pull it up.

"No!" he screamed. He turned his face away, hid it in his long-fingered doctor's hands. "No!"

"Then say we have tomorrow."

"Yes," he whispered.

"Louder."

"Yes. Yes. We have tomorrow."

18

THE PHONE RANG.

''HELLO?'' MARTHA WAS BREATHLESS AS SHE picked it up.

"Hey ho. What do you know?" Her father's voice, chipper and filled with distant static, was too loud in her ear.

"Hi, Dad." Martha was disappointed but wasn't sure whom she had been expecting. "How are you?"

"In the pink. When the cat's away, the mice will play."

"Oh." Martha thought a moment. "Do you mean Jane is out of town?"

Jane was her father's wife and mother of Martha's two stepsisters.

"Your E.S.M."—Marvin's abbreviation for Evil Stepmother—"and her chicks have flown the proverbial coop."

"You're alone? Where is everybody?"

"Here today, gone tomorrow. But, out of sight, out of mind." He waited for her response and receiving none, continued, "I've sent them all away. To a fat farm—excuse me, a spa—in Arizona."

"The girls too?"

"Frankly, Chickadee, glad to see them go. A man's home is his castle. Except when the queen is busy refeathering her nest. One more fabric swatch and I was going off the deep end."

"She's remodeling—again."

"Still. Perpetually. She can no longer see the forest for the trees."

"So—"

Martha never knew what to say to her father. After their dates stopped, later in her life when she was in high school, he suddenly did quite well financially. Then he married Jane, who was only ten years older than Martha and a yoga instructor with big breasts and muscular legs. Jane had lots of dark curly hair, on her head, on her arms, even on her toes. Even to sixteen-year-old Martha, it was obvious that Jane was the exact opposite of the cool-colored Dolly. Jane came with two little girls, Tanya and Traci, dark and curly like their mother and only a year apart. Martha thought of them as a set, like nested mixing bowls, one only slightly larger than the other. They were much younger than Martha.

"How did the girls get out of school?"

"Pay enough for private school, you get to have your cake and eat it too." He sighed. "A fool and his money . . . so, what are you doing tomorrow?"

She had plenty to do, but nothing to tell him. "Nothing."

"As usual. Well, thought I'd take a busman's holiday and come see my number one daughter."

"Great. Really? Great." Martha felt surprised and warmly grateful that he wanted to come. "I thought you were enjoying your time alone."

"A little bit of a good thing goes a long way. I'll rent a car, stay in a hotel, the usual drill. Be there about two o'clock. *Auf Wiedersehen. Adios. Au revoir.*"

He hung up.

Martha stood by the phone table, unsure of what to do next. When her father had gotten married, he had called Martha and asked her the same question.

"What are you doing tomorrow?"

"Nothing."

"As usual. Good. I'm getting married. Wanna come?" He began singing, "I'm getting married in the morning. Ding-dong, the bells are gonna chime."

"Who to?" Martha asked over his joyful crooning.

"Jane, Jane, Jane," he launched into a new warble, "the most wonderful girl in the world—"

"When?" Martha was sixteen. Her mother was crazy. Her stepfather had a surprising backhand. Her father didn't call much anymore.

"Eleven o'clock, with lunch afterward. In the woods, behind the River Road Unitarian Church."

"Okay. Okay."

"*Adios. Auf Wiedersehen. Au revoir.*"

Martha had met Jane only once before, at her father's office. Martha was there to use his Xerox machine to copy a very long term paper. She had copied only three of the sixty-one pages when the huge, putty-colored machine had run out of paper. Martha found a new ream of paper, but she couldn't figure out how to load the paper tray and couldn't bother the chain-smoking word processing secretary. In the end, she gave up and turned in her original.

"Did you do it?" Her father looked up as she passed his office door.

"Sure," she lied.

"Great. Hey, Chickadee, this is Jane."

The woman sitting in the chair facing his desk turned around. She smiled, hard, at Martha. The twisting in the chair forced her white blouse to pull against her C cups. Martha saw her father sigh and smile at them.

"Hi." Martha nodded.

"I've heard a lot about you," Jane said.

"You have?"

"Number one daughter." Jane kept smiling. "He told me you're a dancer."

"I quit," Martha said.

"When?" Marvin looked annoyed, but Martha didn't know if it was because she quit or because Jane looked disappointed.

"About six months ago. Too much school work." What a relief not to be the worst ballerina in the class anymore.

"Too bad." Jane looked at Marvin with a frown. "I wanted Martha to teach my girls a thing or two."

"No problem," Marvin said. "Martha will get her ducks in a row, won't you?"

"Sure, Dad." She nodded her head stupidly and darted from the office, banging loudly against the green metal trash can on her way out.

Martha was overdressed for her father's wedding. Everyone else was in nice jeans, turtlenecks, casual blazers. She wore a slim, strapless party dress and a light velvet jacket borrowed from Audrey with pale shimmery stockings. The dress kept slipping down her flat chest and she kept pulling it up under her arms. It was cold in the woods and her nose was red and running. She dug in the tiny pocket of the fancy jacket, hoping Audrey had left a tissue, even a used one, but found only lint. Her new and first pair of true high heels sunk into the soft, muddy March earth. She looked with dismay at the crust forming around her delicate suede toes.

The girls, Tanya and Traci, were only five and six, angels in pink corduroy and royal blue berets, holding the first yellow daffodils of spring. Other than her father, Martha didn't know anyone there. There were only a handful of adults. They all seemed happy and old friends with each other. No one said a thing to Martha.

The ceremony was long and adapted from some American Indian rite of ancestral connection. There was a lot of walking in circles by her father and Jane and the official, either a minister or a judge, Martha wasn't sure. The guests stood in a semicircle around them, except the little girls, who flanked their mother. Martha stood awkwardly, freezing, with a big space between her and the strangers from her father's life on

either side. Her father's secretary looked over at her during the proce-
dure and shook her head, slightly. Martha blanched, took a deep breath.
Was her strapless, useless bra showing? Was there a leaf in her hair,
snot on her upper lip? She pulled her dress up with one hand and put
the other hand over her nose. She couldn't stand like that forever, so
she put her hand down and ducked her head. She hoped she looked
like she was overcome with emotion.

When it was over, everyone walked down to the parking lot. Martha's mother had dropped her off, angrily staring at Marvin's new red
Mercedes.

"Hmmpf" was all she said before she drove away.

Her father, Jane, and the girls got in his car. His friends got in theirs.
Martha stood in the parking lot and waited, not wanting to bother her
father on his special day. But finally, when it looked like she would be
left behind—her father had his car started and his seat belt on—she
waved at him and walked up to his window.

"Should I . . . ride with you?" she asked.

He looked puzzled for a moment, seemed surprised that she was
there. "Why walk when you can ride? Why ride when you can fly?"

Martha smiled at him. She laughed a little. Her father smiled back.

"Get in. Get in. Time's a'wastin'."

Martha squeezed in the back next to the little girls. Tanya, or Traci,
the one who was closest, moved way over so her leg and Martha's
wouldn't touch. The girls held their flowers in front of their faces and
turned to each other, foreheads touching. They giggled.

"Don't mind them," Jane said from the front seat. "They have their
own language."

When she got out of the Mercedes she saw the mud her shoes had
left on the carpet. She tried to scrape it out with the side of one ruined
shoe and only smeared it.

At lunch she sat next to the little girls on the end of a row, with no one on her other side. There were toasts and jokes and Martha watched her father and Jane kiss. Jane put her tongue in Marvin's mouth. Her father came up to her after the meal.

"Chickadee, you look like something the cat dragged in. You'll like Jane, you will. She's the salt of the earth. We're gonna be one big happy family." He put his arm briefly around Martha's shoulders. She could smell the scotch on his breath. There was lipstick on his jaw.

"When's your mom coming to get you?" he asked.

"I thought you were taking me home."

"Can't. Wish I could. We have to make hay while the sun shines. Drop the girls off, get on that big, white bird. We've got two tickets to paradise."

"I'll call her."

Martha didn't have twenty cents for the pay phone. She looked so stricken standing in the maroon carpeted hallway between the bathrooms that the maître d', a young guy with long hair in a ponytail, smiled at her gently and let her use his phone. Martha fantasized about him for the next month.

It was Lars who came to pick her up. Her mother was too busy in the garden, pulling weeds. Martha knew it would be a bad night. She was right. Her mother was furious at her from the moment she walked in the door.

"Your shoes! You've ruined your new shoes."

"It was outside. I didn't know it was outside."

"This is ridiculous. I don't know why I buy you things."

"I'm sorry."

"Look at your face. Look at you. What did people think?"

"I thought—you said—"

"I know, I know what they think: I'm a terrible mother. I let my child run around like this. Ridiculous, inappropriate. It's freezing outside."

"I looked fine."

"Ridiculous." Dolly turned to Lars, her eyes puddling up and spilling over with those becoming tears. "I've tried. I've tried to be the best mother I could. I've had to work every day since my children were born. If you knew what I've been through."

Lars squeezed Dolly in his starchy tuber arms and looked over her head at Martha.

"Go change your clothes," he said in his best "I'm your father" voice. "Then come down and apologize to your mother."

Martha did as she was told. She was too tired to fight.

Martha was glad her father was coming to visit, but the timing was terrible. She needed to concentrate on keeping her job with Dr. Hamilton. Things weren't going great with Reuben. It wasn't Jewel's weekend, but she'd have to call and trade this one for next.

Still, she couldn't tell him not to come. And, on the good side, she couldn't wait for him to see her muscles—she'd been working out with Reuben for months. He had to notice a difference, appreciate the strength in her legs. Last time she'd been at their house, three years ago, Jane hadn't looked so great. She wasn't aging well, even with all the yoga. Martha was glad it was hot. She could wear shorts. It had been a long time since Marvin had visited. She would clean, have the cushions on her blue couch dry-cleaned; Reuben wasn't very careful with his food and drinks and crumbs. They would go out to dinner and talk. It was just that she had so much on her mind right now.

She called Reuben, to tell him and invite him to dinner.

"Hi . . . it's Martha," she said.

"I know it's you." He chuckled. "What's up?"

"My dad's coming to visit. He just called. Tomorrow. Want to come to dinner?"

"Your dad? You've never said anything about your dad."

"Sure. Marvin. Married to Jane."

"Yeah. I know his name, but—I just didn't know that you were close enough to visit."

"We are. Sure."

"That's great. I'd love to meet your dad. You know, I'm a big family man."

"I know."

"Hey." Reuben sounded warmer than he had in a week. "About the other day. I'm sorry if I was hard on you."

"That's okay. You weren't."

"Been taking those vitamins?"

"You bet." She wondered where the bottle was. "I feel much better. Calmer."

"Great. What are you doing later?"

"I have to work tonight."

"Oh yeah. Shoot. You should get yourself a day job."

"Maybe I will."

"I'll help you look for something."

"Would you, Reuben? Really?"

19

MARTHA, DRESSED IN THE ACHINGLY FAMILIAR
NAVY BLUE, FELT THE ANXIETY ABOUT HER
father's visit drain away. In its place hovered an agitated despair. She couldn't let tonight be her last night with Dr. Hamilton. That afternoon she had done her homework. She had gone to the library and read and studied Naomi Wolf's *Beauty Myth*, *Autobiography of a Face*, feminist articles, and fashion magazines. She was prepared. But she sat in her chair without saying anything. She was afraid that whatever she said wouldn't be good enough. So she waited for him to speak, to tell her how it was going to be.

Dr. Hamilton sat with a bemused expression on his face. He was waiting too. They were both aware of the little buzz of the air conditioner, the rhythmic rolling of the ocean outside, the silence between them stacking up like bricks, each breath another slap of mortar.

Finally, Dr. Hamilton thumped the arms of his chair with both hands. Martha jumped. He cleared his throat.

"So, Martha . . . say something. You wanted this night."

Not just this night, Martha thought. She said, "My father's coming to visit."

"Your father? The supportive one." He wasn't usually sarcastic. "I'm glad for you if you are, but—"

He was ready to dismiss her. Martha leaped into the pause. "Women get their idea of beauty from their fathers—I think. I think the father, or primary male caregiver, is the most important source for a woman's self-image."

"That's an interesting theory."

"Yes. I think women—mothers—can have an effect, but definitely secondary."

"You've found a subject we haven't touched upon."

"Well—we've talked about attractiveness as sexuality. And of course sexuality, on a primal level, is about survival of the species. A basic drive to continue—to perpetuate—" She paused, watching Dr. Hamilton's face. He was looking at his hands, held together in his lap.

"So—" she continued, "it stands to reason that a girl's first idea of sexuality would come from the first sexual object in her life, her father. And how he responds to her—the way in which he recognizes her appearance and responds to it positively will define how she sees herself as an attractive, therefore sexual, therefore able to carry on the human race, kind of person." Martha stopped. She was aware she was breathing hard, panting as if she'd run a race. Her chest moved up and down inside her blueness. She realized that Dr. Hamilton was aware of her chest as well. He was watching it. She coughed, curved her shoulders inward, retreating into the enormous sweatshirt. Then she thought, maybe they can help, and she sat up straight, pushing her small breasts forward until they were obvious bumps in the blue.

But Dr. Hamilton looked away. "You thought this up yourself?" He seemed more amused than impressed.

"I read about it. But I spent today thinking about it. After my father called."

"I see. Well. It's not a new idea to me."

"Oh. Do you have children? A daughter?" Martha thought of the blonde woman at the Halloween party.

"No. I'm not married. Never have been."

"I'm sorry I asked. I know I wasn't supposed to."

"It doesn't matter."

Martha knew this was the end then. Never before had he revealed anything of himself. Usually it was Martha who spilled too much, left her family, her childhood, her past lying in puddles between them.

"Well," Martha began, too brightly, "in my case, having two fathers—or less than two, but more than one—I—well, and having been treated so differently by each of them—" She had worked so hard on the first part of her general theory, she hadn't given much thought to its personal application. But then he asked.

"How?"

"Excuse me?"

"How did they treat you so differently?"

She didn't want to tell him, but she knew people were fascinated by stories of weird childhoods. She hoped he was too. So she took a deep breath. "My first stepfather, Lars, not the man my mother's married to now, used to lurk in my bedroom door. He always managed to show up just when I was getting dressed in the morning or undressed for bed. Lars never touched me. He never molested me, you know, like you read in the tabloids in the grocery store. But he . . . he made me aware of my body in a new way. I don't even know if he liked what he saw. It never seemed to make any difference when he pushed me around."

"Your stepfather pushed you around?"

"When I was rude, talked back."

"What did he do?"

She had been right; he was interested in the dirt. "He would slap me, push me off the bench at the kitchen table. He only really hurt me once." She thought of her fat lip, her bruised hip and shoulder.

Dr. Hamilton was angry. Angry for her. "How old were you?" he demanded.

"Sixteen, seventeen. I was big."

"You're tiny now. You must've been smaller then.

"I'm not tiny. I'm tall for a woman."

Dr. Hamilton opened and closed his fingers. She remembered them wrapped around her arm. He shook his head slowly with great effort. He reminded her of an elephant at the zoo, one leg chained, rocking back and forth.

"Is this something you've brought up just to keep me here?"

"No. I didn't mean . . . I mean, it's nothing."

"The guy should be in jail."

Martha didn't want to cry inside her hood, but one tear slid from her eye down her cheek. It itched.

Dr. Hamilton leaned toward her. He lifted his hands in her direction, then put them down again. "Do you think of yourself as Scheherazade? Can you tell enough tales to keep me from killing you?"

Martha said nothing. She felt somehow gratified. She'd been right all along. That was what he meant by the end. Martha didn't feel afraid. She tilted her head to one side.

"How?"

"How what?"

"How will you kill me?"

He laughed, his ripping, plaintive noises hurting Martha's ears and her heart.

"What's so funny?"

"Sorry," he said, "sorry. You're just so funny. All this time together and you still think—I'm not going to kill you."

She saw tears in his eyes.

He continued, quietly, "I just no longer care to discuss beauty. Discussion doesn't help. Knowledge is only worthwhile in the abstract. Not in real life. And it is time for me to get real."

"I want to finish this."

"It's done."

"No, I need more time."

"Martha," Dr. Hamilton said, closing his eyes, "I will miss you. You

are the one thing that I will miss. You are—have been—refreshing. But
you need to move on. You need to have your own life. I thought—
sometimes I dreamed—"

"What?"

"It doesn't matter," he said for the second time that night. "You can't
do any more for me."

"I can."

"You can't."

"I'm not ready to go."

"Martha. Martha. All right. I can't seem to let you go either. We will
each have our weekend. Your father will come. I will do whatever I do.
Then one more, we can have only one more evening. And then it will
be done, no matter what you say. I must get on with it."

"Get on with what?"

"Let's please just quit for tonight. I can't talk to you anymore."

Martha could only nod.

"I'll see you Tuesday. I will give you your money and we will say
good-bye."

He seemed so tired of her, so ready for her to go, that Martha sprang
from her chair. She ran to the bathroom and slammed the door so she
wouldn't have to see him go.

Friday at 2:00 the house was spotless. The night before Martha had
done what she wanted. She'd gotten one more night. She could do it
again. Today she felt good—better. Tuesday wouldn't be the end.

And so she was ready for her father's coming. She had made her
father's favorite foods, beef Stroganoff and cauliflower pudding. She
had traded weekends with Allen so that Jewel could come this afternoon instead of next week.

Martha put on nice shorts and a sleeveless sky blue silk tank top that
Reuben had given her. She braided her hair away, out of her face. She
put on mascara, forcing herself to look in the medicine chest mirror.

She wished she was shorter, rounder. Her arms and shoulders looked bony, not muscular. Her breasts were nonexistent in the loose top. She felt as she always did with her dad, angular, pointy, all hard corners and elbows.

But when Allen came she could see the approval in his face. He looked her up and down with his lips pressed tight together.

"That's a pretty color for you," he said.

"Thank you." Martha blushed and smiled, feeling rosy.

"Where's, uh, Reuben?" Allen asked.

"He's coming by after work. For dinner."

Jewel got out of the car and nodded at her mother. "You look pretty, Mom. You do."

"Yeah. You do," Allen said. "Guess this guy's good for you."

He hesitated, not wanting to get back in the car, wanting to say something else. But Martha turned to Jewel.

"You look nice too."

Jewel was wearing a new dress that Martha had given her, dark red, that brought out the pink in her cheeks. Allen watched Martha and Jewel go into the house before he got in his car and drove away.

3:30. No sign of Marvin. Jewel and Martha baked a lemon cake, also Marvin's favorite.

5:00. Reuben knocked on the door with his special knock. He brought flowers, six white gladioli, and Martha thought maybe her luck was changing. She decided Reuben wouldn't look so bad at seventy. She set the table. Reuben and Jewel played Bugs Bunny Bingo on the living room rug.

At 6:30 they sat down to eat. Martha wasn't hungry, but Reuben made a fuss over all the food.

"You don't like this kind of stuff," Martha snapped finally. "Sour cream, cheese sauce, white pasta. It's terrible."

"Tastes good," said Jewel.

"Sure does. Once in a while, it's great."

"Can I have some more?" asked Jewel.

"What about your diet?" Martha asked, handing Jewel the bowl.

"We're not dieting anymore."

"Why not?"

" 'Cause it's not good for the baby." Jewel spoke without thinking and then winced and put one sticky hand over her mouth. "Oops. I wasn't supposed to say anything."

"Susan's pregnant?" Martha asked. "Well. Great. Congratulations to her. To all of you."

At 8:30 Martha put Jewel to bed. She came upstairs and sat down on the immaculate couch.

"Did you try the airlines?" Reuben asked.

"I don't know what flight, even what airline he was coming on."

"What hotel does he usually stay in?"

"I don't remember. He was only here once." Martha shook her head. "He's always late. He never once has been on time. When I got married, I told him the wedding was a half hour earlier than it really was. He still barely made it."

"That's why you're so prompt."

"I guess."

At 11, Reuben suggested she call his home in Washington, D.C.

"It's two o'clock in the morning there."

"So? If he's hurt or something we'd better know."

Martha had to look up her father's home number in her slim, black address book. A sleepy Jane answered the phone.

"Hullo?"

"Jane. It's Martha."

"Martha." There was a pause. "Are you okay?"

"I'm fine. It's dad. I mean . . ."

"What about him? He's right here in bed, snoring away." Jane stopped, then Martha heard her gasp. "You mean he didn't call you?"

"No."

"We came home early. He decided not to go to California. He said he missed his girls."

Martha hadn't thought he could hurt her anymore. "Oh."

"I'm sorry."

"No, no. That's okay. I'm just glad he's not in the hospital or something."

She told Jane not to wake him, so she hung up without speaking to him. Reuben shook his head.

"I don't know, Martha. You and your family—it's so fucked up, excuse me, but it is."

He had never used that word in front of her before. "I . . . I know." She watched his face. She could see his estimation of her lessen. If her own father found her of no consequence, not important enough to even call, how could Reuben have any respect for her?

"I hate him," Martha said and surprised herself. She had never even thought that before. But when she looked at Reuben's face, she despised her father.

"Don't say that," Reuben reprimanded her.

"It's true. I only just realized it."

"Don't say that. Don't even think it. He's your father. Your family. You're mad at him, but he's still your father."

"He's a jerk."

"Who knows what happened today. He'll call you tomorrow."

"Why are you defending him? You've never even met him. You sat here with me all day waiting for him." She looked at him. "Do you find this threatening? Does it make you think about your son? The times you've stood him up?"

"Hey! I know you're upset. It's late. I'm going."

"Don't go."

"Yeah, right."

So at midnight she said good-bye to Reuben. She wanted him to stay, tried to convince him with her bare arms and silk-covered skin, but he wouldn't, not with Jewel there. He got angry with her again for persisting.

"It's not right. It's . . . it's indecent. I'll see you Monday."

He pushed her arms away, didn't kiss her, and ran to his car as if escaping.

Martha stood by the front door. Allen had hated her father. Allen had stood by her. But Allen was asleep in bed with Susan. And Susan was pregnant.

Martha went downstairs and tiptoed into Jewel's room. Jewel's breath was loud and even in the dark. The room smelled like a child, uncomplicated and familiar. Martha lay down on her back on the floor in her daughter's room, on the plush pink carpet. She began to cry and the tears bubbled from her eyes, cascaded over her cheekbones and into her ears. She sobbed silently, not wanting to wake her child, not able to leave and be any more alone.

20

"YOU ARE SUCH A CRAB!" JEWEL WAS SCREECHING, HER FACE RED AND DISTORTED with frustration.

"I am not!" Martha felt her own face as red.

"You are, you are, you are! I want to go home!"

"Your father's not going to let you have candy for breakfast either."

"He will. He does. He does everything I want!"

"Well, too bad for him."

"I want to go home."

"This is your home."

"I want to go to my real home. I don't want to come here anymore. I don't even like you. I hate you!"

"Don't you talk that way to me." In her anger Martha could hear her mother's voice. "I will not be spoken to that way."

"I don't care. I hate you. I hate you! I hate you! No wonder Grandpa didn't come here. You're such a crab!"

Martha's anger galloped forward like Bambi running from the forest fire. "He has nothing to do with this!" she exploded at her daughter. "Nothing!"

Jewel's eyes narrowed and her cheeks swelled with animosity.

"Even Reuben." The words slid from her mouth.

"What about Reuben?"

"He doesn't like you. He's just going out with you because you're white."

"What?"

"That's what Mom—Susan—said. She said you're just something different for him. Dad agreed. Why else would he be going out with you?"

Martha's rage glued her teeth together. She breathed through her clenched grimace, unable to speak, to move. Of course that's what they thought. Of course it was true. Why else would Reuben go out with her? Hadn't even Dr. Hamilton said as much? And Jewel had never called Susan "mom" before. She let go and screamed. Her hands flew from her, knocking the carton of milk to the floor. The puddle spread toward Jewel's feet.

"Mom!"

Martha didn't care. She picked up the carton and began to fling milk all over the kitchen. She poured it on the counters, the table, over the stove, everywhere. Her perfect spotless kitchen dripped with frosty white liquid.

She had never been anything. She never would be anything. She was like a glass of milk. Boring, of dubious benefit, and white, white, white. She left a nasty film on the inside of your mouth. Martha stood in the middle of her wet kitchen floor and cried. She sobbed.

"I want to go home," Jewel said. She was crying too.

Martha looked at Jewel's frightened face and felt terribly, wickedly guilty and that made her angry all over again.

"I'll take you home. You want to go home? Back to your nice plump 'mom.' She never gets mad. She never even does anything wrong. Come on, we're leaving."

Jewel didn't move.

"I mean it! Get in the car."

Martha ran downstairs to the rosy pink bedroom and threw Jewel's things into her little suitcase. She took the stairs up two at a time. Jewel was standing by the front door.

"I said, Get in the car. I've got your stuff."

The drive over to the west side was silent, except for Martha cursing at the traffic.

As they pulled up in front of the house, Jewel looked at her mother. "Mom?" Jewel was crying.

"You call me," Martha said. "How about that? You call me when you want to see me."

She leaned across and opened Jewel's door. Jewel got out, snorting with tears. Martha closed the door behind her daughter. She watched until the front door opened and Susan pulled Jewel into her plump bosom.

Martha sped away. Her hands were shaking. She opened both windows, but she could barely breathe. She held her mouth open in the wind, but she couldn't get enough air. She swerved in and out of traffic on the freeway, then abruptly cut across three lanes of cars and exited.

She would go to the health club. She would work out. Her neck was stiff. Her head was hurting. She needed to sweat. Susan was fat. This baby would make her fatter. Martha would wear shorts and cropped tops that showed off her flat stomach. She had had Jewel so young. Susan was probably thirty-five and plump to begin with. Martha raced up Gower past the Paramount Studio gate. She could look like a movie star. She swung into the Hollywood Spa's pink stucco parking structure and into a parking place, right in front. She laughed. There were wonderful things in store for her.

Saturday mornings at the club were busy, crowded with all the working stiffs who couldn't make it during the week. Martha sauntered into the women's locker room. She belonged here. She knew the drill. She unlocked her turquoise locker and put on her expensive, matching pur-

ple Lycra outfit. It made her hair look wilder, redder. She laced her
expensive sneakers, grabbed her towel, and went out into the swarm of
sweating bodies.

She strutted into her usual place in the weight room, conscious of a
gray-haired man's appreciative staring. She threw her towel over the
bar and began.

Lying on her back, holding twenty pounds in each arm, she suddenly
heard Reuben's voice. How wonderful, she thought; how glad he'll be
that I'm here.

He laughed. Then Martha heard a responding female laugh. She lowered her weights and sat up. Reuben was across the weight room, helping a young Latina with a machine. She saw the way the woman looked
at him. The woman was lush, round, the color of a Sugar Daddy. She
wore black workout clothes that made her dark eyes look liquid. It was
Sharon. Sharon from the barbecue; Sharon whose sister had gone out
with one of Reuben's cousins. Martha relaxed. She was practically
family.

She got up and started toward them. She wiped her neck with her
towel. Then she saw Reuben lean down and kiss Sharon on the mouth.
He had never kissed Martha in the club. He had never run his hand
down her smooth long hair and let it rest at the high curve of her butt.
She didn't have smooth hair and there was almost no curve to her butt
at all. He had never shook his head, looking into her eyes at the sheer
wonder of her.

"Reuben?" Martha said.

He turned and it was in that moment she really knew. He looked
caught. He had the eyes of a rabbit in the road at that last moment
when it's too late to brake, too late to run.

"Martha, what are you doing here?"

"Working out. Hi, Sharon."

"*Hola.*" Sharon's voice was as glossy as her hair.

Martha walked away.

"Wait," Reuben said.

"For what?"

He didn't come after her. "I'll call you," he said finally, with no remorse, only resignation.

"Okay." Martha continued out the door of the weight room, through the club. She winked at the gray-haired man on the treadmill. She couldn't remember ever winking at anyone before. He grinned and nodded. She walked on.

In the locker room, she found her clothes and shoes, her car keys sitting on the bench, her locker door wide open. She had never put them away. She felt so grateful that they were still there. She looked around at the other women in the room, in various stages of undress and redress.

"Thank you," she said. No one looked at her, so she said it again, louder, "Thank you."

A few women looked at her and quickly looked away. Martha smiled and realized she was crying. She gathered up her things and left, still wearing the atrocious purple spandex.

She got in her car and drove. She didn't want to go home. There was milk all over the floor. She drove west again, winding her way down Sunset Boulevard. November, Thanksgiving next week, and the heat and the smog were as oppressive as August. The foothills to her right were faded, bleached away in the thick chalk sky. She watched a long-haired rock and roller and his spiky girlfriend window-shopping at a fancy guitar store. She could tell from their scrunched faces and the way they squeezed their skinny bodies together that they were broke. The instruments in this window existed only in their dreams. She knew people came to L.A. to make it. This was the place. This was it. She had come here for college. She had wanted to go far from home and UCLA was the only school that would take her. Her high school grades were terrible, but her SATs were good and they needed to fill their out-of-state quota. And then she hadn't even graduated. She slept with Allen, got pregnant, got married, and left.

She liked driving. She could be happy in her little blue car. No one could see her purple thighs spreading on the seat. No one cared if she was crying. She had known that Reuben was going to leave. She had known it would happen soon. She had been expecting it. Just not today. Today she hadn't been prepared. She didn't think it was really anything specific she had done. She thought of lying on the floor at the gym and winced. She thought of begging him to stay and fuck her, and groaned out loud. But she didn't think it was really that. It was the way she looked. Not because she was white, as in Caucasian, but because she was too white. White and pale, wintry, even the freckles on her arms were just a dimmer shade of eggshell. She wasn't beautiful. She wasn't soft. She was all angles and bones, her big teeth more white in her bloodless face. She looked down at her hand on the steering wheel. It seemed at first to belong to an albino, but as she looked it became transparent. She was so white, she had become a ghost. She noticed how the people in other cars stared at her. Their eyes widened; she detected tentative fear in their nostrils, their open mouths. They had never seen a ghost driving before. They convinced themselves it was a Hollywood prank. That was the problem with Los Angeles; there was no magic left to believe in. Too much of it had been purposefully manufactured.

Without really realizing it, she drove all the way to Malibu. She delighted in scaring the other drivers. She stuck her tongue out. Shook her head. Howled at the filtered circle of sun.

The Belle Noche was busy too. Martha pulled in, but her customary spot was taken. She parked out on the Pacific Coast Highway. She paused for a moment before getting out of the car; she had only her exercise clothes on. But then she remembered she was a ghost. Clothes didn't matter on a ghost.

She opened her car door and got out. She stood just off the shoulder, on the edge of the highway blacktop. A Jeep, filled with young people, was coming toward her. She was aware they couldn't see her; she wondered what it would feel like when they passed through her. Would there be a bump or a tug on whatever shred of human body was left? But they missed her. They passed so close that her hair was pulled in the wake, her thighs jiggled with the vibration. They hadn't even seen her.

Inside her familiar hotel, no one spoke to her. A different clerk was at the desk. He didn't even look up. No one saw her as she sauntered through the lobby and onto the elevator. She got out on her floor and walked to her room. The door was ajar. When is a door not a door? Did Jewel know that joke? It didn't matter. Susan would tell it to her.

She slipped into the room without opening the door any further. She hoped he was here. She knew he couldn't see her, but she believed he'd sense her existence.

The bed was unmade. The room was a mess. A suitcase lay open on the floor, filled with a woman's clothes. Martha stumbled, dizzy, and sat in her beige chair. It thumped against the carpeted floor. Not the blonde, she thought, it can't be the blonde.

"Honey?" A man's voice from the bathroom. "Honey? Zat you?"

It wasn't Dr. Hamilton. Someone else had their room. The man came out of the bathroom, wrapped in a towel, halfway shaved.

"Who the hell are you?" he asked.

Martha sat still. He couldn't see her. She was nothing more than a presence, an idea of a person.

"I said, who the fuck are you?" He waited, but got no answer. "Get out. I'm calling security."

Martha stood. She looked at the man, nondescript in every way. Some gray hair, but not too much. A face, but just a face. A little over-weight, but not really. And she realized he saw her because he was a ghost too. He was as absent as she was, nothing really, totally transparent.

"Okay," she said, "I'm leaving."

She felt sad for him, still holding on to the trappings of real life: shaving, bathing. She wondered if he'd still be there Tuesday night when she came to see Dr. Hamilton.

She went to the double glass doors leading out to the balcony and pushed them open. She had never been on the balcony before. The beach and ocean were right below her, only two stories down. It was nothing for a ghost. She wondered if the wind would carry her, if she could sail over the ocean, hover above the white caps.

"What are you doing?" Her fellow ghost was yelling at her.

He should try it, she thought, give up the corporeal world. She climbed up on the stucco balcony wall, spread her arms, and floated.

It was over too soon. She fell hard, landed with a clumsy, palpable bump on her hip and thigh. For a moment she was confused, disoriented.

"Jesus Christ!" The man upstairs leaned over the balcony and shouted down at her, "Are you all right?"

She was fine but suddenly too solid and disappointed, terribly disappointed. She had wanted to fly.

"I'm calling the cops," the guy shouted.

Martha looked up at him. His shaving cream dripped off one cheek and fell onto the sand, right next to her no longer spooky hand.

"I'm fine," she said.

"I'm calling—calling—somebody." He disappeared.

Martha didn't want to be caught outside Dr. Hamilton's hotel. She stood and jogged tenderly through the sand, around the hotel, and back to her blue car.

Driving home she saw a guy, tan and blonde, wearing shorts and hiking boots and a bright blue T-shirt, come out of 7–11 carrying a cup of coffee. He looked handsome, rugged and attractively dangerous, drinking coffee at 6 P.M. Why did he want to stay up? Where would he go tonight? What would he talk about and with whom? She wanted a man who would drink strong coffee at six o'clock. A man who wasn't afraid of espresso. That would be a man, a coffee-drinking man. Forget Reuben and his carrot juice.

But when she put the key in her front door lock, the back of her neck tingled where Reuben had first kissed her. Opening the door she got an overwhelming whiff of spoiled milk. She was too real, not a ghost anymore. Ghosts aren't annoyed by things that stink. Her answering machine was blinking. Her heart lifted to her throat. Reuben had called; Reuben would apologize. She pushed the "play" button, impatient for the short message to rewind.

"Martha." It was Allen. "What the hell is going on with you? Jewel says you poured milk all over the place and screamed at her. I want an explanation."

"Fuck you," she said out loud. She didn't often use that kind of language, but today it seemed appropriate. "Fuck you, Allen."

She wanted to call him and say it to him over the phone, but her address book was in the kitchen and she had to clean to get to it.

She went downstairs to her bedroom, stripped off the too bright exercise clothes, and wadded them into the wicker trash basket by her dresser. She put on baggy shorts and her soft, soft holey T-shirt and dragged out her rain boots, ten years old, brought from back east where it rained sometimes.

Upstairs, she waded through the puddles of congealing milk to the broom closet for the mop and bucket. She began to clean, and as she pushed the yellow-handled mop she sang, "Heaven, I'm in Heaven. And my heart beats so that I can hardly speak. . . ."

21

WHEN SHE WOKE UP THE NEXT MORNING, SHE WAS SORE ALL OVER. HER HIP WAS COVERED with a dark purple and blue bruise the size of a dinner plate. Her wrist hurt. And her neck. She tried to sit and then quit trying; it hurt too much. But she smiled when she remembered how the keen sea breeze had felt against her face and the true faith she had had in her own ability to fly.

Her phone was ringing. Allen, she figured, still angry. Or Reuben, she thought just in time. Just before the answering machine clicked in, she was able to reach with one painful arm and pick up her bedside phone.

"Hello?"

"Martha?" It was Dr. Hamilton. "I hope I'm not waking you."

"No, no. Of course not." She had no idea what time it was.

"Um . . . how was your visit with your father?"

"He didn't come. His wife came home early."

"Oh. I see."

He paused. There was a noise in the background, a buzzing, almost screeching.

"Where are you?" Martha asked. It was hard to imagine him anywhere but the Belle Noche hotel. Why had she gone there yesterday? Of course he didn't live there. She must've been out of her mind.

"I'm at my office," he said. He sounded grateful to have to answer a question. "They're doing some construction."

"On Sunday?"

"I'll shut the door. Hold on a moment, please."

Martha heard the creak of his desk chair, then the thud of a door closing. The construction noises went away.

"Is that better?" he asked, picking up the phone again.

"Yes. Thank you."

Another pause. Another odd noise started, a huffing and every now and then a little withheld squeak.

"Now what?" Martha said.

There was a louder huff and a wet snort. Martha realized Dr. Hamilton was crying. Idiot, she told herself.

"Dr. Hamilton? What? What is it?"

"It's over," he said finally.

"What?"

"I'm calling to ask you, to tell you, not to come Tuesday night. I don't want you there."

"Will you be there?"

"Well—yes, but I have something else to do."

"I'll come."

"No."

"But—"

"No."

"I thought—"

"I said no. You may not come. I'll tell the manager not to let you in."

"He will. He's a friend of mine." But Martha knew he wouldn't. He wasn't a friend, just someone she saw often, like a checker at the grocery store. He wouldn't risk his job for her. Suddenly, she knew Dr. Hamilton had someone else. There was another woman to fit into the blue envelope.

"There's someone else," she said flatly.

"What?"

"Will she wear my clothes? My hood? Or did you make her new ones?"

"What are you talking about?"

"You've found another woman to talk to you. Smarter. Better read. More like you."

"Oh, Martha. There isn't anyone else. There never could be."

"Then why—"

"Don't you know? Can't you guess?"

"What? What?"

He was silent, not crying, only silent. She wanted him to talk about her some more, to tell her again there could never be anyone like her. But then why was he ending it?

"Well," she said, hearing her mother's voice in her own, "maybe we could have lunch sometime."

"No."

"At separate tables, with a screen between us, back to back." She tried to make it a joke. She wanted him to know how much she wanted to continue their work. "I'll wear your blue costume out in public." She paused. "If that's what you want."

Don't leave me, she thought, don't leave me.

"That won't be necessary," he said with a finality that made it true. "There won't be any lunches. I'm not sorry to never meet you face to face—"

"You're not?"

"No.

"Not even curious?"

"No. Why should I be?"

That stopped Martha, stopped her where she breathed, hurt more than her father's snore or Reuben's kiss. "Oh."

"Thank you, Martha."

He hung up. Martha stared at her princess phone. She couldn't let it end like this. She forced her irritated body out of bed and up her stairs. In her book she had paper clipped the original ad, the precise rectangle with Dr. Hamilton's request and office phone number. She found it, picked up the phone, and dialed.

His phone rang and rang and rang. Where was he? She listened to it ring, the intermittent sound of frustration, and knew he was listening too. He was there. He knew it was her and was too disgusted by her to even let her beg. She hung up, this time more gently.

Martha sat down on the hard chair by the phone. The bruise on her hip throbbed. This was it then. Suddenly she was angry, furious, rabid with hate for Dr. Hamilton and Reuben. Before they'd been there she had been happy. She had her routine, her little house, her trips to the market, the YMCA, and Winchell's. It was all spoiled. She looked down at her blue couch and screamed. She threw the cushions across the room. There was a lamp that Allen had given her for their first wedding anniversary. She picked it up, yanked the cord from the socket, and smashed the lamp on her hardwood floor. There was a photo, framed in a tacky silver frame, of her father, Jane, and the girls. Why had she kept it? Why did she display it? She grabbed the photo and tossed it like a Frisbee. It sailed across the room and hit the wall with a crack, then fell to the floor, broken in a million tiny pieces. She was in a fury of destruction. Anything any one had ever given her was useless now.

The last object she broke was a misshapen clay pot that Jewel had made her in art camp one summer. Just as the pot left her hand, Martha screamed, "No!" Not that, not that. But it was too late; she had thrown it without thinking and now it was broken. She had loved that pot. Imprints of Jewel's tiny fingers were frozen in the hard orange clay, a crude flower scratched on the front with a toothpick. On the bottom it said, "I love mommy. J.W." Martha crawled on her knees across the floor littered with shards and remnants of her things. She didn't mind the ache in her hip; she didn't mind the scratches on her knees from the broken glass. She picked up the pieces of the broken pot, but they crumbled in her fingers. Martha began to cry.

She sat on the floor and sobbed. She looked at her hands, white skin powdered with orange dust; the dirt lined every wrinkle, her hands looked so old. She pushed back the sleeve of her nightgown and saw the skin on the inside of her arm, dry and cracked like a mosaic of eggshells. She was old.

She got up, went downstairs, and took the full-length mirror Reuben had given her off her bedroom door. She brought it upstairs into the kitchen, where the morning light was strong and clear. She leaned it against the side of her kitchen table. Then, standing in her bright morning room, she took off her nightgown and faced herself, wholly naked in the mirror.

Tears continued down her face, unnoticed. They dripped off her jaw and fell on her bare breasts. She saw the bruise on her hip. She saw another bruise on her shoulder. She saw her skinny shapeless thighs and little old man butt. She saw each of her ribs outlined and the bones of her hips thrust forward from all her recent dieting. She looked sharp and tough, her bones too obvious. And everywhere she was freckled and white and hairy.

She was ugly. No wonder they all had left her. Her father, her mother, her stepfather, her husband, her daughter, her boyfriend, her employer.

She turned to the sink and threw up. And retching she remembered the eight thousand dollars in her underwear drawer. She had the money. She would buy new clothes, go to a tanning salon, have breast implants and a tummy tuck. She would put collagen in her lips.

She turned back to the mirror, the taste of vomit bitter in her mouth, and stepped closer. She inspected her face. She saw the wrinkles beginning on her forehead. She saw the softening of her jaw line. She saw the scar from chicken pox when she was seven and the crow's-feet just starting to walk. She didn't have much time.

She would see a plastic surgeon. She would have it all redone in a better way. When she first met Allen and they started sleeping together she had relaxed for a moment. She remembered a hazy month of long mornings in bed and watching television unclothed that was warm and comfortable. But after Allen had said he loved her, then he wanted her to change. He asked her to blow-dry her hair to get rid of the curl. He didn't like her clothes and bought her khaki pants, crewneck sweaters, loafers like his own. He teased her about her nose; it was straight, no cute little pug. She was wispy, he said, not athletic enough. Her skin was too pale, so she used bronzers and tans that came in a bottle and turned the palms of her hands and the tops of her feet orange. She had tried hard to please him. As she had tried to please Reuben and Lars and her mother and even Jewel.

Only Dr. Hamilton was different. In the beginning she had wanted to tell him what he wanted to hear, but it hadn't worked. He had always known she was faking it. And so she had learned to say what she thought, whatever it was. It surprised her that she knew what she thought, but she usually did. Safe in her blue nonentity, she didn't care about his opinion. If he couldn't see her, she was safe.

Too late, now. Too late. She should have tried harder. Whatever she had done, it hadn't been enough. He didn't want her anymore either, and he didn't even know how ugly she was.

But it was Sunday. She couldn't see a doctor on Sunday. She left her house the way it was and her body, bruised and dusty, and climbed back into her bed. If she could just get through today, she would take care of everything tomorrow. She was a good sleeper. She could wait.

2
2

MONDAY MORNING, MARTHA WAS FILLED WITH
PURPOSE. SHE THREW ON ANY OLD CLOTHES;
jeans ripped and paint-spattered from three years ago when she painted
Jewel's room; a black T-shirt faded to gray with a hole under one arm;
clogs, scuffed and worn and out of fashion. She didn't even brush her
hair, but let it hang long and wild down her back. She was starting over.
She wouldn't keep these kinds of clothes anymore. She'd be tailored
and put together and perfectly groomed.

She took the eight thousand dollars from its hiding place among her
bras and panties and stuffed it, all of it, into her front pocket. It was a
wad of cash, a real wad, and she liked the way it felt. She had money.
She would be beautiful soon.

She walked gingerly through her destroyed living room, her clogs
crunching on the broken glass and bits of broken things. She didn't
lock her front door. It wasn't necessary. She had the eight thousand
dollars. She didn't care about anything else.

But once in her car, Martha didn't know where to go to get beautiful.
She pulled over on the side of the road leading from her house and
thought. She needed a plastic surgeon. She needed immediate help. She

didn't have time to stop and look someone up in the phone book or call her gynecologist for a referral.

Cedars-Sinai appeared like a vision in her mind. The hospital of the stars, large, dark brick, and imposing. It was where she had given birth to Jewel. A nurse had told her that Demi Moore was in labor down the hall. Martha didn't care at the time, groaning and grunting, afraid of the next contraction and wanting them to come faster and faster so she could get it over with. Martha couldn't care less about Demi Moore. She wanted a refund from her Lamaze class, she wanted drugs, she wanted Allen to die. Afterward, Allen used it as part of the story he told of the birth, "Martha had Jewel right next to Demi Moore."

Cedars was filled with plastic surgeons. She decided to drive to the twin office buildings next to the hospital, look at the black board with the doctors' names in precise white letters, and pick one that sounded good. Maybe there would be one she'd heard of or read about in the paper. It was the place to start.

She started across town, down the curving road past Silver Lake. It was just a reservoir, not a lake, man-made with cement sides. It was surrounded by a fence topped with barbed wire. To have a view of this artificial oasis was coveted and expensive. Her neighborhood was ugly. The sky was colorless and hazy with smog; there were too many low beige stucco apartment buildings with brown dirt lawns and bent chain-link fences. A Mexican woman sat on her stoop, her skinny brown calves bowed from her stomach's weight; she wore a polyester skirt and mismatched sleeveless top with the straps of her black bra showing. A child, still in his G.I. Joe pajamas, dark hair askew, ran in the dusty yard with a stick and a broken plastic car. What had once seemed unique, now gave her the creeps.

She crossed onto Beverly Boulevard and entered Koreatown. Korean faces, narrow and flat, yellow tinged, stared at her from every corner. She saw an old man squatting on the sidewalk. He held one nostril and blew his nose onto the street. Then he spit on top of it. The light turned

green and Martha watched him in the rearview mirror as he wiped his
hand on his pants.

People were disgusting, she thought, and she was one of them. She
looked down at her thighs expanding on the seat. Her jeans looked
dirty. She thought she smelled. She sniffled, her nose clogged and thick
from all of yesterday's crying. She didn't have a tissue; she never had a
tissue and she had sometimes used her hand. She was as gross as he
was.

Her hands were shaking. She burped and tasted vomit mixed with
toothpaste in her throat. Her eyes were full again, full of salty seawater,
full of herself.

A low, black hardtop sports car pulled up next to her. Martha looked
over. A young L.A. guy was driving. His hair was short and styled; he
wore a white sweatshirt in his air-conditioning. He glanced at Martha.
She stared at him. She knew he was going to visit his mom and dad in
the valley. She knew what dinner at their house was like. He frowned
and smiled at the same time at her; his eyes went up and down, took
in her small blue car, her frizzy hair. He looked away and gunned his
engine. Martha wanted to call to him, wait, wait for me. Soon I'll be
just what you want. She wanted to go home with him. Life would be
simple. She would have a car phone. She would have backyard barbe-
cues with chips and dip and cans of beer, pasta salad, and hot dogs.
She would love his mother, even though sometimes she drove Martha
crazy. They would go to all the most popular movies. Wait, she called
after him, wait.

Beverly Boulevard left Koreatown and crossed Larchmont. Suddenly
it was green. The lawns were green, there were real trees, and the
houses were big. Hancock Park was where the Orthodox Jews lived, big
houses with lovely lawns; it was as much like back east as Los Angeles
got. On Fridays and Saturday mornings you'd see the families walking
to temple, the men wearing suits and wide-brimmed hats, the strings
of their prayer shawls hanging out the sides of their suit jackets. The

women covered their hair, dressed up but not in high heels. The children trailed along behind them, the little boys with yarmulkes and long sideburns.

Today it was quiet. She left that neighborhood and entered the shopping district. Trendy eateries, expensive women's clothing, hair salons, she was almost there. The squat imposing bricks of the hospital and the identical office towers were just ahead, faded in the dirty air. Mecca, salvation, the Emerald City. Martha imagined standing before the congenial round-faced doctor. "I want to be beautiful," she would say. "Simply beautiful." He would smile, pat her hand, and step behind the curtain. It wouldn't take long, it wouldn't hurt, and she would have everything she wanted.

She passed the hospital once but didn't want to pay to park. She had no other money than her eight thousand dollars and she had plans for it. So she drove around behind the hospital into a neighborhood of small, Spanish-style homes with patches of lawn and sprinkler systems. She parked and got out of her car, checking the wad in her front pocket. She read the parking sign, "Two-hour parking Mon. thru Fri." Would she be here more than two hours? She wasn't sure, but she wouldn't mind getting a ticket.

She walked down the neat sidewalk toward the hospital. She heard a rhythmic thumping and looked up the driveway of a trim yellow house. A young man, in shorts and a sleeveless undershirt, well built and wearing boxing gloves, was hitting a punching bag in his garage. She stopped to watch. He was young and squarely handsome. His red leather gloves blurred in her eyes and she felt herself begin to cry again.

The man saw her and stopped hitting. Martha didn't move.

"Are you okay?" he called.

Martha wanted to say, Help me, I'm ugly. Help me, I'm ugly. But she only looked at the beige sidewalk, the color and texture of her vomit.

"Hey," the guy said, "has something happened?"

"No." Martha shook her head. "Nothing's happened. Nothing at all."

He took a step toward her. Martha took a step away.

"What's the matter?" he asked.

He was nice, so goddamn nice, and Martha ached toward him. She wanted him to put his arms around her and smooth the hair back from her face. "You looked so beautiful," she said. "I was just struck with how beautiful you looked with your red gloves."

He blushed, but he was pleased. He raised his hands, palms toward her, a shrug, a gesture of pleasurable confusion.

"Wait till I come back," Martha said, smiling. "You'll see. It'll be a whole new me."

"I didn't know the old one," he said.

"Just wait."

Martha turned and ran down the street. She knew it would take longer than an afternoon; she hadn't meant wait until I come back today. She thought she would change her appearance and come back when it was done, when she was transformed, emerged from the chrysalis of her ugly self, spectacular, lovely, and lovable.

The lobby of the Cedars-Sinai office tower was crowded. Old ladies with walkers and African American attendants; old men in enormous rectangular sunglasses and brown pants that hung straight from their waists over shriveled butts and legs; pregnant women; pale men with the dusty hair and tentative movements of the very ill. Martha relaxed. She felt hidden here, simply unattractive, not hideous.

She walked to the directory. She felt a sinking despair in her stomach. The doctors were listed alphabetically, not by specialty. She wouldn't know if the name she picked was that of a plastic surgeon or a urologist. She looked around. There was an information desk, but Martha couldn't talk to the woman sitting there. She was everything Martha was not; she had bronze hair and maroon fingernails, matching lipstick. Martha couldn't ask her which doctor would make her beautiful. Martha turned back to the board. She would read every name and look for one that sounded familiar or distinguished or just right.

Martha read down the columns. Suddenly, she gasped. There was Dr. Hamilton's name. Dr. Aaron Hamilton. She had never thought he'd be here; she never thought of him as a medical doctor, more as a psychologist or a research scientist. She read his name again. Just that, just reading the even white letters, caused her breath to come faster. He was here, somewhere in this building. She read his office number, 804. Now she had the courage to face the well-coiffed information woman.

"Excuse me," Martha said.

"Yes, dear?" The woman surprised Martha by sounding nicer than she looked.

"Dr. Hamilton, Dr. Aaron Hamilton—is that—is he a psychiatrist?"

"No." The woman smiled sympathetically at Martha. "You must have him confused with another doctor. Dr. Hamilton is a plastic surgeon. He's quite well-known. Famous, in some circles."

"Oh." Martha was stunned. "Thank you."

"Peppermint?" the volunteer asked and offered Martha a basket filled with candies.

Martha took one, knowing that her breath was horrendous, vomit and barely brushed teeth. She took another and nodded her thanks.

She walked to the bank of elevators and pushed the arrow pointing up. She felt betrayed. Dr. Hamilton had used her to talk about beauty when he was obviously already an expert. Tummy tucks and liposuction, nose jobs, chin lifts; he knew what made a woman beautiful. He knew what women wanted. He saw beautiful women every day and made them even more stunning. What could she possibly have told him that he didn't already know? Martha felt her toes curl with humiliation. She could hear Dr. Hamilton laughing at her as he left the desert-colored hotel room and drove back to his mansion in Beverly Hills. He laughed, chuckled mightily about the theories she spouted, the idea that she could know any more about beauty than he did.

Once, driving in the car with her mother, going home from the local swimming pool, Martha had looked down at her white and freckled thighs stuck to the green vinyl seat and asked her mother, "Why? Why do I look this way? Why am I so pale? Why is my hair so curly? Why am I taller than most girls? Why don't I look like Audrey?"

"It's your father's fault," Dolly said and laughed. "You'd better ask him."

And she had. "Am I pretty, Daddy?"

And her father had replied, "Remember, Sport, beauty is only skin deep—if you get my drift."

Martha did. She understood the basic answer to her question.

Dr. Hamilton's door was just like every other door on the floor. The hall was quiet; the brown and beige patterned carpet, clean and thick. She opened his door. An older receptionist in a nurse's uniform was talking on the phone, barely visible behind a counter. A nicely dressed woman sat in the waiting room with her head bent over a sailboat magazine. Martha entered and let the door close behind her. The woman reading the magazine glanced momentarily at Martha. The woman's face was horribly disfigured, burned, the skin puckered and tight, the planes of the cheeks dissolving into the nose and forehead. Before the woman looked away, Martha saw the pain in her eyes, her guilty hatred for Martha, her fear, her resignation at her own fate.

The receptionist looked up. "May I help you?"

Martha looked past the receptionist at the closed door of the examining room.

"This is Dr. Hamilton's office. Which office are you looking for?" The receptionist was nice but direct.

Martha shook her head. "Sorry," she whispered. She didn't want Dr. Hamilton, if he was there, to hear her voice. "Sorry." She turned and ran out.

In the lobby, she found the pay phone. She didn't have any change so she used Allen's calling card.

The phone on the other end rang, once, twice, three times, then: "Hello?" When Dolly answered the phone you could hear Missouri in her voice.

"Mom?" Martha's voice was small.

"Martha? That you? How are you? Oh my, you don't know what I've been going through here. I've been—"

Martha interrupted, "I broke up with my boyfriend."

"Well," Dolly said, just like Martha's grandmother, just like a Pruitt, "well, don't I know all about that." She laughed. "I've been having a time with your stepfather. This damn fishing club he belongs to. Since he retired he's been driving me nuts, you know, and when he joined this club I thought good, get him out of the house. But now. We can't go to Orlando with the Becks on Friday 'cause he's got a fishing club meeting. We can't play bridge next Tuesday with the Olsons 'cause he's goin' fishing. And, Martha, the house is full of fish. We got fish in the freezer, fish in the deep freeze in the garage, and I got fish soup, fish cakes, and fish to fry in the fridge. I'm turning into a friggin' fish!"

"Oh," Martha said and sighed. "Mom—Mom—"

"How's Jewel?"

"Fine. Mom, I don't know what I'm doing."

"You mean about Christmas?"

"No, no, but—"

"Listen, your sister's not feeling well. She's come down with a terrible flu. They think it might be pneumonia. Stu and I think we'll just have to go there this year. You're not upset, are you?"

"No."

"Good. I knew you'd understand. You get Jewel over to your house Christmas Eve. You know, through all my divorces I never did give up having you kids with me. I don't see why Jewel lives with Allen."

"I know."

"It was so hard. I worked, I took care of you and your sister. I wasn't a very good mother, I know that, but I did the best I could. I did."

"You were great, Mom. You were."

"Oh, I don't know. I'm sorry we're not gonna be there for Christmas, but Audrey and those five kids of hers need us more. I wish you and Jewel would come to Salt Lake."

"I can't, Mom, I can't. Mom, I'm in—"

"I spent the worst Christmas of my life alone with you and Audrey, that Christmas after Lars left. Remember? You set the toe of your sock on fire trying to keep warm by the fire. It was cold. I was—well, I was miserable. But I never let on in front of you and your sister. I bet you never even knew how miserable I was."

Martha had known, only too well. Lars had tried to burn the house down. After years of taking care of Dolly during her psychotic episodes, he had one of his own. Martha was awakened one night by the sound of Dolly and Lars arguing, fighting, screaming at one another. There was a crash and Martha ran to her mother's room. Lars stood there in his red and white striped pajamas, looking like a large, demented, stubbly child. His hair stood up, his face was red, his tongue poked around his lips. He had pushed Dolly's antique dresser over on its face.

"There," he said with satisfaction.

Dolly sat on the edge of the bed. "What do you think you're doing?" she asked. She sounded like his mother.

Lars laughed. "It's time there were some changes around here."

He vaulted over the prone chest of drawers and slid on his bare feet down the hall carpet and on down the stairs. Dolly looked at Martha and raised her eyebrows angrily. Martha ran after Lars. He darted through the kitchen and down the basement steps. Martha tiptoed down after him.

He opened the fuse box. He picked up a wrench and a screwdriver.

"What are you doing?" Martha echoed her mother.

"Now, Martha, this is none of your business."

"But—"

"You used to be so sweet. When you were little and I was first coming around, you did what I asked you to do. Your mother did what I told her. Times have changed."

He unscrewed the panel on the fuse box. He stuck the screwdriver into the mass of wires. There were sparks and he jumped back, shocked. Then he was at it again, this time with the wrench.

"What are you doing?" Martha pleaded for an answer.

"I'm gonna burn this goddamn house right to the ground."

More sparks, but when he couldn't get it to do what he wanted it to do, he picked up the hammer and pounded on the wires and plastic switches until everything was broken. The lights flickered and went out. Martha was afraid in the dark. Lars found a flashlight and switched it on. He held it under his face. His flesh had sagged over the years; his big features drooped and in the stark shadows of the flashlight beam there were huge gaps in his face. Martha backed away from him.

"Come here, Martha. We're going to have a fire."

"No."

"Martha, little Martha. Not so little anymore." He picked up a clump of rags. "Come on. We're going to the garage."

Martha didn't want to, but she felt she had to follow him. As they crossed the kitchen, Martha could hear her mother singing upstairs. Why is she singing, Martha wondered, why is she singing?

"Mom? You okay?"

The singing stopped, so Martha knew she'd heard her, but Dolly didn't answer.

In the garage, Lars put the rags in a cardboard box and poured on lighter fuel from next to the barbecue grill. He danced around the box in his little boy pajamas, like he was playing Indians or fairies in the woods. When the can of lighter fluid was empty, he dropped it on the ground. He went to the shelf above the barbecue grill and picked up the box of matches.

"I'm not stupid, Martha." His voice was matter of fact. "I know the words for fire. Burning, flames, inferno, pyre, combust, blaze, conflagration. You see? Your mother wouldn't even ask me."

He turned the flashlight onto Martha. She was aware of her short T-shirt nightgown, her messy hair. Lars growled from somewhere deep. He put his hand on Martha's hair. "Like your hair," he whispered. "Combustion! This house has become an inferno; it doesn't need me to light the match. But I will."

He opened the box of matches. "Shit!" he said.

The box was empty. He began looking for other matches. He ran into the kitchen but couldn't find any on the shelf behind the stove. He pulled the silverware drawer out too far and it tipped and the silverware tumbled and clanked to the clean floor. He rolled up a piece of newspaper and then tried to light the stove, but it had an electronic ignition and he had destroyed the electricity.

He walked out of the kitchen, through the living room, and out the front door. He sat down on the steps outside. He put his head in his hands.

"I never should have given up smoking," he said, and he laughed. "It was your mother made me give it up."

Martha stood next to him, stood there until the sun came up and Dolly came downstairs with her suitcase packed looking fresh and lovely as always.

Martha and her mother moved in with Audrey. The gas furnace broke and they spent Christmas huddled around the tiny Danish fireplace. Dolly had spent the day crying, not about Lars but about her house, her dresser, his lack of respect. Martha and Audrey had consoled Dolly, cooked her special foods, decorated the entire house, gone to the grocery store, and filled her a stocking. She didn't have presents for either of the girls; she just couldn't manage it.

The day after Christmas, Lars had shown up, groveling. Dolly had been overjoyed. They went home like nothing had ever happened and

Dolly talked the skinny electrician who came to fix the fuse box into taking Martha out. Bad breath and bad sex had definitely rounded out that holiday season.

"Sure, Mom," Martha said into the phone. "I'll be okay." She hung up, turned away from the phone. Dolly would not be standing here in dirty jeans and a ratty T-shirt. Reuben would not have left Dolly. Dr. Hamilton would not have fired Dolly. Jewel would not prefer Susan to Dolly. Martha had never wanted anyone but Dolly.

23

THE YOUNG FOUR-SIDED GUY WITH THE PUNCHING
BAG CAME OUT OF HIS YELLOW HOUSE AS MARTHA
walked by.

"Hey," he called to her. "Hey. Let me see."

"What?" Martha slowed and turned to him.

"You don't look any different," he said. "I was watching for you."

"Oh . . . oh, I'm sorry."

"You don't have to apologize to me. Where'd you go? I thought maybe you were gonna have your hair cut or something."

"No. No. I was looking for a doctor, that's all."

"You don't need a doctor, do you?"

Martha didn't know what to say.

"Are you sick?" he continued.

"No."

"That's good. Well—" he paused.

Martha looked at him. He was cute. He had a Jeep parked in the driveway. He was probably twenty-three years old.

"Are you an actor?" Martha asked.

"Yeah." He was pleased. "How'd you know?"

Martha tossed her hair. She pretended she was one of the best waitresses at the Sweet Spot. She arched her back, pushing her perky breasts forward.

"I could tell," she said.

She glanced at him sideways. All she wanted was for him to ask, just ask her. He did.

"Wanna come in? Have a beer?"

"Isn't it a little early?"

"Breakfast of champions."

She laughed at the old joke. "Sure."

"What's your name?"

"Rosie," she said. "Sad, but true."

"It's a great name," he said, "with your red hair and all. I'm Mitch. Short for Mitchell."

Rosie leaned against his kitchen counter and ran the cold opening of the beer bottle around her mouth. Rosie watched him watching her. Rosie put her hand on his well-developed biceps. Rosie pulled him to her and kissed him. He tasted like beer. He was a good kisser, wet and sloppy. Rosie put a finger in his mouth as they kissed and drew a moist trail across his cheek. Rosie led him to bed.

His sheets were tangled, the bed unmade for days, perhaps forever. The noon sun was gray, filtered through his dusty window shades. Martha never thought of her own orgasm but prolonged his as long as Rosie could.

With his face buried in her hair he said, "Jesus. You are something."

What something did that mean, she wondered. What kind of something was he talking about.

When her mother was going through the worst of her nervous breakdown, Martha had been sixteen. A late bloomer, she was hovering on the cliff of womanhood. She was well aware that she was tall, flat-chested, and too skinny. She was shy and never spoke in class, never said much to anyone, giggled nervously when spoken to. She had lost her virginity the year before to a dropout she'd met in the school parking lot who touched her arm when he spoke to her.

At home, Lars and Audrey competed with each other to take the best care of Dolly. Audrey told Martha she couldn't talk to anyone on the phone. Lars told Martha not to ask for anything, to eat what was on the table, to step quietly. Martha did as she was told. She tiptoed in her house. Marvin called it "walking on eggshells," said he always had around Dolly. Martha knew this time what he meant.

One night, she'd been working late on homework. Her mother and Lars were in the kitchen where they often sat at night after the dishes were done. Sometimes they played cards. Martha got up from a boring biology book and wandered to the kitchen. She was hungry, distracted, her mind filled with single cells and symbiosis. Dolly sat in the rocking chair, her legs crossed, a cigarette in one graceful hand. She looked beautiful, sexy, as she laughed low in her throat and put out her free hand to touch Lars on the knee. He sat next to her, perched on the bench of the picnic table, and gazed at her. Martha was struck with the romance of the picture.

She ducked in quietly and went to the refrigerator. She nodded shyly, made shy by her mother's elegance, and opened the fruit drawer for an apple.

She took one and smiled at her mother. Her mother's face changed, fell; she looked puzzled, frightened.

"Lars?" Dolly asked. "Lars?"

Martha froze.

"Yes, Dolly, what is it?" Lars sounded calm, like a doctor.

"Who is that?" Dolly pointed at Martha. "Who is that girl?"

"That's Martha," Lars said.

"Who is Martha?"

"Dolly, Dolly." Lars wasn't chiding her; he was trying to change the subject.

"I don't know any Martha. I don't know anyone named Martha. Who is that girl? What is she doing in our house? Who is she!"

Martha fled, ran through the living room, up the stairs, into her small bedroom. She looked at her face in her closet mirror. She looked the same as always. She heard her mother's voice again. "Who is that girl?"

Martha crept into her bottom bunk and curled her long legs against her stomach. She kept her hands on her face, stroking her nose, her cheeks, her wet eyes. She was someone. She was a real person, a tangible object. She could smell and taste and feel. She was there.

Mitchell used two condoms. It was late afternoon when they finished and his phone had rung a dozen times. They had heard his friends and girlfriends on the answering machine. There had even been a knock at his door.

They were sitting at the kitchen table drinking the beer they hadn't finished earlier when his roommate came in. Mitch looked embarrassed; his shirt was open. Martha was flushed, barefoot, and had curls of hair stuck to her neck.

The roommate wore a white shirt and a tie. A salesman, Martha figured, or a computer nerd.

"Doug," Mitchell said, self-conscious but a gentleman, "this is Rosie."

"Hi," Martha said. "I was just going."

She went into Mitch's room to find her clogs. She saw his wallet on the dresser and took out a twenty-dollar bill. She needed it, a little something besides her eight thousand.

At the door, they kissed again.

"Bye," Martha said. "Thank you."

He laughed. "I'll call you. Gimme your number. I'll call you."

"I'm old enough to be your sister," Martha said.

She kissed him hard and pressed her body against his, pushing the top of her thigh against his groin. He groaned.

"Don't go."

It was what she wanted to hear. She left.

Martha got in her small car. She didn't know where to go but she knew she was gone, she was out of here, she would never be back.

Mitch had been her final farewell. The eight thousand and twenty dollars in her pocket was her ticket and her passport. Men didn't care if you were beautiful, not for sex, not the first time. Mitch had hands that were small and damp when he took off his red boxing gloves. He bit his nails. She could smell him. She rolled down her window and let the warm air blow him away.

She turned right on Beverly Boulevard, heading west, into the sun. The smog had turned the sunset blood red, a stain in the sky shaped like licks of flame.

If she never went back, what would happen to her little house? Allen would sell it, eventually. He would take a few things from it for Jewel to keep and sell the rest. She thought about the mess. Allen would think there'd been foul play, that Martha had been raped, abducted, left in a ditch off the freeway with wide silver electrician's tape wrapped around her mouth and wrists. Susan would be angry because Allen would be upset and Jewel would be frightened. Martha knew what it felt like to be pregnant and want your husband's, Allen's, entire attention.

Too bad, Martha thought, I should've left a note.

The sun melted, liquified, stretched along the horizon and then melted away. Martha switched on her headlights. They illuminated the road in front of her, the color of raw cookie dough, and made the rest of the world seem darker. She turned them off again. She looked over at the red BMW next to her. The woman talked on a car phone, smiled at something that was said. She was hurrying home, couldn't wait to be there. Martha pulled over behind her. She wanted to ride in her wake.

If Dr. Hamilton tried to reach her, she would be gone, her number no longer in service. If he wanted to ask her just one more thing, he wouldn't know where she was. But there weren't any more questions. He told her there was nothing left to talk about. She had said everything she could and it wasn't enough. It never could be. The woman in his waiting room had agreed with her.

Her hands were shaking as if she'd had too much coffee. But she hadn't; she hadn't had any coffee or eaten anything all day or yesterday either. She was hungry suddenly, ravenous, and craved a cheeseburger, French fries, and a vanilla milk shake. She wanted grease and carbohydrates and thought of Reuben. She thought of his smooth caramel skin and the way his pubic hair didn't curl as much as most people's. She thought of the smell of his breath in the morning. She wanted her mother. She wanted Dolly to tell her how to get through this, Dolly who had so much experience with leaving.

She let the woman on the car phone get away and pulled into a gas station with a minimarket. She was hungry. She envisioned Hostess cupcakes, Twinkies, Three Musketeer bars. It had been a very long time since she'd eaten anything. She wanted something good but not good for her.

Martha parked to one side, away from the pumps. She got out of her car. She could see two boys in service station gray inside. She could see the metal rack of junk food. Her mouth watered.

Another car pulled in, a late-model Camaro with wide tires and darkly tinted windows. A young guy and a girl got out and skipped into the store before her. One of the guys in gray came out and began filling their car with gas.

It was bright inside; the fluorescent lights buzzed and turned the skin on her arms an alien green. The young couple stood at the counter talking to the attendant. He was their friend. Martha looked at the girl. She was strawberry blonde and pretty, wearing a nice pair of tight black jeans and expensive high-heeled boots. She had on a leather jacket, and her hair was straight and brushed until every strand was shining and clear. She was spinning on her boot heels, twisting first to the Camaro driver, then to the attendant. Martha couldn't buy the junk food she wanted. She was too embarrassed. She couldn't buy doughnuts, cupcakes, potato chips in front of them. She got a bottle of water that she didn't want from the refrigerator case and stood behind them. She waited.

The other attendant returned, and the four friends talked together, ignoring her.

Martha waited and stared out the window. A pickup truck pulled in, battered white, with an older bald man at the wheel. The rotating neon gas station sign reflected on the man's shiny scalp, on and off, on and off, like a blinking yellow light at an empty intersection. The man reached in the back of his pickup. Martha tensed, ready for a shotgun, an Uzi, a roll of dynamite. But it was just a gas can, dirty green plastic. The man gave it to the attendant to fill, then leaned against his truck and lit a cigarette. He threw the hot match to the ground.

"Fuckin' idiot!" she heard the guy behind the counter say. "Gonna catch us all on fire."

The Camaro driver laughed, not sure if it was possible. The girl bit her lip. She was frightened.

Martha watched the attendant step hard on the match, grind it into the blacktop, and step away from the man to the other side of the pump.

When the can was filled, the man paid, put the can in the back of his truck, and drove away, cigarette still hanging from his lip.

"Asshole," the attendant said as he came back into the store. His face was white. "Shit."

Martha watched the girl put her hand on his dirty arm. The guy behind the counter shook his head. All three smiled at him, glad he was safe, agreeing the bald man had been crazy.

Martha looked at the attendant's face. He was young and pimple-chinned. Eyes too close together, eyebrows growing across his nose in a straight line. He smiled at his friends with crooked teeth. They laughed, relaxing. The girl put her arm through the attendant's. He was her boyfriend, Martha realized, surprised, not the driver of the Camaro. The girl leaned her head on the attendant's shoulder, kissed his greasy grease monkey's neck.

Martha grabbed a bag of chips and a package of Hostess cupcakes.

She put Mitch's twenty-dollar bill on the counter. The guy rang it up, gave her her change, and smiled at her.

Sitting in her blue car at the gas station, eating corn chips, Martha was suddenly struck with the idea of someone knowing her, knowing her so well that they didn't see her anymore. Someone knowing more than the outside of her so that seeing her wouldn't matter. She knew, all at once, that was what beauty truly meant.

Dr. Hamilton. He knew her, but he didn't see her. Did he see anyone? Could he see anyone? She thought of his patient in the waiting room, the way the woman sat hunched away from the door and Martha's interested eyes. Martha had seen the puckered flesh on the woman's hand, the pinkie bent unnaturally. Would anyone ever be able to know her, the real her, or only her healed remains?

The bald man jumped into her mind. The dirty green gas can in the back of his truck, the ardent ember on the end of his cigarette. The green can under the hotel room table. The white towels. The bandaged woman. The green gas can in the back of the truck. The cigarette. The attendant in gray and his words, "He's gonna catch himself on fire," and Dr. Hamilton's, "I'm not going to hurt you."

And in a flash, a spark, a flame, she knew. She knew what Dr. Hamilton was going to do, could already be doing. How far would he go to study the importance of beauty? She knew him. He would go too far. Unable to talk about it anymore, he would want to experience what his patients felt, firsthand. To learn to see their beauty.

Martha jumped from her car, leaving the door open, and ran to the phone. What if she was too late? What if the ambulance had come, his colleagues already shaken their heads and turned away?

She called information. She got his office number; it was all information had. She looked at the dark sky. Was he still there? Could he still be there? She didn't know what time it was.

The phone rang and rang, then, amazingly, he answered.

"Dr. Hamilton."

"Dr. Hamilton." She couldn't keep the relief from her voice.

"Martha?" He didn't sound unhappy to hear from her.

"Yes. Yes, it's me. Dr. Hamilton . . . are you okay? I mean . . . I thought . . ." She felt like an idiot. She shouldn't have called; she didn't know what to say. He was a reasonable man, a plastic surgeon. "I'm sorry—"

"Martha," he interrupted as a semi pulled into the gas station behind her, "where are you?"

"I . . ." She tried to laugh. "I don't know exactly."

"Are you all right?" When she didn't answer right away, he contin- ued, urgently, "Martha, answer me."

He was worried about her. She smiled. "I have to see you," she said.

"Why?"

"I know what you're going to do to yourself," she said, surprised at the pride in her voice. "I've figured it out. You left too many clues."

"Martha—"

"I have something to tell you. Something important. See me, or I'll call the hotel, the police, your lawyer."

"My lawyer?"

"I met him at a party." She couldn't remember his name, but it didn't matter. She heard Dr. Hamilton sigh.

"Can you get to the hotel?" he asked.

"Yes," she said. "What time is it?"

"Almost nine."

"I won't be there until ten."

"I'll wait."

"Don't do anything." She was strong. She demanded his safety. He had to listen.

"I won't. I promise. Martha?"

"Yes?"

"Hurry."

Martha drove as fast as she could. She couldn't wait to see him. Her heart lifted. The souls of her feet felt light, tingling, as if they'd been brushed with a baby's hairbrush. She drove with just her toes pressing on the pedals.

She had already assumed the secure safety of her navy anonymity. She flew on the roads now. She wasn't in anyone's way; she wasn't a bad driver. She moved smoothly, used her turn signal. Martha weaved and dodged among the other cars effortlessly. She was perfectly in tune with driving.

At the Belle Noche, she parked in her usual spot and ran into the lobby, her ugly clogs clacking on the Mexican tile. Her friend was there at the desk. He smiled at her, looked her up and down.

"Been painting?"

"What? Oh, well, what a day."

The night manager shrugged politely, without commitment either way. "You're late tonight."

"Yes. I am. Is he—" Martha was suddenly worried. Where was Dr. Hamilton? How would he know she was there and ready.

"I'll buzz him—tell him you're here. He's waiting in the other room."

"Oh, oh. Good. Of course."

She took the key and went up.

In the bathroom she suddenly felt nauseous. She crouched on the white tile floor in her underwear. Her bra strap slid down a shoulder. The cotton of her underpants had pulled away from the waistband. She was afraid. She was sweating. She wanted to take a shower, but there wasn't time.

What would it be like to burn? She couldn't think of any men, only women who were burned at the stake. Joan of Arc, the witches of Salem, women with long hair and soft skin. She would pop and crackle; the grease would flare; her body's fat would sizzle like a strip of bacon in a Sunday morning kitchen.

There was a knock at the room's door. For the first time, Martha wasn't ready.

"Just a minute," she called. She hurried, struggled with her blue costume. Her stomach lurched and gurgled.

He knocked again.

"I'm coming," she called. "Almost."

She tucked her hair in and pulled on the hood. She ran to the chair and sat.

"Come in," she called. Silently, to herself, she said it over and over again; come in, come in, come in, come in, come in.

He entered. He looked wounded and afraid. He carried a legal-sized manila envelope.

"Martha," he said. He put the envelope on the table and sat, gingerly, tentatively, on the chair across from her.

Martha saw the green can and the two white towels, not under the table as usual but sitting on the dresser. She felt herself shaking.

Dr. Hamilton put his face in his long clean hands. He rubbed his eyes, put the heels of his hands on his forehead, and then dragged them down his face. Martha watched him. He looked up at the ceiling, away from her, anywhere but at her blue form.

"I think I owe you something," he began. "I know you're curious about me. I thought I should answer some of your questions."

"Next time," Martha said.

"Very clever." Dr. Hamilton smiled at the ceiling. "But there won't be a next time, Martha. Martha—"

He started to say something more, then closed his mouth, then opened it again. Martha watched the freshness of his lips, his tongue on his teeth.

"Reuben dumped me," Martha said. "He left me for someone else. Someone prettier. My father stood me up. I had to call his wife in Washington to find out he wasn't coming. I've had a terrible fight with my daughter."

She was pleading with him, trying to make him understand why she was there, why she wanted him whole and safe and constant every Tuesday, Wednesday, and Thursday night, even more, as much as she could get.

He frowned, his hands opened and closed, then he reached for the envelope. He picked it up, opened it, and pulled out a stack of 8" X 10" black-and-white photographs.

"Maybe this will explain. Can you see them?" he asked, handing them to her. "Shall I direct the light for you?"

"It's fine."

Martha turned the photos over in her lap. She caught her breath like a hiccup. The first was a picture of a woman's face or what was left of it, terribly burned, gaping moments of puckered flesh, the eyelashes gone, the nose missing, no lips. This one was much worse than the woman she had seen in the waiting room. She looked at the next photo. Worse again. The woman in the picture looked directly into the camera lens, her lidless eyes filled with tears of pain, of hate, of fear. Martha felt her own eyes fill. She took a deep gulp of air. She turned another picture over. It was the full-figure shot of a naked woman, the pubic hair singed away; the breasts like blackened gourds, pumpkins left outside until they turn black with rot. Martha began to cry. Picture after picture of women who had no beauty left, nothing to be seen. They were alive, but their eyes told Martha they weren't happy about it. She let the photos slide from her lap and fall to the floor. Martha cried. Her hood grew wet, the gauze in front of her face stuck to her nose and cheeks. Dr. Hamilton let Martha sob.

"I'm sorry. But I wanted you to know," he said finally.

"They're all women."

"Yes. There are some men, but as I said, it's different for men. It will be different for me."

"I don't understand," she said. "Not at all." He looked disappointed, but she didn't care. "Why?"

"You mean, why do it? Because I must."

Martha kept crying. She hated each of them, in every picture, all the careless women who had smoked in bed, who let the morning frying pan catch on fire, allowed the ugly boyfriend to hurt them, who had driven Dr. Hamilton to this. But Dr. Hamilton wasn't like them, not yet.

"I had a thought." She sniffed, wiped her eyes through the hood, straightened her shoulders. "About beauty."

"It's a little late."

"No," she said, "it's not." She took a chance, hoped he would answer what she needed to hear. "Dr. Hamilton, do you know me? I mean, intimately. Don't you really know me?"

Dr. Hamilton closed his eyes, grimaced in a terrible smile of distress and despair. "Yes. I know you. I know all about you. I know the way you smell. I know the way you laugh when you're nervous. I know what frightens you, calms you. I know the sound of your breath when you have a new idea."

"What about how I look?"

"I don't care how you look. I don't. Because I know you, even inside that ridiculous, enormous blue thing that I make you wear, you show through. It's you I see."

"It doesn't matter what I look like."

"No. You are simply Martha."

She realized she loved to hear him say her name. His quiet words gave her voice strength. "Then why does it matter what these women look like?" She indicated the photos lying on the floor around her feet. "They're alive, isn't that enough?"

"Would you want to live if you looked like this?" Dr. Hamilton sounded disgusted. He picked up a photo. "Would you? Wouldn't you rather be dead? I gave this woman back her eyelids so she could close them at night and sleep, but I couldn't give her a morning to wake up to. Her children screamed when they saw her. Her husband couldn't eat dinner at the same table. What have I done? Why have I saved her? I haven't really saved her from anything."

"You have. You just said you don't care what I look like. That you believe in my beauty, just because you know me. We adapt. We get used to looking at things. After a while her husband will learn to enjoy the sound of her voice, the way she feels in the dark, the favorite dish she cooks for him, just like he did before."

"Will he?"

"Of course. He must. He must or there's no hope for anyone. Anyone who has an accident, who gets fat, who gets old."

Dr. Hamilton shrugged, but Martha wouldn't let him agree with her. It wasn't hopeless. He had to see that.

She stood in the dark hotel room. Slowly, finger by finger, she pulled the dark blue glove from her right hand. Her hand looked small and shocking in the dim light. Martha shuddered but continued. He will see me, she thought, see that I am ugly and that he doesn't care. He can't care. Her bare fingers reached for the gloved ones, tugged the other glove off. She put both hands on the bottom of her soggy hood and began to lift.

Dr. Hamilton cried out. She looked at him. He was staring at her hands. She let go of the hood and held her two hands out to him, palms up, offering them to him.

He fell forward from his chair onto his knees in front of her. He leaned his face against one open palm. With her other hand she touched his hair. He groaned.

Suddenly, she pushed him away. She grabbed the green gas can and ran to the sliding glass doors and opened them.

"No!" Dr. Hamilton was shouting from the floor.

Martha flung the can as far as she could, as hard as she could, off the balcony. It was the same flight the ghost Martha had taken off that balcony just two days before. Martha watched the can. It went farther than she had, landed closer to the sea. The cheap green plastic split and the gas poured out into the sand. Martha turned to Dr. Hamilton triumphantly. She knew he could get more, anywhere, but this time, for tonight she had kept him whole.

"Watch, Dr. Hamilton," Martha said. "Watch."

Her hands went to her hood again, began to lift. Dr. Hamilton backed away from her.

"Don't," he said.

"Why not?" she asked. "You know me. You would know me anywhere. No matter what I look like."

She pulled the hood from her face, but in that instant when her eyes were covered, Dr. Hamilton ran, bounded out the door and away from the revelation of her.

"No!" It was her turn to scream.

She ran after him, down the hall. "Wait!"

She flung open the stairway door and shouted down, "Don't go. Please don't go."

She heard his footsteps below, his hard loafers hitting the cement stairs. "Wait."

He was gone. He had heard her, but he ran away. He heard her, but he was afraid to see her and he had left, running down the stairs.

2
4

SHE LAY, SHEERLY NAKED, ON THE HOTEL BED
IN THE COMPLETE AND UTTER DARKNESS. SHE
felt the quilted bedspread with every nerve. She felt exposed in the
blackness, as if a doctor's fluorescent light shone on her body, reflecting
white off the steel gurney of her daydreams.

Her doctor. Dr. Hamilton. She had been unafraid to show herself to
him. And now, in the dark so dark she was one of the blind, she studied
herself for flaws and found she didn't care. She had not been able to
save Dr. Hamilton, but she had done the best she could, that anyone
could. She missed Jewel, felt her arms ache for her daughter's soft skin,
and knew she had made a mess of that. She realized she was completely
alone and wondered, as if from a great distance, about her life and why
she wasn't worried about it.

She heard a keycard slide through the slot in the room door. She lay
still, even though she knew she should get up or get under the covers.
It was a member of the hotel staff, she supposed, who knew that Dr.
Hamilton never stayed the night. Maybe it was the blonde receptionist
who had come to take a catnap.

The person came to the bed and stood beside her.

Still she couldn't move. She lay on her stomach. She could pretend sleep, then wake, alarmed and angry. She could jump up, act the terrified woman, pull the bedspread up around her breasts like Doris Day finding Rock Hudson in her boudoir.

"Martha."

It was one word spoken low and quietly, but it shouted everything to her.

She rolled over and put her arms up.

Dr. Hamilton found them in the dark and sunk into them. He kissed her collarbone, her neck, but not her lips. She looked for him, but she couldn't see him. It was too dark to recognize his face, but she knew his smell, and his shirt felt soft and crisp, just the way it always looked.

"I wish," she began and stopped.

"What?" he asked. "Tell me."

"I wish that I could be burned," she said and felt him shudder and then freeze. "I wish that I would be burned so badly, the worst case you've ever seen. I would be your greatest challenge. You would take the skin from my inner thigh and build me a nose, an ear, two new lips. You, only you, could make me whole."

"Don't say that." He whispered it, low in his throat, immediately. "Never say that."

"I want to be your favorite."

He pulled away from her. She was unafraid. She reached up toward the lamp above the bed. He stopped her.

Then his hands moved over her body, starting at her face. He felt her forehead, her eyebrows, the bridge of her nose, the plains of her cheeks. His hands found her lips, pushed inside and felt her teeth and her tongue.

He continued. She was a topographical map, her hills and valleys giving him directions. She strove to be what he wanted, a place he wanted to go. He put one hand on either side of her waist, his thumbs nearly touching in the middle. His hands continued down, charting her obvious hip bones, her thighs, her knees, the freckled calves, and finally her feet.

"You are beautiful," he said.

"It doesn't matter," Martha replied, and felt a surge in her heart that it was true. "It doesn't matter."

"No," he said, "it doesn't."

She looked down at his unlit and indistinct figure beside her on the bed and realized that was how she usually looked to him. Without expression, without form. And he was here anyway.

She heard his shoes fall to the thick carpet. He stretched his lanky length along hers, his chin in her hair. She rolled over to him and pulled apart the loosely knotted professional tie. She unbuttoned the blue shirt. He wasn't wearing an undershirt and Martha was surprised to find that so appealing; the thought of the shirt against his bare flesh made him seem both brave and vulnerable. His chest was broad without the uncomfortable, chastising hardness of Reuben's. There was more hair than she expected.

She urged her naked chest against his. She could hear a heart beating, his or hers, she wasn't sure. His breath was soft in her face and slightly medicinal, a doctor smell.

Then she couldn't wait and neither could he. She pulled at his belt; he helped and stood momentarily to kick his pants off. His mouth found hers perfectly in the dark. His hands continued their explorations.

Now she was more than just a country, or even a continent. In a dark so dark that she couldn't see her own body, she became an entire universe. Unable to see anything at all, she finally felt like she could see herself.

Afterward, he held her small fist in his hand, held it so tightly that he hurt her. She didn't want to move. She didn't want to look forward to the curtains opening in the morning or backward to the photos still lying on the floor. She didn't want to wonder if Dr. Hamilton loved her, if he would stay, if she could make up with Jewel, if she would go to Salt Lake City for Christmas. It all seemed unimportant compared to herself.

She curled against Dr. Hamilton's side, her head in the space between his chin and shoulder, and fell asleep.

The grove of pines was green and fragrant in the clean summer sun. Martha squeezed her eyes shut. She was her nine-year-old self; blazing fiery braids, long freckled legs in cutoffs, sunburned shoulders. She rose on her tiptoes, squinted through the branches. She could see them, but they couldn't see her. She was the best at hide-and-seek. She was excellent at hiding. She absorbed and was absorbed by her surroundings. She disappeared. No one could ever find her.

From her hiding place, she watched the other children. They seemed small and fleshy, more solid than she. She swung from the tapering limb of her pine tree. Her feet left the ground and she felt she flew.

Dolly tripped through the woods, looking glamorous in her high heels and slim skirt. She called for Martha and smiled, her red lips a cardinal of color in the woods.

A girl danced by. She looked like Jewel; bright-eyed, hair glittering in the sunlight, she was effervescent. It was Audrey. She turned in a circle, looking for Martha. Then she and Dolly ran off together, after the other children, leaving the clearing empty, the free space open for Martha.

Martha let her feet land in the soft pine needles. She stepped out from among the trees into the blinding sunlight. She stood still and straight.

"Ollie Ollie In Come Free!"